Destroyer Rising

Also by Eric R. Asher

Keep track of Eric's new releases by receiving an email on release day. It's fast and easy to sign up for Eric's mailing list, and you'll also get an ebook copy of the subscriber exclusive anthology, *Whispers of War.*
Go here to get started: www.ericrasher.com

The Steamborn Trilogy:

Steamborn
Steamforged
Steamsworn

The Vesik Series:
(Recommended for Ages 17+)

Days Gone Bad
Wolves and the River of Stone
Winter's Demon
This Broken World
Destroyer Rising
Rattle the Bones
Witch Queen's War – coming fall 2017*

*Want to receive an email on the day this book releases? Sign up for Eric's mailing list.
www.ericrasher.com

Mason Dixon – Monster Hunter:

Episode One
Episode Two – coming summer 2017*

*Want to receive an email on the day this book releases? Sign up for Eric's mailing list.

Destroyer Rising

Eric R. Asher

Edited by Laura Matheson
Cover typography by Indie Solutions by Murphy Rae
Cover design ©Phatpuppyart.com – Claudia McKinney

There is always hope in the shadows.

Acknowledgements

To all my readers, thank you.

Thank you to The Patrons of Death's Door.

Thank you to my editor, Laura Matheson, who found a great many comma splices, she didn't find this one.

CHAPTER ONE

I T WAS THE nightmares. That was the worst part of having a million screaming voices inside my head, because they weren't really nightmares. They were the dreams and hopes of a million lost souls. They took over what little sleep I could get, replacing my thoughts with their own. Every night filled me with visions of lives and homes and cities that no longer existed, annihilated in Hern's gambit. I could not escape them.

I left another dreamscape behind as my eyes flew open. The pounding in my chest wasn't my own fear, not really; it was the fear of a father's final moments as he watched a blinding light swallow his family before the world went white.

"You okay?"

I glanced up at the perilously stacked old books on the table beside me. Foster sat on top of them, his brow furrowed and his black and white Atlas moth wings slowly flexing behind him.

"Yeah."

"It's been weeks," he said. "I thought it would get better by now."

"You didn't tell me Cara was married to Glenn, Foster."

The fairy looked away.

"And don't tell me he couldn't have stopped it." I narrowed my eyes. "What did you expect me to do? Just forget it happened? Just forget how half the people I trust with my life conveniently forgot to mention their relation to Glenn?"

"I meant the nightmares," Foster said, shifting on his perch, "not the rise of Falias."

I grimaced and leaned forward, rubbing my eyes with the palms of my hands.

"Have you found anything in the older texts?" he asked.

"No. I've been trying to find a way to free Vicky before … you know."

"You might need to help yourself before you can help her. How can you think clearly if you have a thousand voices in your head at once, and no sleep?"

I reached out and dragged the Black Book across the oak coffee table. It was an old tome, dripping with forbidden things and rituals I wished I could un-see, but it also seemed the most likely place to find out more about Vicky's fate. Foster was right, I wasn't going to be sleeping any more, so I might as well get more research done.

"I talked to Sam," Foster said. "They still haven't found Vassili. There were traces of him in Phoenix, but the trail went cold."

I stared at the book.

"You can't hide up here forever," Foster said. "Mom will be pissed if you don't get over it soon."

"Yeah, right."

I looked up when the air moved beside me, and I watched Foster glide down the aisle of books and vanish into the stairwell. He was still my friend, goddammit. I just needed some proof he wasn't waiting to ambush me with something even more dangerous than Cara had: Gwynn Ap Nudd, the Fae King, husband to one of my grandfather-clock-dwelling fairies.

Foster was her son, and he hadn't told me.

I ground my teeth and turned the page of the Black Book. The text on the tanned parchment wavered for a moment before coming back into focus. Several pages were like that, and each fell after a passage about the Burning Lands. Every time it felt like I was getting closer, a pale symbol marked one of those pages. Koda thought it could be an old code, and possibly a map to a dark thing known as the Book that Bleeds. That was months past, though, and none of us had found mention of it. Not in the vampires' archives, not in my collection, not anywhere. Something was hidden inside that tome, and if it could help Vicky, I had to figure out what.

CHAPTER TWO

I STOOD UP and stretched after staring at the Black Book for another hour, wrinkling my nose at the rather sharp reminder that I hadn't showered in two days. I stashed the Black Book in a safe place: Zola's old trunk with enough wards on it to hide Irish whiskey from a fairy. Scrounging through a duffel bag on the other leather chair in my reading nook turned up a clean shirt. I let it fall open and laughed when the fangs and hollow sockets of a vampire's skull greeted me.

I changed shirts and slapped on some fresh deodorant before walking to the other end of the room and starting down the stairs. I'd stared at those books and manuscripts for weeks, and still I couldn't find a definitive way to free Vicky from her fate. All I knew for sure was that I needed to find the devil who held the contract, and burn them both to ash. For that, I'd need demons, magic, and a hell of a lot of luck.

I had a demon who I called friend, and I had magic, and … I tripped on the last step, flailed, and flopped onto a lumpy green rug. The rug growled, shook its butt, and let me slam the rest of the way to the floor. Bubbles gave me a put-upon look as she shuffled away and vanished into the cu siths' lair.

Food. I need food, I thought as I pushed off the floor. Even the cu siths were grumpy with all the tension around the shop. Although it might have something to do with Peanut being gone most nights to guard Ashley's coven, too. I scooped up a bag of Frank's beef jerky and walked toward the front of the store, glancing at the grandfather clock before pushing through the saloon-style doors.

"Morning," Frank said, sorting the amber stones on the counter.

"Inventory?" I asked. I popped a chunk of fiery beef jerky into my mouth and began to wonder if that was the best thing to eat for breakfast.

Frank pushed a Frappuccino toward me. "Heard you stomping around up there. Thought you could use one."

I nodded and unscrewed the cap.

"We're low on amber again," Frank said. "I set up a call with Robert. Took some talking to get him to agree to come down."

"Still worried about the military?"

Frank returned to sorting the amber. "What did he do?"

"Robert?" I asked.

"Yeah, you've seen him when the police walk by the windows, right? I saw that look on a dozen ex-cons back in the old days. What did Robert ever do that he'd be afraid of a military presence?"

I frowned. "I don't know, exactly, but Zola trusts him."

Frank looked up at me. "That's a strong supporter, yeah, but wouldn't you like to know? We have enough shit to deal with right now without something else blowing up." He stacked the gemstones into a little tray before carrying it across the shop.

I spun the tablet around that Frank had insisted on buying to track the inventory and looked over the numbers for the month. I whistled at the bottom line.

"Things have picked up with the tourists," Frank said. "Not that you'd have noticed, with your head stuck in the library all day."

"I know. There's a lot of research to be done." I needed to give Frank another raise.

"Why not head over to the Pit later? Vik won't mind if you use the archives."

My gaze wandered to the back room and the grandfather clock. *Because I want to keep an eye on things,* I thought. Really, though, it had been weeks, and the fairies hadn't done anything out of the ordinary. Maybe that's what was bugging me, wondering what would come next.

"I'm going down to Trailhead for lunch with Sam," Frank said. "You mind covering for me? Before you head down to the Pit?"

"Not at all."

Frank nodded to himself and slid the trays into the display. "We need to restock the tourist items, if you're up for it."

"Will do."

Frank picked his keys up off the counter and rattled them a couple times in his palm before he walked toward the door. He paused with his hand on the knob. "And Damian?"

He didn't say any more until I looked at him.

"Work shit out with Foster before I kill you both."

The bell on the door jingled as he left.

I took a deep breath, watching his bald head bounce by the front windows. "Don't I know it," I muttered. I lifted a cardboard box of miscellaneous junk off the countertop and walked to the tourist section.

It felt good, right even, to be stocking and straightening the shelves again. I pulled a snow globe, of all things, from the top shelf and frowned at the broken Gateway Arch inside. We'd need to return that to the supplier. I shook the glass orb and watched the silver pieces swirl around the cityscape, clicking and tumbling as they went. A vision flashed through my mind, a torrent of power unleashed by the Old Man and the Fae, sending entire cities into oblivion. I shivered and my knuckles whitened on the base of the globe. Falias had appeared in that maelstrom, before the souls had swarmed Vicky and before I had peeled them off her with my necromancy.

Vicky.

I was sure Happy would have let me know if he'd learned anything new about Vicky, but I closed my eyes and pushed my aura out anyway. The experience didn't give me a sense of travel like it used to. The slightest effort told me where the bear was.

"Have you heard anything?" I asked.

The panda raised his head and looked directly at me from his perch inside the birdcage. *From Mike?* His voice boomed in his panda form. *I have not heard from the Smith in days.*

"Do you think he's okay?"

I can't fully express the unnerving oddity of having a ghost panda laugh at you. Happy's skull-rattling chuckle faded. *He is a fire demon within the Burning Lands. I am certain he is well.*

"How's Vicky?" The question died on my lips and turned to a scream as golden light blinded me.

Damian! Damian, answer me!

The bear's voice cut through the storm of screams and terror in my head for only a moment, and then chaos reigned.

Gold turned to ash, and ash to darkness, as a monstrosity that could not be real blasted my mind. Hunched and looming, with long, silver teeth. Its entire body squirmed and writhed, promising death to all who dared near it.

Light swallowed the awful vision. The nightmare of a thousand dying souls replaced it. The fire, the loss, the light. I didn't know if it was flames or tears that burned my face, but it felt like my skull was coming apart at the seams. And then the vision was gone. Only darkness remained.

CHAPTER THREE

"D AMIAN!"

I'd heard that voice before somewhere.

"What's wrong? Answer me!"

Something shifted me, and I remembered the fire and the screams. My eyes flashed open. Foster's colossus-sized face was no more than an inch away.

"Foster?" I asked, surprised to see the concern etched into his forehead.

"Are you okay?" Foster stood up and glanced at something above me. "You hit hard and wouldn't wake up."

"Hit what …" I trailed off as I tried to sit up. The world tilted sideways and nausea threatened to overwhelm me. I touched the throbbing back of my head, and cursed at the pain and the blood.

"Don't move. I'll get Aideen."

I wasn't going to argue.

I stayed down, closed my eyes and waited, pondering the odd silver-toothed vision that had bared its fangs before the souls had put me on the floor. I groaned when someone lifted my shoulder.

Aideen cursed. "Damian, what did you do?"

"Fell down." I smacked my lips together. My head felt funny.

"He almost scalped himself on that broken snow globe," Foster said.

"Hold him still."

Gentle fingers prodded the wound on the back of my head, but it still hurt like a bitch. I winced.

"Brace yourself," Aideen said. She didn't give any more warning than that. *"Socius Sanation!"*

I grunted as the darkness lost to pale white light that brightened into a sun. I felt every shift of the skin on my scalp as Aideen's magic pulled the wound closed, lessening the throbbing in my head.

I opened my eyes and squinted at the sunlight. "How'd you get to me so fast?"

"Happy," Foster said. "He would have come himself, but he's tracking something with Vicky."

"No, he's not. I saw him at the birdcage."

"Likely an old impression," Aideen said as she inspected the healed wound on my head.

"A ghost image of a … ghost?"

"Yes," she said with a small laugh. "Exactly that."

"My head still doesn't feel right," I said, pushing myself off the floor and wobbling to my feet.

"Give it time. It should straighten out soon."

"Thanks." I squinted and shuffled to the back room, tossing a bag of popcorn into the microwave before flopping onto the green couch. It wasn't more than a minute before something large and furry slammed onto the wood floor beside me. I scratched the cu sith's ruff and sighed.

✦　✦　✦

IT WAS THE burning that woke me. The acrid stench of ... "Popcorn! Shit!" The room devolved into shouting fairies and a barking cu sith as I tried to battle the flames leaping out of the microwave.

"How long did you leave that in?" Foster shouted.

I smacked at the button on the corner of the door until it swung open with a pop. A gout of flame leapt out and singed my arm before I hopped back. *"Minas Glaciatto!"* A small torrent of ice flashed into the microwave, sending flaming bits of popcorn all over the room.

Foster cursed. "It's on fire, you idiot! Put it out!"

"Oh my god," I shouted. "I'm on fire!"

"Was that the door?" Aideen asked as she surveyed the smoldering popcorn strewn about the room.

"I don't know! I'm on fire!" I beat at the blackened popcorn on my shoulder and jeans and finally managed to brush off my singed arm hair.

"Damian, please. I've seen you much more on fire than that."

A full-sized, fully armored Aideen stepped through the saloon-style doors, leaving Foster and me to deal with the mess.

I stomped on the last few bits of fiery popcorn with Foster's help before I looked up and met his eyes. He grinned and I laughed.

I turned back to the microwave. "You've met your end today micro—" I yelped as I grabbed the edge to pick it up and throw it away. The metal scorched my fingers. I blasted it with another ice incantation before smashing it into the trash can and cursing at great length.

"I think it's broken," Foster said.

I took a deep breath. "We needed a new microwave anyway. You know that damn thing burned a chimichanga? How do you burn a frozen chimichanga?"

I pushed the doors to the front open and eyed the guests I didn't realize were there. Alan stood beside a light brown-haired woman with enough gauze wrapped around her arms to supply a small hospital. I gave the werewolf a nod before climbing onto the stool behind the counter.

"Please excuse our dramatic host," Aideen said, turning to our guests.

"You're Aideen, right?" the woman asked. She looked nervous, but she hid it behind a drawn brow, like she expected the fairy to lash out at her.

"I am," Aideen said with a nod.

"You're … full sized."

A warm, white glow that emitted no luminescence enveloped the fairy before she snapped into a much smaller size.

"We have found it to be helpful keeping the tourists in line."

"And it's good for business," I said.

Aideen sighed. "Can we help you find anything?"

"I'm actually here to see Damian. I have something from … a friend."

I beat down the last smoldering ember on my sleeve and frowned. I leaned forward when the woman's words sank in. "And you needed a werewolf bodyguard to bring it here?"

"Need is a strong word," she said.

"Ouch," Alan said, casting me a small smile.

"Ha!" I glanced at her bandages again. She'd either had surgery, or she was a blood mage. "You're …" I narrowed my eyes. "Beth, right? Elizabeth?"

"Just Beth, yes."

Another blood mage. Cornelius's apprentice, yes, but when I thought about the damage that video had done, my tolerance for blood mages wasn't at an all-time high. I took a deep breath and shook my head. What could she possibly be bringing into my shop? "Well, what is it?"

Beth glanced at Aideen, but she didn't speak. She hesitated before nodding twice. "It's a book."

I glanced at Alan and Aideen before settling my gaze on Beth. "Let's go upstairs. We'll have a bit more privacy."

"I will keep watch over the store," Aideen said. She grimaced and looked away, and I felt the guilt gnawing at my brain.

I started for the back room, making sure that Alan and Beth were following me. Peanut trotted along at my heel, and I ruffled the fur on his head. "He's a lot more calm than Bubbles, usually. That's the one you really need to—"

The saloon-style doors burst open, and Bubbles charged through, knocking me into the edge of the counter and sending me to the floor with a curse. I watched upside down as Bubbles sailed into Alan's arms, landing with her paws around his neck. He grunted and spat, trying to get away from her enormous pink tongue.

I dragged myself back onto my feet just in time for Bubbles to charge back at me. The impact slammed me into the wall before she vanished into the back again. If I'd felt bad before, now it felt like the entire room spun around me.

Beth released a sharp laugh. I looked up at her and sighed, and her mouth snapped closed.

"No respect," I muttered, standing up again and brushing myself off. I looked over the top of the door and nodded. "Alright, they're both back in their hole."

"How far under the shop have they dug?" Alan asked.

"Straight to hell, I think."

"What?" Beth asked, following us through the saloon-style doors. I caught her staring at the old grandfather clock, ticking in the relative silence. Bubbles and Peanut scratched at the floor beneath us.

I pointed at the jagged hole in the wall. "They carved out a den. It's …"

"Huge," Alan said. "At least the building didn't collapse yet."

I flashed the werewolf a grin. "So optimistic with that 'yet,' Alan. Come on." I started up the staircase, turned at the landing by the back door, and led Beth and Alan the rest of the way up the carpeted steps.

"So, what did Koda send you over here with?"

I looked back when Beth didn't respond. She still stood at the end of the bookshelves, staring up at the hall of tomes that ran from one end of the building to the other. Maybe she'd be one of those not-so-bad blood mages. Ashley liked her, and that spoke volumes in my book.

"Beth?" I said, lowering myself onto one of the wide dark leather chairs around the low oak table. Alan pulled up another chair. Beth paused by the section of shelves that held two dozen of our oldest books on Wiccans. She started to reach for one, and then stopped.

"Beth?" I said.

"Sorry. I just … you have more books on witches than I

expected."

I squinted and nodded as I tried to remember the number. "I think we have about two hundred and sixty of them now. You're welcome to borrow them, outside of a few of the more dangerous volumes."

She stood in one place and stared at me until I started to fidget. I don't mind eye contact, but damn, not blinking is unnerving. The moment passed and she hurried down the aisle. "Thank you. That's very generous." She dropped into one of the open chairs, and pushed down on the deep leather.

"Good for naps," Alan said, stretching his legs out with a lazy smile.

I gave Alan a slow nod. "You've learned my most secret of secrets. You can never leave here alive."

"Just ignore him," Alan said. "He has a terrible sense of humor."

Beth gave the werewolf a somewhat nervous smile and unfolded her purse. Golden light filled the void within, and I sat up straighter.

I cursed when the light exploded in the dimly lit nook into a blinding gold sun. "What did you bring into this house?" I held up my hand, ready to call a shield. When nothing happened, I reached for the shelf beside me.

"Oh, not that thing," Alan said as I picked up a brown, shriveled ear.

I held it in my palm and reached out to Beth.

"What is it?" she asked.

"A silence charm. No one will hear us."

"What's it made out of?" She asked, pressing her palm against it with less hesitation than I'd expected. The fleshy ear pressed into our palms, and Beth twitched.

Alan took her left hand and the world fell silent.

"No one can hear us now," I said. "Tell me, what is this?" I nodded at the book.

Beth frowned at the glowing tome. "Koda said it's the Book of Blood."

I froze. "To unlock the Book that Bleeds?" But Koda had said nothing. Had he found it? Was this the key to the Black Book? "That's a lost text. That book is legend. It can't be real. It was mentioned in the Black Book, but I never thought … the Book of Blood … it's like a key or something, right?"

"Yes," she said.

No one spoke again until Beth broke the silence. "Koda said to unite it with the Black Book. That's all I know."

I spun around to the wall. Below the shelf was an ancient trunk, warded against all who were not bonded to it. Only Zola and I could see it and open it. Beth leaned forward to keep her hand against the silence charm.

When I turned back to the table with the Black Book in my hand, Beth sucked in a breath.

"That's it?" she asked.

I nodded and ran a hand over the rough leather. I sat the book on the table and leaned back. Beth frowned and tried to pull away from it.

"I'm sorry," I said, leaning forward and shifting the book to the opposite edge of the table. "I didn't realize how much it was bothering you."

Beth let go of Alan's hand and held out the golden book. I slid it from her grip and gasped. The golden glow swelled and brightened until it felt like it might burn my hand. I shouted, and dropped the book and the silence charm as a thousand voices burst to life inside my head. They still screamed, even so far from tragedy. I whispered "quiet" over and over again as the voices created a horrible screaming silence all their own.

Sound rushed back into the room.

Alan stood beside me as the cacophony relented. "Are you okay? Is it the souls?"

"Souls?" Beth asked.

"You don't have to tell her that," I said through gritted teeth.

Alan continued as though I hadn't spoken a word. "The souls of those who died at Gettysburg attacked Vicky, the little ghost." He paused and frowned. "Attacked may be the wrong word, but they swarmed her. Damian took them away."

"How do you 'take' them …" Her brow creased and she trailed off.

"Yeah," I said. "I have some extra voices in my head now. Sometimes it's worse than others." I cringed at a sudden lance of pain before taking a deep breath.

"Better?" Alan asked.

"Yes, thanks." I turned my focus back books. "No sense waiting."

Before Beth or Alan could say anything else, I grabbed the Book of Blood and slammed it onto the Black Book. It slowly sank into the Black Book, and instead of the rough leather and terrible sense of foreboding, a nightmare sat in its place.

"By the …" Alan's voice trailed off. We all stared at the leather tome. It wasn't black. It wasn't golden. It was a mottled, scaled mess that dripped a constant thread of blood.

I picked it up carefully, half expecting it to kill me on the spot. Horror warred with fascination and I cracked the book open. Pages turned, and nothing came to kill us. I suppose Koda would have warned us if it was deadly simply to utilize it, but then again he hadn't told me he had the Book of Blood.

"The Book that Bleeds ... bleeds?" I asked, watching a trail of blood drip from the book's spine. It didn't leave a mark or a stain where it fell.

"That's the creepiest thing I've ever seen," Beth said.

I watched the blood and ground my teeth together. "I've seen it before." I looked at Alan and then back to the book. "It's like Vicky in Cromlech Glen, when she was first ... when she ..."

I didn't have to say it. Alan and I knew Vicky's story, and I was willing to bet Beth did too.

I flipped through the pages. "There's more text than there was before." I flipped through another chunk of the book, finding one of the last pages I knew had been marked before. "Timewalkers?" I skimmed through it faster. "There's a chapter on the Burning Lands. This isn't even the same book anymore." I turned the pages more and more frantically. "I need to find Koda." I slumped into the chair and stared. Devils. The Abyss. The Wandering War. Page after page with new words and twisted things. I let the book bleed all over my leg as I reached for the pile of aged manuscripts on the shelf. I had to compare the notes. This is where the answers *had* to be.

"Come," Alan said. "He will be busy for a great deal of time."

Some part of me acknowledged their departure, but this ... this was everything.

CHAPTER FOUR

A VOICE REGISTERED somewhere in the back of my mind, but I could only stare at one of the unlocked pages of the Book that Bleeds. A detailed accounting for a Key of the Dead, a dagger like the one hidden in the chest at my feet.

"Damian?"

I glanced up. Aideen hovered above the table for a moment and then landed with a tiny whumpf. "Edgar is here. He would like to speak with you."

I nodded slowly. "Okay. I wouldn't mind speaking to him about a few things either."

Aideen glided back down the stairs.

"What do you think he wants?" Foster asked from his perch on the shelf behind me.

"I didn't know you were there."

"Yeah, well, someone has to stab you if you go crazy from whatever's in that book."

I smiled and turned my gaze back to the Key of the Dead incantations before closing the book and covering it in a sloppy pile of manuscripts. "Foster, it says a Key of the Dead can open a Hellgate or let you step into a bloodstone."

"Why would you ever want to step into a bloodstone?" Foster muttered. "Cozy up to a trapped demon? Sounds brilliant."

"You're speaking to each other again?"

Neither of us gave Edgar a response. Foster hopped down onto the table and we both watched the man walking toward us. His normally immaculate suit looked worn, but he still carried himself with authority. Edgar's face was drawn beneath the bowler that perched at a low angle on his head. I guessed he'd lost a good fifteen pounds, and the man hadn't had it to lose.

"How is Falias?" I asked.

Edgar let himself collapse into one of the deep leather chairs before pulling off his bowler with a sigh. Without the shadow of the hat, his sandy face was disturbingly close to skeletal.

"It is … it is chaos."

"Hern?" I asked.

Edgar shook his head. "He's been underground since Gettysburg. I don't know when we'll see him again. I'm more concerned with Gwynn Ap Nudd."

"Why?"

Edgar eyed Foster. "Where are your loyalties, on your honor?"

"I suppose I deserved that," Foster muttered before sitting down and folding his legs beneath him. "To my family first, my friends second, and my people third. Thank you for not questioning me in front of another Fae."

I stared at the fairy. "That's it? We just had to ask him a question on his honor?"

Edgar nodded. "Though an honor-bound fairy could still lie if he had no honor." Foster scowled and Edgar continued. "It does make me wonder why you didn't tell Damian about

Gwynn Ap Nudd and your mother. Did she explicitly tell you to keep silent?"

"No," Foster said, "but I do not wish to continue these questions."

"Tell me why," I said as I leaned forward. "I have to know, Foster."

He glanced up at me and then looked away. "I thought you and Sam would be safer not knowing."

I flopped back into my chair. Did he say that, knowing it was the only answer I wanted to hear? Or was I getting too paranoid for my own good? Maybe the voices in my head were wreaking more havoc than I realized. The mere thought of them brought a cacophony to my ears like that of a screaming stadium filled with people.

I watched Foster while he flexed his black and white Atlas moth wings. "Thank you."

He froze, and then gave me a nod.

"What of Falias?" I said, turning my attention back to Edgar.

Edgar stared at me for a moment before releasing a sigh. "Gwynn Ap Nudd, Glenn, has appeared there almost daily. He's been helping to rebuild Falias on this plane. You've seen the pictures on the news, I'm sure."

I had. The city seemed to grow. Buildings rose in sections, almost like a living thing. "The builders don't show up on film."

"Only because they don't want to," Foster said.

Edgar nodded at the fairy and crossed his legs. "Foster is correct. The government is still flying drones over the area, but the Fae are invisible to them unless they choose not to be."

"Why do the buildings show up, then?" I asked. "Cara said

they're built with Fae magic."

"They are," Foster said quietly. "It means Glenn wants the buildings to be seen, and he wants humanity to understand the power they have."

"Indeed," Edgar said. "Enough power to grow buildings back before their very eyes. On one hand, I can't blame him. The decision to drop bombs on Falias when it appeared was poor and misguided."

I'd heard about that too. The bombs had vanished before they could detonate. Who the hell knows where they ended up? "Glenn could have considered that an act of war."

Edgar blew out a short breath. "Considering his posturing, I'm sure he does."

"What do you mean?" Foster asked. "They haven't been showing themselves on video."

Edgar grimaced. "No, they haven't, but they've been threatening any military presence that comes within a mile of the city's borders. Not aggressively, mind you, but when men with guns see a twenty-foot-tall Green Man rise from the earth, well, it leaves an impression."

"Glenn brought the Green Men here?"

"No ..." a small voice whispered from above us.

I glanced up to find Aideen perched on the highest bookshelf. She hopped off and glided down to the table. At first, I was irritated she'd been spying on our conversation, but I remembered Foster's words and suspected her loyalties were much the same.

"Aideen," Edgar said. "You did not need to hide from us."

"I have no desire to upset Damian further."

"You haven't told him?" Edgar said with a half frown.

"Told me what?"

"Is it safe to speak here?" he asked, looking at Aideen.

"Yes, it is only us."

Edgar inclined his head and turned to me. "Aideen has been an agent of the Watchers for decades."

I sank into my chair, appalled at the idea, and somehow not surprised.

"I have a long history with necromancers," Edgar said, his gaze studying my face. "My experience is perhaps deeper than any other member of the Watchers. I am sorry for the accusations and hostilities I brought upon you as a Watcher, especially those that weren't deserved."

I narrowed my eyes. "Explain what that means."

Edgar frowned slightly, but he didn't comment on my tone. "Aideen told me many years ago that you were a noble soul. Zola did too, but I had long assumed she was the only exception to the rule. I trusted her and Philip in the Civil War, only to see Philip follow a path from which there was no return."

Things began clicking together in my mind, and my eyes snapped to Aideen. "You've been spying on Cara. Fucking hell, you've been spying on Glenn!"

"Quiet," Edgar hissed. "We may be alone, but his ears are many."

"No one will hear," Aideen said. Her hands glowed with a dim white light. "I have silenced this space."

Edgar met my gaze and held it, his black eyes boring into my own. "And now you hold the darkest necromantic text known to this world. Damian, with the knowledge inside the Book that Bleeds, you will be perceived as a threat to everyone."

I glanced at Aideen.

"I had to tell him," she said. "Edgar is no threat to Koda. He won't tell anyone else."

"You shouldn't have," Foster said.

Aideen's posture stiffened at his words.

"Koda is an old friend," Edgar said. "I would never harm him, or any member of the Society of Flame. They are invaluable, and impartial. I understand his concern."

I didn't say a word. If I was a threat to Glenn, that meant I was a threat to Hern, and maybe it meant I could harness enough power to free Vicky.

Edgar crossed his arms. "Tread lightly. Your alliances with the Old God, Aeros, the Ghost Pack, and Gaia are well known. You felled Prosperine and Azzazoth, and the dispatching of Ezekiel has created a backlash among the immortals. That says nothing of Mike and his ghost, or Ashley's mastery of the Blade of the Stone. And Samantha? Frank? The Piasa Bird? With Nixie's allies behind you, the River Pack, and the Demon Sword, there isn't a being on this plane who won't see you as a threat."

"What are the Green Men?" I asked, letting Edgar's words pass unchallenged.

"Enforcers," Aideen said.

"Yeah," Foster said. "Like the trolls from the Burning Lands we faced in Gettysburg."

I remembered the fiery, lumbering creatures. I remembered skewering them with an art so powerful it still made me cringe to think of it. Despite that aversion, I longed to do it again. "Are they like the legends? Leaves and vines and bark given life?"

"I don't believe that is the legend, exactly," Aideen said.

"But yes, they are all of those things."

"May I see it?" Edgar asked.

His question confused me at first, but I realized he could only mean the Book that Bleeds. I lifted the pile of manuscripts to reveal the tome. Edgar stared at it for a moment.

"A very long time ago, that was known as the Book of the Dead. It still brings dread to my heart."

I frowned and looked at Edgar. "I would have thought that would be all hieroglyphs, no?"

"It is much older than ancient Egypt, Damian. It is a living thing in its own right, evolving as the magics recorded within its pages evolve. A practitioner who speaks only Mayan would see the entire text in his native tongue. You see only the incantations and words with no meaning to your language in their native form because that is how they function."

The scope and precision it would take to create so complex a magic gave me chills.

"Tread lightly, Damian. Your allies have the power to shape the world, or destroy it."

CHAPTER FIVE

I STAYED UPSTAIRS after Edgar left. Aideen and Foster returned to the shop when the bells chimed, signaling the late arrival of a customer. Bubbles settled onto my feet, her massive form threatening to cut off the circulation in my toes, but I didn't make the cu sith move.

I was flipping through the Book that Bleeds, hunting for more information on the devils of the Burning Lands, when I found the end of the Wandering War. The Nameless King, slain by Gwynn Ap Nudd. An etching sat on the page, dripping and red with the same blood that seeped from the book itself.

Hern kneeled before Gwynn Ap Nudd, a severed head held high in the victor's hand. Beneath the etching, the story continued.

It was then the hand of Gaia was lost to the Fae, but not lost to the world. It sought a new master, a descendent of its owner, the beginning of the Anubis bloodline. Her power remained inside the realm, trapped within the hand and scattered across the Abyss, but her body would forever rest in the New World. A man would build his house upon her bones, never truly understanding why he *must* build upon the riverbanks. For all time, an immortal stands guard over Gaia, for when she awakens, the world of men will be forever changed.

"That can't be ..." I stared at the passage and read it again and again. I slid the page of a manuscript into the book and refocused on my search for the devils. I would ask Gaia about her resting place when I stepped into the Abyss again.

Two chapters later, I found a short passage about the Burning Lands. It was one of several realms that sat beside the reality I took for granted. Each was blocked by a Seal, except for those that weren't. The book didn't define Seals very clearly. One passage described them as physical barriers, while others were wholly focused on ley line energy. What followed caught my attention.

It is a long-held belief that a Seal can be created only by an immortal or an Old God, but that is not entirely true. The truth is always fluid. A being or beings can, with enough power, reforge a broken Seal or create one anew, bringing to light a shield or a punishment against an entire realm.

"Damian," Aideen said, pulling my attention away from the Book that Bleeds. She frowned. "What?"

I shook my head and closed the book on another manuscript. "I don't know, maybe nothing."

She took a deep breath. "I understand why you don't trust us—though I hope one day you'll understand we had no choice—but please, go see Koda. This is beyond us all."

"I don't even know where to find him right now."

Aideen looked away for a moment before she met my gaze.

"Go to the restored church off Main Street. He will find you there."

I crossed my arms and narrowed my eyes. "Were you just talking to him?"

She nodded. "He has been away for his safety, and yours. Please, talk to him, Damian. We may be able to trust Edgar, but not the other Watchers. Koda can't be seen here."

Aideen had never steered me wrong. She may have helped hold Cara's ruses together, but she'd never lied to me directly. At least not that I knew. No matter how angry I was with her and Foster, I still trusted them with my life. Maybe that was a mistake.

I frowned and gave a sharp nod. "I'll be there tonight at ten o'clock."

✦   ✦   ✦

THERE WAS ANOTHER call I needed to make before visiting Koda. I stared at the page before me and waited. The phone rang four times before the receiver clicked and an old New Orleans accent sounded across the speaker.

"What is it, boy?"

"Zola, I have the Book that Bleeds."

Silence greeted my words. What seemed like a minute passed by before she asked, "How?"

"Koda. He gave me the key. I need your help. I've already found information on the Burning Lands and Timewalkers. This thing could have some of the answers we've been looking for. There's … there's something you need to see."

"And it may pose more questions than we're prepared for," Zola said.

"Are you coming?"

"Yes, let me tell Vik what's happening, and Ah will see you shortly."

The phone went dead. She was definitely still at the Pit if she was talking to Vik. That meant she'd be up in twenty minutes, maybe thirty at the most. It gave me more time to stare at the monstrous tome.

✦   ✦   ✦

"THAT IS ... DISTURBING," Zola said, watching the blood pool on the table only to run off and vanish. I ran my hand through the stream and held it up.

"It doesn't stick to anything. It's like the blood on Vicky's hands. Do you remember that?"

"Yes, boy, Ah remember. Show me what you've found."

"I'm not even sure what I've found," I said as I turned the tome toward Zola. She settled onto the edge of one of the leather chairs.

"*Daemon Exilium.*" Zola spoke the words and then leaned closer to the book. "It's Latin, but Ah can read this page as if Ah've spoken the language all my life. Be wary of what you read aloud. Some of these phrases may be incantations."

"Will that allow us to banish a demon?" I asked, pointing to the phrase *Excutio Daemonium.*

Zola's eyes trailed down the page. She shook her head. "Not in the way you hope. Ah don't believe anything can banish the Destroyer from Vicky's body."

"Only what Mike said? Burning the devil that holds her contract?"

"Contract," Zola snorted. "That makes it sound like some

ridiculous religious hokum. It means a devil has bonded her aura to Vicky's, allowing a piece of herself to cross into our plane."

"I know, I just hoped ..."

"We must always hope."

We spent the next few hours shoulder to shoulder, comparing manuscripts until it was time to meet Koda. Zola stayed behind, though she expected to be gone by the time I returned. Her finger traced the words in the book, her nose an inch away from the pooling blood as I left.

CHAPTER SIX

I T WAS FALL again, and the chill in the air made me wish I'd grabbed a jacket. It'd been warm earlier, but the weather in Saint Charles was nothing if not inconsistent. I followed the brick sidewalk along the cobblestone street.

A National Guard personnel carrier rumbled by. Somber faces drifted past and I nodded to the only soldier who met my eyes. The military presence in my hometown was an awful thing, even if I understood why they were there. I wondered if they'd still be there if the military understood how outmatched they were against the Fae.

I slid my hands into my pockets, longing to feel the weight of the pepperbox against my hip, but not crazy enough to carry it with the Guardsmen around. There were a few drunks wandering in the lamp-lit street, and a handful of tourists, but nothing like it was before the rise of Falias. I hoped things would get back to normal, but some part of me knew it would never be quite the same.

A few steps off Main Street, a pale stone path led me into the shadows. Stone benches sat to either side of the carefully laid rocks and a low tree canopy hung over it all. What seemed at first an old church—but was actually a more recently built replica—waited at the far end of the walk, before the path reached the next street.

ERIC R. ASHER

I paused at the bronze historic marker laid in a large stone beside the log church. Vertical timbers filled with mortar formed the outer walls. It was far different from a traditional log cabin. The angle of the steeple rested on horizontal boards, and a bell waited by the wooden cross.

Ten pews—benches, really—I could scarcely make out in the shadowed room lined the interior, roughly cut from a light wood. I took six steps to the front of the small church and sat on the edge of the right pew.

Lanterns hung from the exposed rafters at the front of the church. They slowly came to life, emitting pale golden flames. I studied the jagged stone floor in the blossoming light.

"Damian."

I glanced up. Koda's pale form stood bathed in the golden light of the lanterns. His hooded robe was the same as ever, hiding part of his face in shadows above the large prayer beads around his neck. I'd known the ghost since I was a kid, and seeing him felt like coming home.

"It's been too long," I said.

"It was … necessary." He gathered his robe and lowered himself onto the pew across the narrow aisle.

"Are we safe here?" I asked, glancing back to the entrance.

He nodded. "I would not have come were it not so. Edgar is aware of my ruse, and Aideen. I did not expect her to stay silent so long. Foster is fortunate to have such an honorable soul at his side.

"Was Zola able to read the book?"

I hesitated, and then said, "Yes."

"I thought as much. The ritual that granted her long life altered her being more than she may realize."

"How so?"

Koda shrugged. "It is a hard thing to say, but she can read a book meant for immortal eyes."

"Should that surprise us?"

Koda tilted his head to one side. "I suppose not. Those were dark times, and her magic was no different."

"What should we expect to find in the book?"

"I do not know, Damian."

I frowned and crossed my arms. "Then why call me here now?"

"For another reason that is perhaps more sinister than anything inside the Book that Bleeds. Tell me, what have you learned from the Fae?"

"What do you mean?" I asked.

"What did they teach you? Did they ask you to perform tricks or magics that even Zola cannot?"

"No ..."

"Are you certain?"

I paused and combed through every memory I could think of: the deadbolt, the healings, all of it. "There was one thing. A few years ago, Cara taught me to use a growth spell on a pitcher plant."

"Indeed," Koda said. "And what did you do with that magic?"

I told him about the pigeons in Forest Park, how I'd vaporized them to stem the tide of my raging vampire sister.

"That is disgusting," Koda said, leaning back.

"Oh, so I should have let Sam kill everyone? That's a better option?"

Koda sighed and rubbed his prayer beads. "This is not the

time, and I did not mean to call your decision into question. You twisted a magic that cannot harm living things, and used it to kill."

His words stopped me cold.

Koda offered me a weak smile from the shadows of his hood. He pushed the edge of it back far enough that I could make out his bald head and soft features. "I heard about the revelation of Cara's husband, Glenn, and the fairies' ... lack of informing you. They have been manipulating you, Damian. Testing you."

"I know," I said as one of the lanterns on the wall flickered. "It makes me suspicious of everyone."

"As well it should."

I eyed the old ghost. "Why didn't you tell me you had the Book of Blood? Why didn't you tell me what was in it?"

"I may be a ghost, but not all of us in the Society of Flame are. I must protect my brothers and sisters above all, even above you. I heard of your plans, your intent to journey into the Burning Lands with the help of the Fallen Smith."

I rubbed my chin and leaned forward. "What of it? If there's a chance to save Vicky, I'm taking it."

"And what will happen while you are gone from this realm, Damian? What moves will be cast because you are no longer able to interfere?"

I ground my teeth because I knew he was right. What if Hern struck out against my friends while I was in the Burning Lands? What if Vassili came for my family? What if Nixie's queen began her war in earnest? I slammed my fist onto the seat of the pew.

"That is why I gave you the book now," Koda said. "The

risk of what it may unlock inside the Black Book is far outweighed by the knowledge we may glean. As to your earlier question—why I did not tell you what was in the Book of Blood—that tome is merely a key to unbind the Book that Bleeds."

"It's a spell?"

Koda frowned and nodded. "In a manner, yes, but it is a book of ghosts and dead things not meant for mortal eyes."

His words drove home something the Old Man had said, *'Welcome to godhood.'* I met Koda's gaze and said, "I'm not mortal anymore?"

"Not in the traditional sense of the word, no. As you are, you will live a million lifetimes."

I almost flinched. "The voices ..."

"The souls will fuel you, unless you find a method to discard them or burn them away. It is not so unlike the souls that sustain Adanaya. You can still die, of course. Ezekiel's death has shown you that."

"Zola isn't crippled by voices and visions."

Koda smiled, but it didn't reach his eyes. "Was that always true? Where did she learn the meditations that control the things you sense with your necromancy and help silence those very voices?"

It made sense when Koda said it. I'd never really put that much thought into it, which probably wouldn't surprise Zola one bit. "So why now?"

"The book?" Koda asked. "I told you, the risk is now outweighed. No one has read the Book that Bleeds in millennia. You are now privy to knowledge that I can only dream of, though I do hope you will share."

I nodded. "Of course."

"Do you know the rumors around that tome, Damian?"

"No."

"It is interesting, said to be the work of an Old God, precursor to the bloodline of Anubis, and perhaps the first necromancer."

Koda held up his hand when I started to speak. "You may bear the title of necromancer, but you *are* something else. No one would argue your skills in the darker arts, but you are not consumed by them. You perform magics that most could not without the sacrifice of a life."

"Their own?"

"Or someone else's," Koda said quietly. "Beware the day you meet a true necromancer, for they are unlike anything that walks this earth."

"What about Zola? Or even Philip?"

"They are, or were, what necromancers became." Koda laced his fingers together and stared at his hands. "There are darker things you have yet to face."

I took a deep breath. "What now?"

"Research," Koda said. "Find what you need to know to free the child, or at least halt the rise of the Destroyer. The demon must be stopped, at any cost."

His words sent a chill down my spine.

"We will meet again, Damian, but I must take my leave. If you need me, tell Aideen. She is our best spy, and her only loyalty lies in Foster. Remember that well." He stood up and squeezed my shoulder.

The lanterns went dark, and Koda was gone.

CHAPTER SEVEN

N O ONE WAITED in the shop when I returned from my rendezvous with Koda. Other than a few moments of shrieking, the voices in my head had been surprisingly quiet. Maybe the old ghost was right, maybe I only needed time to adjust. It hadn't been as bad the past week, except for that morning.

The Book that Bleeds waited where I'd left it, a steady trail of ghostly blood pooling on the table and dripping to the floor, only to vanish. I threw myself into that tome. Page after page of things waited, things that made Philip Pinkerton look like a harmless child and spoke of creatures in the Abyss that could devour a demon whole. If any of our enemies had had this book, we might not have survived this long.

The second passage on Timewalkers caught me off guard. It described how a vampire could bind itself to a demon, each overriding the bonds of any master with something called a Devil's Knot. The knot could control hellfire and—

"Damian?"

"Hmm?" I asked, without looking up from the fascinating, terrifying passage. I winced at my sore back as I leaned forward, following a sentence onto the next page. I didn't give much thought to the fact no one but the fairies should have been in the shop.

"Something's happening." The voice cracked, and I realized Vicky stood across the table from me. My head snapped up.

Gouts of darkness surrounded her eyes and ran down her cheeks, as though she'd put on half a pound of eyeliner and then cried for days.

"What the hell?" I hissed as I jumped out of my chair to touch the darkness on her face. It felt rough beneath my fingertips, as if something had burned her and the skin had scarred over.

"*Foster!*" My voice broke as I fought the panic back down. I wasn't sure if the fairies were in their clock, but I hoped to hell they were.

Foster swooped up into the second floor a moment later and flashed into his seven-foot form, sword drawn. Aideen followed close behind.

"Vicky?" Foster said. He sucked in a breath when the girl turned to look at him. "Nudd be damned, what happened?"

"It is starting," Aideen said as she hurried around Foster, pushing his wings to the side so she could crouch beside Vicky. "She looks like a teenager now. Her spirit is old enough to make the transition."

"I don't want to change," Vicky said between short breaths.

"I thought we had more time," I said. "Mike and I haven't finished planning the hunt. He's still in the Burning Lands, and I can't reach him."

"It doesn't matter," Foster said. "You have to go soon, or there's not going to be a point in trying."

"We need Cara," Aideen said. "If anyone knows how to slow it, she will."

I squeezed my forehead, running my fingertips up into my

hairline. It didn't matter if we weren't talking on a regular basis. Vicky was infinitely more important than whatever trust issues I had at that moment. "Get her."

Aideen nodded and ran back through the hall of books and down the stairs, using her full-sized form to hop down the flights in two bounds.

"I can hear the fires talking to me," Vicky whispered. "They say awful things, Damian. They say I should have let the Fae in Falias die. It would have stopped the war."

"The Fae will always fight," Foster said. "They aren't so different from humans in that regard." He looked back at me. "We need Mike."

"Can we wait for him? Or do we just chase him down in the Burning Lands?"

Foster glanced at Vicky and then back to me. "Build a carefully laid plan, or dive in head first? Why did you even ask?" It should have been funny, but his voice was flat.

Vicky wavered on her feet and reached out to the nearest bookshelf.

"You okay?" I asked.

Her head twitched to the side and she winced. "Oww. I don't … I don't feel right."

I raised my Sight, and stared in horror as the golden glow I was so used to seeing around her soured and grew deep with reds and blacks and darkness.

Vicky stilled as the miasma surged. She stood like the old vampires—unmoving, unbreathing—until a voice screeched through the void that made me want to claw my ears out. "Why do you battle the inevitable, Anubis-son?"

Vicky's head turned toward me, but there was nothing left

of her in those eyes. Infinite black pits stared through me.

"Who are you?" I whispered. My heart flailed in my chest.

"I am …" Her lips curled into a smile. "Prosperine."

Images of the battle at Stones River roared back into my mind, and the voices in my head screamed with me. Carter and Maggie dying, the soulsword, the final blow, Philip's escape. When the golden cries inside my head died out, Prosperine spoke again.

"You cannot kill what is not mortal, necromancer. I have come to take this child, and in your failure you—"

I held out my hand and screamed, *"Excutio Daemonium!"* Golden light flashed across the table, slamming Vicky into the bookshelves with a terrible thud and dropping her to the floor. Golden drifts of power rose from my hand, and the thick scent of burned hair filled my nostrils. My skin bore red welts where the power had torn through me and seared the hair from my other arm.

"Are you *mad?*" Cara shouted as she breached the stairs with Aideen. "We have *no* idea what the spells in that book do! You could have killed her!"

"Nothing can kill the Destroyer," I said quietly as I crouched down and rolled Vicky over. She was breathing normally now. I frowned at the burn near her shoulder. Beneath her scorched shirt lay an intricate pattern of scars, not unlike a Celtic knot.

"That was a soulart," Foster said. "It was blinding."

"I need Mike and Hugh. We can't wait any more." I scooped Vicky up and sat her down gently in one of the chairs. She made a whimpering sound and curled up into a ball.

I focused my Sight and studied the golden flow of her aura.

None of the awful red and black stains remained. "Whatever grip Prosperine had, it's gone now."

"Check her eyes," Cara said.

Ever so gently, I lifted one of her eyelids. I could see the white of her eye again, but flecks of blackness remained.

"It has begun," Cara said.

"We need answers," I said, turning back to the Book that Bleeds. "Get Hugh and bring him here. I'm going into the Burning Lands."

"Where's Happy?" Vicky whispered.

I glanced up at the fairies. Foster offered a shrug.

"Call him," Cara said. "He is her guardian as much as we are, if not more so."

I closed my eyes and pushed my aura out. The bear misted into my vision a moment later. "Happy, something's happened to Vicky. Come quick."

The room shook with the heavy bark of the ghost panda as he materialized in the shop. I watched the bear shift and become the man, Shiawase.

"I feared her time may be growing short," Shiawase said. "It is a wonder she has lasted so long against the rising darkness."

"Do you know what to do?" Foster asked.

Shiawase shook his head. "Had I known what to do, it would have been done long ago. The answers wait in the Burning Lands. Where is Mike the Demon?"

"He's already crossed over," I said.

"Can the Ghost Pack reach him?"

I gave a brief shake of my head. "Carter tried a week ago. They tracked Mike to a fortress in the waste before they lost all trace of him."

Shiawase looked down at Vicky and ran a hand across her head. "She could track him. Her powers are magnified a hundred fold inside that realm. I have been hesitant to let her venture back into those lands, but now I fear the choice has been taken from us."

"The ghosts and Vicky can cross over," Cara said, "but how do you expect to get Damian there without Mike?"

"I have to ask Gaia," I said, before Shiawase could answer. I stepped around the table and crouched down, pulling the trunk out of the back wall. Gaia's gray hand waited beside the Key of the Dead and the bloodstone. The hand felt cold in my grasp. I stared at the fairies and Shiawase. "Watch her."

I stepped into the Abyss.

✦ ✦ ✦

BLACKNESS AND COLD surrounded me in the depths of that lost realm. Stars wavered into my vision before the blasted images of Old Gods and tentacle-laden creatures out of nightmare rose beside my path.

"Gaia," I said, watching the golden motes of light drift down to the severed hand, forming the outline of her spirit.

"Welcome, my friend. Where might I take you today?"

"I need to get to the Burning Lands."

Gaia frowned and looked away. "Would it not be best to consult Mike the Demon?"

I couldn't stop a small smile. That was what we called Mike all the time, and now even Gaia was using the name. "He's already in the Burning Lands and we have no way to contact him."

"Truly? The dead wolves cannot reach the Fallen Smith?"

"No."

Gaia's brow wrinkled. "What is his purpose, to go so deep into those lands?"

"He was hunting for the devil that holds Vicky's contract."

"Ah, one of the ancient accords. He means to break it?"

"We all do."

"I cannot take a mortal through the old ways, Damian, but I believe you may survive with the army of souls at your side." She raised my left hand and placed hers on top of it. "I will make the journey with you, but understand you will be alone in the Burning Lands until you find your friends. I do not know where the broken Seal may take you and my hand cannot summon me through it. It will be up to you and Mike the Demon to find a way back.

"Do you wish to prepare, or shall I take you now?"

"I need to prepare. Take me back to the shop please."

"As you wish. Take my hand when you are ready, and I will walk you into the Seal."

The Abyss bowed and twisted in my vision, and then I was back in my reading nook, staring at the fairies.

CHAPTER EIGHT

"**C**AN YOU GET to the Burning Lands?" I asked, glancing between Foster and Aideen.

"In theory, yes," Aideen said, "but we would need a gateway, or a tool like the hand."

"We need to leave soon," I said. "Tomorrow at the latest."

Foster looked back to Aideen.

She shook her head. "I'm sorry, I don't see any way for us to do that without Glenn's help."

"Shit," Foster said. "That's not an option. If Damian's gone, we don't want it broadcast to all the Fae."

"Where's Cara?" I asked.

"She left to find Hugh," Foster said.

I nodded. "Vicky can travel with Happy." I looked down at the sleeping girl and the samurai beside her.

"Yes," he said, inclining his head with a bob of his topknot. "I can travel between the worlds, but is it so wise to take the child into the Burning Lands?"

"If fighting a devil is anything like fighting a demon, Vicky might be our strongest weapon."

"She could be a deadly adversary if Prosperine is able to consume her in full," Aideen said. "Are you ready to strike her down if you must?"

"No," I said as I closed my eyes and sighed.

"Yes," Shiawase said. "I will not abandon her to the destiny of the Destroyer.

I turned and stared at the samurai. There was a sadness that lingered on his face, but more than anything, the crease of his brow spoke of his fierceness. It was a stark contrast to the hand he ran over Vicky's hair.

A black whorl opened behind Foster, and a surprised-looking werewolf fell out of it. Hugh grunted as he hit the floor, barely catching himself in a three-point landing. Cara stepped through behind him.

Hugh looked up at Cara. "A bit more warning would not be unwelcome."

"We have more important things to attend to than your motion sickness, wolf."

It was cold, if not untrue, but Hugh didn't seem phased. He stood up and laid a hand on the back of the nearest chair. "Cara has told me you intend to enter the Burning Lands."

"Yes." I glanced at Vicky, and Hugh's eyes followed mine.

He sucked in a breath before crossing his arms and bowing his head. "You intend to hunt?"

"I intend to kill her devil in creative and violent ways."

Hugh smiled. "It is a noble sentiment Damian, but this is not a journey to be made alone."

"Gaia is taking me through the Seal. It's the only way." I didn't blink as I said the last. I held Hugh's gaze. I couldn't tell him why with Cara standing in the room, but I hoped he'd understand that we couldn't explain anything more right then.

"I will be with him," Shiawase said. "So long as Vicky remains herself, she will be able to fight alongside us."

Hugh nodded. "It is when she becomes something else that

I fear for us all. The child is tied to Damian, who is tied to the Ghost Pack, who are tied to the River Pack. What could a creature of the Burning Lands do with that bond?"

I stared at the werewolf. The thought hadn't crossed my mind. "Could Prosperine use that bond?"

Foster hissed.

"It is a unique scenario," Cara said. "I don't know what is possible and what is not. I would think the Seal, even broken, would protect the River Pack from any physical harm, so long as Prosperine remains in the Burning Lands."

Hugh eyed the fairies before turning his attention back to me. "This is a battle for Carter and Maggie, Damian. They deserve blood, and more, from that creature."

The pack marks on my arm burned with Hugh's words, and I curled my hands into fists.

"Vicky is one of the Harrowers," Hugh said. "She is as much a part of the Ghost Pack as any wolf. Fight beside them. You will not be able to convince them otherwise."

"They may not be safe around me."

Hugh smiled. "A wolf does not fear death, and a dead wolf, well … what greater honor is there than fighting for your family? Than dying for them?"

"Gaia will keep me connected to this realm," I said, not acknowledging the pang in my chest at his words. My gaze didn't waver from Hugh.

He frowned slightly—and it would have been easy to miss if I wasn't looking for it—before nodding.

"I'll do what I can to report back through the Ghost Pack. My bond with Vicky and my bond with the pack may be affected by the Seal."

"That is good, brother. I feel better knowing you are able to come back at a moment's notice."

Hugh was perceptive as hell.

I glanced at the fairies and asked, "Can I carry my weapons with me?"

"Those that have been blessed by the Fae should make the journey," Aideen said. "Others may be lost to the Abyss. Crossing through the Seal is not so simple as walking through the Abyss with Gaia."

"That's why I asked."

Hugh slid into the last empty chair. "What is your plan? Why did you need me here?"

"Can you and Alan keep watch over everyone? If I *am* tied up in the Burning Lands and can't return when you need me, or Sam, or Ashley, or—"

Hugh held up his hand. "We will help where we can."

"Damian." Cara's voice was quiet.

I turned to look at her, and met her blazing green eyes.

"We will keep watch here as well. We can't travel through a broken Seal without Glenn's help, and I have no wish for him to know you're absent."

I looked down at Vicky. Her breathing was even and the blackened scars on her face had shrunk. "I'll be back as soon as I can." I looked back up at her, the fairy I'd come to call Mom, the fairy whose lie had cut me to the bone. "And thank you."

She nodded and turned away, marching up the aisle and down the stairs in her full-sized form.

Vicky whined and kicked out her leg before she fell still again. I looked at Foster when he turned away from the stairs.

He shrugged and snapped into his smaller form before

gliding onto the table. "I don't know whose side she's on," he whispered.

"That is … disturbing," Hugh said under his breath.

Shiawase laid a hand on Vicky's head. "It is not our concern now. Whether we remain here or travel to the Burning Lands will play no role in her decision."

I pulled my phone out and texted Zola and Sam. "Shop at 10?"

Sam replied with an almost immediate 'Yes.' It took a minute for Zola's response to come through, but I finally got, "Yes. I told you last week to stop typing at me, boy."

I smiled and laid the phone down. "Zola will be here in the morning with Sam. From there …" I trailed off when Vicky twitched again and groaned. I clenched my hands into fists.

"Peace," Hugh said. "Be at peace until you can release her. We will stay vigilant in your absence, though your friends and family can take care of themselves."

"I know," I said, stuffing the Book that Bleeds into a backpack along with Gaia's hand and my focus—the hilt of an old Scottish claymore. Never knew when you might need to run something through with a soulsword. "Thank you. All of you. I'll see you after we get some sleep, Foster. Aideen."

"I will remain here with Vicky," Shiawase said. "If anything should happen, I will lock her inside of your ghost circle."

"That would hold her?" I asked, honestly curious.

"For a time. Ward is perhaps more prepared than you realize. There is little he builds without more than one purpose."

"Where is he?"

"Last I heard from the Old Man," Hugh said, "they were all in Falias, helping with the reconstruction."

"Has he seen Glenn?" Foster asked.

"Not that I am aware of. Do not forget how large the city is. One could wander for days and never find themselves."

"Ward fought to protect Falias when Ezekiel destroyed it," Aideen said. "I imagine he is safe from anything Glenn might do."

I slid the straps of the backpack over my shoulder. "Okay then. Anything else? Or are we calling it a night?"

Hugh stood up and stretched. "I will return to Howell Island to discuss matters with Alan come morning. Journey well."

Hugh extended his arm and we traded grips, palms to forearms.

"I will wait here as the bear," Shiawase said. "It brings her comfort, and I fear she will need that when she awakens." Before anyone could respond, the samurai blurred and distorted, his ghost becoming the familiar shape of a giant panda. He hadn't moved from the chair before he changed, and now the ghost panda was awkwardly seated in the leather chair. His somewhat stubby hind legs shot straight out while his front legs clawed at the air.

I snorted a laugh and the bear froze. He chuffed and rolled onto the floor in absolute silence, settling in below Vicky's feet.

Something sniffed at the top of the stairs. Bubbles waited, her eyes just peeking above the top step. Her tail whipped back and forth twice before she bounded down the aisle, dodging the fairies and werewolf so she could stand beside the ghost panda. Bubbles cocked her head to the side, and then dropped to the ground. She rested her muzzle on Happy's back and wiggled her bristly green butt into a more comfortable spot.

I looked around at everyone. "Until the morning then."

✦   ✦   ✦

I CLIMBED OUT of my '32 Ford Victoria and shambled up the stairs to my apartment. It was late, and I was tired, but that didn't stop me from laying out the Book that Bleeds on the oak coffee table.

After a few minutes, I walked to the old green fridge and pulled out a pack of frozen chimichangas. I pulled them out when the microwave dinged and made my way back to the couch.

It was another hour before I found the passage. I wanted to scream, and jump, and celebrate, but then I dug in to what I was really reading. It seemed so promising. A devil could be struck down by hellfire, immolated. There was a huge caveat after that. One of two things happened to any creature bonded to the devil. They either died with the devil, or became it.

My fists shook as I clenched them. I finally turned the page.

"Devils and Timewalkers?" I said, confused at the correlation in the next heading.

The only bonded beings known to have survived the destruction of a devil are those with a bond to Timewalker. The Timewalker magics are far older than the Burning Lands, heralding from a time before the Great War of the Abyss. What makes them truly extraordinary is the ability of these magics to function on any known species.

I read on, but the book didn't do much to clarify what I'd read. A later passage described an unstoppable soldier, and it took me a minute to realize it was describing a vampiric zombie. Where would we even find a Timewalker? If Vicky was bonded to one, could we destroy her devil? Or would she still burn up along with the damned thing?

Possibilities blurred with risks and dark thoughts crept up into my head. I slid the page of a manuscript in to mark the passage and leaned back, resting my arm on the backpack. I needed to sleep, and I cringed when I looked at the clock. Tomorrow was going to be hell.

CHAPTER NINE

THE ALARM ON my phone woke me up with a series of trumpets and a crash of cymbals. I almost smashed the damned thing on general principle. A stuttering zombie shuffle carried me to the shower, Frappuccino in hand.

Mornings like this always felt surreal. It was my normal routine, same food, same drinks, same shower, same everything, but I knew the end of the day might leave my world changed forever. There was nothing I could do to stop it. It reminded me of one of Hugh's sayings: "No matter the trial you face, do not lose the peace and rhythm of life."

It irritated me, how that wolf could say something one day that didn't make a damn bit of sense, and then a year later … poof, oh, that's what he meant.

I pulled my jeans on, along with a clean vampire-skull T-shirt. Vicky had taken to buying them for me whenever she came across one. She had money, and I wasn't sure I wanted to know where it came from. Happy had told me not to worry about it, so I didn't. I had six of the T-shirts now. I tucked an extra one into my backpack, along with two more Frappuccinos and a bag of Frank's beef jerky. I slid extra speed loaders for the pepperbox into the front pocket.

I glanced at the clock on the microwave. It was only two where Nixie was in Europe. I could definitely make it there and back to the shop on time. She might be busy, or not even home, or I might land on some unsuspecting visitor's head, or maybe Glenn wasn't really in Falias and he'd be waiting to—

"Screw it." I pulled Gaia's hand out of my backpack before hooking the shoulder straps over my arms. The dead hand felt frigid in my grasp before the fingers flexed and laced in with my own like an old friend. The wood paneling on my walls flickered, and then there was only darkness.

"You have returned quickly," Gaia said.

She'd spoken before I could so much as make out a pale dot in the infinite darkness. That was unusual, but not unwelcome.

"I thought I'd go see Nixie before …" I paused as the pale, glowing path lit beneath my feet and Gaia took form. "Before we go into the Burning Lands."

"You fear you may not return," Gaia said, her breathy voice almost a song in the silence.

I didn't answer. I'd be an idiot to think this was going to go off without a hitch.

"You've grown wiser in the short time I've known you."

One of the great Leviathans rose up beside us as we continued forward. I couldn't be sure if it was Croatoan—the awful creature the Old Man had fought centuries before—but it was enormous, its tentacles barely moving, trapped in the distorted time of the Abyss. I watched the massive beak as we neared the thing. It cracked open wide enough to see the trio of slimy beaks within it, beneath a great black eye. I shivered and looked away, and by the time I glanced back, the entirety of the beast was already gone.

"Gaia," I said, thinking back to the Book that Bleeds. "Do you know where your body is?"

"I do, young one."

I looked at the flowing golden light of her hair and studied the side of her face. "Is it beneath Rivercene? Are you the Guardian there?"

Gaia's steps hesitated. "I do not know if I could give my imprisonment such a noble name, Damian. I am trapped within that place for all time, though my spirit is free to roam the Abyss.

"That's wrong," I said. "Then the innkeeper, she's your prison guard?"

"Oh, no. She is a very old friend. It would do well to be kind to that creature, for she is not what she seems."

"She's an immortal," I said. "Like Edgar, like Ezekiel was."

"Ezekiel," Gaia said, tilting her head to one side. "I suppose, in a way they are similar, but she would never kill that which did not deserve to die."

A frisson of adrenaline wracked my spine as the reality of holding Gaia's hand within the Abyss slammed into me. All she had to do was let go, and that would be the end of me. "Why did you never abandon Philip or Ezekiel here?"

"You already know that answer."

"Whatever binds you makes you happy to serve the bloodline of Anubis."

She nodded slowly. "That is part of it I suppose, but I am not a cruel being." Gaia slowed to a stop. "We are here once more."

"Do you remember being free?"

Gaia looked up into the infinite stars of the Abyss before lowering her gaze to mine. "A great Fae cursed me to this life, binding my very spirit into the world. Were I to be free, I do not know what would happen. I remember a time before my shackling, but it is dim, and it is distant."

I looked down at our hands and turned them over. "Have you always had the power to wander the Abyss?"

"No. That I remember quite clearly. A piece of my body needed to be severed and sustained by a terrible soulart. The kind of magic that will outlive its practitioner, and perhaps its very world."

"Thank you for talking about it," I said. "I know it can't be easy."

"It is not a difficult thing, either. I have had a great many centuries to accept my fate."

I frowned and looked into the darkness before nodding. "I'll be back soon. I have to be at Death's Door by ten."

Gaia released my hand, and I fell.

✦ ✦ ✦

TORCHLIGHT GREETED ME as my feet slammed into the floor. I stumbled two steps and snatched Gaia's hand from the air before it hit the ground. I stuffed the severed limb into my backpack, squinting against the light. The stone tiles were a stark contrast to the soft path through the Abyss.

Gaia's aim had gotten better. I stood directly in front of the door to the room Nixie had been staying in. The same room where I'd stayed with her after my appearance in the Royal Court. I glanced behind me at the monolithic statues that doubled as pillars to either side of the hall.

The waterfall cascaded across the door. I hoped that meant Nixie was here, and I wasn't about to step into some newfangled Fae trap that would turn me into a deadbolt. As soon as I came within three steps of the door, the waterfall cut off and the door clicked.

The door cracked open slightly. "Who's there?"

"You ordered a pizza?" I shouted back.

The door swung inward and Nixie stared at me. Her hair was shorter, barely to her waist now, and her eyes sparkled in the torchlight. "Damian? Why are you here?"

"I have an hour to kill before I head to the Burning Lands."

Her eyes narrowed. "Come in." She stepped back into the room and I followed her inside.

I closed the door behind me and heard the waterfall start up again. Nixie settled onto an ornately carved chair by a stone table.

"Are we safe to talk here?" I asked.

"As safe as we can be. Glenn is in Falias from what I understand, and the Queen has not been seen here in over a month."

"Cara?"

"What?" Nixie asked. "Oh, no, I mean the queen of the undines."

She hadn't so much as hugged me after I mentioned the Burning Lands. I guess she already understood what I was getting myself into.

"I will not pretend to be happy about this, Damian. Things with the Queen have been ... there were several deaths before her faithful left this place. Having you in an uncertain situation is not ideal."

She sounded cold, calculating. I wasn't sure what to say. "I'm sorry," was all I mustered.

She shook her head. "Did you hear from Mike?"

"No," I said, sliding out the chair beside her after setting my backpack on the table. "Vicky ... something's happened."

She sat up straighter. "What? What happened to the child?"

I told her the story of the black scars and the demon's voice. It was the incantation I used that caused her to cross her arms.

"You banished a demon? How? Where did you learn that?"

I unzipped the backpack and slid out the Book that Bleeds.

"Nudd's balls," Nixie said. "How in the world did you get that?"

"You know what it is?"

She nodded. "The Book that Bleeds is a thing of old stories. The kind of tales we use to terrorize our young." Nixie leaned forward and reached towards the book before pausing. "Do you understand what could have happened if Ezekiel or Philip had ever gotten their hands on this?"

"I've only read part of it, but yeah, I get the gist."

She frowned slightly and met my gaze with her crystalline blue eyes. "What do you intend to do in the Burning Lands?"

"Find Mike. Find Vicky's devil, and destroy Prosperine utterly. It should break the bond."

"It could kill the child."

"Maybe not." I pried the book open at the latest manuscript I'd stuck between the pages. "Look at this. It says that something bound to a demon can survive its destruction if it, in turn, is bound to a Timewalker." I went on, running through another page of text. "I don't know what a Devil's Knot is, though."

"It's a ward," Nixie said. "You are gambling with a great many lives, Damian. You have to understand that you could fail. Vicky could lose to Prosperine, and the Destroyer would be reborn into this realm."

"That's …" I sighed and slouched into my chair. "That's why I wanted to see you. In case things went sideways and I didn't make it back."

Nixie's eyes flicked rapidly to the side. "What do you mean?"

"In case something happens, I had to tell you I love you."

"Damian, I don't like this. Don't think like that. You have to come back."

I didn't say anything more on it. I closed the Book that Bleeds and slid it back into my pack. Nixie watched the trail of blood as it ran from the table and then vanished into the ether.

"How are the witches?"

She inhaled and exhaled through her nose. "It has been quiet since we thwarted the tidal wave. The Queen is still scheming, and we don't know what she'll do next. There have been deaths, though, on both sides."

"Who?"

"No one you know, but friends."

"I'm sorry," I said, reaching out and taking her hand. She squeezed it before letting go.

"Did you hear of the witch that attacked Alan and the blood mage yesterday?"

"What?" I snapped. "Alan? Is he okay? Hugh didn't mention it. And what blood mage?" My brain clicked over before Nixie spoke.

"Her name is Elizabeth. She is loyal to Ashley's coven, apprentice to Cornelius."

"She … I met her yesterday."

"Did you know she is a friend of Alexandra's?"

"No."

"Alexandra trusts her, enough that she smuggled a very dangerous weapon to the blood mage."

"What kind of weapon?" I asked. "Is that the best idea?"

"One could ask the same of the book you brought into this place."

"Touché."

Nixie smiled. "There is a rumor that the first of the dark-touched has been sighted in the west."

"Where?"

"The deserts of Arizona. That is not as important as what I have to say. Use your connection with Ashley to ally yourself with Elizabeth. The blood mages are not many, but they are powerful.

"How have the tensions been with Falias and the common-ers?"

"Well," I said, "the government hasn't tried bombing it again, so I guess there's that. We still have a military presence in every major city. You know how it is. People fear what they don't understand."

"They have a right to," Nixie said. "They lost more than a million souls to the rise of Falias. Those people died in a heartbeat, making the war with the Fae already one of the most costly in humanity's memory."

"The souls aren't so lost." The cacophony of voices rose in the back of my mind at the mere mention of their existence.

"You hear them now, don't you?"

I nodded.

"Let me see the book, Damian."

I tilted my head to the side, shrugged, and then pulled it out again.

Nixie sighed and opened the pages. "Show me what you'd read of the Timewalkers, and maybe we can find a way to save the child."

We poured over the pages until the hour was almost past.

"I will find Ward," Nixie said. "He may not like the idea of helping to create a Timewalker, but it may be our only chance to save Vicky."

I nodded. "Thank you."

"You understand she may die with the devil? You cannot lose yourself if that happens, Damian. There is too much left for you to do."

I stood up and slid the backpack over my shoulders. Nixie leaned forward and wrapped her arms around me, pressing her soft lips to my own before releasing me.

"Be careful, Damian."

"You too, Nix."

I laced my fingers into Gaia's and returned to the Abyss.

CHAPTER TEN

GAIA'S AIM WAS less accurate on the other side of my journey. I materialized about five feet above the landing on the stairs in Death's Door and squealed before slamming into the floor.

"Oww."

"Damian!"

I looked up toward the top of the stairs. Sam stared down at me, concern plain on her face.

"The boy is nothing if not graceful," Zola said, stepping up beside my sister.

"He's almost as graceful as a drunk groomsman."

"Hilarious," I said, slowly marching up the steps. "You're both hilarious." I paused at the top, surprised to see the upstairs empty. "Where's Vicky? And Happy, for that matter."

I made my way down to the end of the books. Frank snored in one of the leather chairs.

"Frank!" I shouted.

He startled awake and flailed, almost spilling himself onto the floor. "Damian. Christ."

I pulled the chest out and holstered the pepperbox under my left arm before eyeing my staff. It would be unwieldy and, considering it came from Glenn, I didn't much trust it at the moment. I left it leaning in the corner, in the gap between the shelves.

"You keep watch over my sister, yeah?"

He gave me a sleepy half-smile. "Sure, like she needs that." He started to doze off again and jerked awake. "Oh, I heard back from Robert. He'll definitely be by this week. Not sure when exactly, but you know if he says he'll be here …"

"He'll be here," I said. Robert was always punctual. I was a little worried about the guy, considering how jumpy he'd been since the military had shown up.

Foster glided over Frank's head, and dove onto the short table. "This may be the best time to go," he said. "Glenn has been seen in Falias, so we know he's distracted."

"Cara says the military is seeking a parlay of sorts," Zola said. "It could be a ruse, Ah suppose, but this is a lull, Damian. You bring hell into the Burning Lands and leave your mark."

"I will," I said with a nod.

"And Ah don't care what you need do, boy. You come back alive." She smacked my shoulder hard enough to make me cringe.

"Cara doesn't have a reason to lie about this, does she?" I whispered.

Foster shook his head. "Either way, it's not like there's a choice. You either break the devil's hold on Vicky, or we have to battle the Destroyer. I'd rather fight Ezekiel again."

"That's the long and short of it," Sam said, slipping between Frank and me, taking a seat on his armrest.

"Are you taking the book?" Zola asked.

I turned around to face her and nodded. "I don't know how long I'll be gone. I haven't had enough time to study it."

"Shouldn't we go with you?" Sam asked. "It's Vicky, Demon. I'd do anything to help her.

I smiled at Sam's somewhat awkward timing for my nickname. "I know. That's why I'm going. One way or another, her
suffering is going to come an end."

"You're taking me with you," Sam said.

"No. Sam, I can't. I need you and Zola and Frank here. I
need to know someone will protect Mom and Dad if this goes
south."

She started to protest, and Zola laid a gnarled old hand on
Sam's shoulder. "Stay with me, Samantha. Help me keep watch
while your brother does this thing."

Sam hesitated, her eyes flashing from Zola to me.

"If anything happens …" I said. "If we don't make it back, I
want to know you all have a fighting chance."

Something crashed below us and one of the cu siths barked
loud enough to rattle my brain. Foster shot down the stairs.

"Nixie's going to go looking for Ward." I unzipped the
backpack and pulled out the Wasser-Münzen. It was my only
connection to Nixie when she was in Faerie, outside of Gaia, at
least. I held the disc out to Zola. "Help her, if you can."

"Why is she looking for Ward?" Zola asked, gently taking
the blue obsidian disc from me and sliding it into her cloak.

Footsteps sounded below us, followed by the chaotic
scrambling of the cu siths' claws on wood.

"The only way that we've found, so far, for Vicky to survive
is a Devil's Knot."

"Ah don't know what that is."

"Timewalker magic."

"*Timewalkers?* Boy, Ah hope you know what you're sticking
your foot in."

"Does he ever?" Sam muttered.

"Just, please, be safe," I said. "I'll be in touch as soon as I'm able."

Sam reached out and hugged me, threatening to crack bones before she finally released me. "Go, save Vicky. Be the hero she deserves."

"Did you just quote—"

"Just go, Demon," Sam said with a small smile.

"Be careful," Frank said. I gave him a nod.

Zola patted my arm. "We'll meet again boy, be it in this life or the next."

I paused at Zola's words before squeezing her shoulder. I turned to leave, hurrying down the steps, half curious what all the racket downstairs had been. Vicky and Happy waited there with an overly excited Bubbles.

"We'll meet you there," Vicky said, ruffling Happy's fur.

"So be it," I said.

She hopped onto the panda's back, and they were gone, sucked into a sickly red and yellow vortex.

Bubbles stopped hopping around and stared at the space where her best panda friend had vanished. She chuffed and flopped onto the floor.

I smiled and turned around. I'd almost reached the back door when a voice spoke.

"Damian, wait."

I paused and glanced behind me. Cara stood there beside Bubbles, running her fingers through the cu sith's fur.

"What is it?" I asked, keeping my voice as even as I could. It was still hard not to bite off every word I spoke to her.

"Take Bubbles with you."

"Why?"

"You'll understand once you're there," she said.

"That sounds promising, or like a very terrible idea."

Cara smiled slightly. "She will be of more use than you may think. The cu siths thrive in different planes. They are truly gifted in the Burning Lands. Peanut will still be here to guard the Coven. Our friends can guard each other without Bubbles."

I hesitated, and then nodded. "Come on, Bubbles. Let's go get a tan."

Bubbles hopped back up onto her paws before slamming her hips against Cara. The fairy stumbled and the cu sith trotted over to me and blinked.

"We'll see you soon, Mom." It slipped out. It was so natural a thing, the nickname I'd used with her for years now.

She gave one small nod. It made me think of my own mom, my real mom, and how I should be telling her and Dad goodbye. That made the chance of not coming home seem too real. I couldn't do it. I glanced back at the shop, taking in the old Formica table and the grandfather clock near the saloon-style doors, and then slipped out the back door.

Foster waited there. I walked past him and Bubbles followed. He sniffed at the air. "Do I smell Frank's beef jerky?"

"Yes, indeed," I said, patting the backpack.

"You're taking insanely spicy jerky … to the Burning Lands?" he said, completely monotone.

"And a cu sith."

Foster sighed. Bubbles snorted and started pacing back to the door. I stood in the parking lot for a time, waiting for Foster to say more. The cu sith had taken to staring at our Faerie deadbolt. She growled, and he insulted her, and then she ran her giant pink tongue over the little screaming face.

"Good dog," I said before turning back to Foster. If he wasn't going to say anything, I was. "Something still bothers me."

"What?" He crossed his arms.

"Something still doesn't sit right with Koda's story. 'The rewards outweigh the risk.' "

"Is that a question?" he asked, relaxing his posture. Maybe he thought I was going to start in about Cara.

"I find it hard to believe Koda kept that book from me for years and suddenly decides to take a risk to help Vicky."

"Koda knows she means a lot to us."

I gave him a half smile. Vicky meant a lot to him too. I remembered what he'd done to that vampire at the mall. I could still hear the sounds of the body being cut in two.

I took a deep breath. "He didn't want the Watchers or the Fae to find out he had the book. Why? What Fae wouldn't want me to have it?"

"All of them?" Foster said with a smirk.

I blew out a breath of laughter. "I guess you're right there."

"Be careful, Damian. I'll do anything I can to protect our friends while you're gone. Don't stay gone too long."

I looked across the gravel lot at my old car and nodded. "I'll be back as soon as I can."

"Good. With Falias in turmoil and the military everywhere, something's going to give."

"Not to mention the dark-touched," I muttered. "Vicky comes first, Foster. We may not have saved her from that goddamned vampire, but I'm saving her from this."

"And if you don't, I will," Foster said quietly.

I nodded before pulling Gaia's hand out of my backpack. I snapped my fingers and Bubbles bounded away from the screeching deadbolt. "Let's go, girl." I wrapped one hand in her ruff and the other I laced into Gaia's fingers. The hand warmed, and the world vanished.

CHAPTER ELEVEN

"**A** CU SITH," Gaia said and, for perhaps the first time, I heard joy in her voice.

My jaw almost unhinged at the sight of Bubbles. She was a beacon of pure golden power in the void of the Abyss.

"This is, uh, Bubbles," I said.

"Bubbles? An odd name for such an ancient creature. You need not hold on to her here, Damian. She will not stray. The bond between you is as plain as the sun."

I let go of the cu sith's ruff and she stiffened for a moment before looking around. Bubbles rubbed up against Gaia's leg, her head near Gaia's chest. I squinted at Bubbles.

"Did she just get bigger?"

"Yes, and she will again when you enter into the Burning Lands. Do not fear her."

"Why would I be afraid of Bubbles? She's like my favorite ankle-biter."

Gaia began walking, and I followed. Bubbles trotted along beside us. "She will not look the same as she does here."

I cursed under my breath. "Is that why Cara sent her with me?"

"What is your mission?"

"To save Vicky."

Gaia smiled. "No, young one. Look at a smaller piece of

what you must do. What will you do when you cross the Seal?"

"I have to find Mike."

"And does Bubbles know the Fallen Smith?"

"Yes," I said. Gaia's knowledge surprised me. Perhaps her long life and unusual history of acquaintances had given her more knowledge than I could imagine.

"She will be a tracker of unparalleled skill inside the Burning Lands. For her to locate a friend will be a simple matter of sniffing the air."

"And then what?" I asked.

"Then you hold on for dear life."

Gaia stepped from the lit path and the Abyss turned sideways. I almost retched at the sudden change in orientation. The stars and lights curved by in a violent, jagged pattern before coming to a jarring halt.

"I apologize, Damian. I should have warned you."

"No problem," I mumbled, leaning heavily on what seemed a very solid Bubbles. "Where are we?" I held my head and waited for the vertigo to pass.

"This is the Seal of Anubis, or what is left of it."

I took a deep breath and opened my eyes. What waited for me there was immeasurable in its size, and made even more surreal by the slight spin of my receding bout of vertigo. The Seal was a mountainous gray stone, with no beginning and no end. A pattern showed, carved deep across its face. Great lines of power sparked and leapt between enormous fractures.

My eyes trailed high, across Celtic knots and whorls and impossibly complex valleys and ribbons of stone. I froze. "It's a ward."

"Yes," Gaia said. "All of the great Seals are such."

"How do we get past it?"

"I would suggest riding the cu sith," Gaia said, as though it was the most obvious thing in the world.

"What?"

"They are not bound by the magics that separate the realms. Cu siths are not so unlike a dragon in that regard."

I glanced at Bubbles. Her head was almost up to my chest. I shrugged and stepped up beside her. Bubbles hunched down like she knew exactly what I needed. I threw my right leg over the cu sith and she stood up. I felt like I was six years old, playing with the neighbor's Mastiff.

"Mike said this would be unpleasant."

"Mike intended to send you through the Seal on a river of hellfire. This … well, this will still be unpleasant. Are you prepared?"

I nodded, trying not to ponder her words too closely.

"I hope we meet again, Damian Valdis Vesik. It has been a pleasure."

Yellow light exploded all around me and Bubbles barked, the sound like a cannon shot. By the time my vision cleared, we were only a few feet from the Seal, on a direct collision course.

I didn't have a chance to yell before we collided with it. My world turned to fire and pain. Bubbles's fur kept me grounded, my fingers wrapped up so tightly in her ruff I had a moment of fear that I was going to hurt her. When my skin started melting away to reveal the muscle and bones beneath, I wasn't so worried about the condition of the cu sith's fur anymore.

Inside the Seal, power filled me past the point of bursting. I was no longer myself. I belonged to the Seal, was part of it, set to burn and writhe and fuel that gateway until nothing but a memory of myself existed. Some part of my brain, a part that perhaps I ignored as best I could, struggled to find a way to harness the infinite force within that broken stone.

I reached up and extended a tiny bit of my aura into the hurricane of lightning and colors that stormed all around us. It was my power, the stuff of gravemakers, souls, and the dead. Something warm and wet slapped into my face and my aura snapped back into place with the shock of the impact.

Bubbles looked back at me, her tongue draped across her forehead, and I could have sworn she scowled at me.

I blinked, and the moment was gone. It was just me, riding a cu sith through the vastness of space until we smashed through the other side of the Seal.

✦   ✦   ✦

FOR A TIME, I couldn't tell if it was me screaming, or if the overwhelming chaos was that of the voices inside my skull. More than ever, it felt as though my head would break open and my life would end at any second. I ground my teeth together and focused on Vicky, focused on the mission, the only thing that mattered.

I glanced down at my arms when I finally managed to sit up, when the pain receded enough to think again. I expected burns and flayed skin and exposed bone, but it was only me, and my previously singed arm hair. The ground was a deep, sandy red, but that I only noticed in passing.

Bubbles chuffed beside me and nudged my back with her nose. I felt shaky as I started checking things over. I still had the backpack. The pepperbox was in its holster. I panicked for a moment when I couldn't find Gaia's hand. Bubbles shifted her bulk to survey the landscape, revealing the hand beneath her feet.

I sighed and stuffed the severed limb into my backpack beside the Book that Bleeds, casually noting that Frank's beef jerky had made the journey too. I zipped the backpack up and looked around.

I couldn't understand what I was looking at. Flickers of lost spirits shot across my vision, sprinting through rolling fields of what appeared to be wheat that shifted in a warm breeze. Two of the monstrous trolls we'd fought at Gettysburg sat peacefully among the hills, watching a strange trio of stubby reptilian armor-plated creatures waddle by.

The crimson sky raged above us, casting the brown vegetation into a bloody light. When the winds picked up, and the wheat shook in earnest, the entire field seemed to catch fire. The trolls stirred, both locking their gazes onto Bubbles and me, but they did not rise.

I started walking to the northeast. At least, I assumed it was the northeast if the sun followed the same path here, but it was impossible to know in this place. I looked down at Bubbles and froze mid-stride.

She sucked her tongue in and cocked her head to the side. Here in the Burning Lands, the bristly green fur I'd grown so accustomed to was red, flickering and fading as a great mane of fire flashed out behind her only to recede to a mere stripe of kindling flame running down her neck.

"What. The. Fuck."

Bubbles blew out a heavy breath and slammed into me with her hips. I reached a hand out on instinct alone and recoiled as my fingers touched the fires. But they didn't burn me. I looked at my palm, and then slowly reached back to the flaming cu sith. Her fur was soft and warm, nothing like the inferno it suggested.

She looked up at me. Her eyes had changed, now more like those of the Ghost Pack than anything else, all sunburst golds and reds. I took a deep breath and shook my head. "You'll know when you get there," I muttered. "Thanks, Cara. But what does a flaming Bubbles do for me?"

A mountain range loomed off to the east, and more trolls waited to the west. "Straight ahead it is," I said, leading the cu sith forward. I walked in silence for a while, Bubbles stomping on any small strange creature she didn't recognize. I didn't blame her. I didn't want to touch anything.

"What are we going to do, Bubbles? Where are we going to find Mike? Or Vicky, for that matter. Happy said they'd be here."

Bubbles barked, slammed her hips up against me, and started running.

"Dammit, Bubbles. Don't run!"

She wasn't really running. It was more of a fast trot, but at her current size I was damn near sprinting to keep up. The cu sith was kind enough to flatten a path through the wheat field, but that still didn't stop me from tripping and stumbling and generally cursing a lot.

Our path took us closer to a troll than I liked when we crested a small hill and rounded a large boulder on top of it. I glanced down. It wasn't a boulder. The troll's dead face sent shivers down my spine. Cracked flesh and empty eye sockets stared into the burning sky. Its body was gone, either eaten or carried away, or perhaps some other great beast had left the head here.

I looked back to our path, at the live troll as it twisted and leaned forward. Its flesh looked like that of a gravemaker—dark rotten bark coated its limbs. Its eyes were different than what we'd seen on our own plane, full of fire and smoke. A dim orange light pulsed inside the troll, flashing out through breaks in its skin like a visible heartbeat. The creature lost interest in us after a time, and turned back to whatever it had buried in the wheat.

"Bubbles, stop!"

The cu sith stopped so fast that I slammed into her furry butt before collapsing across her braided tail. She glanced back and then flopped onto the ground.

I raised my arm to take a closer look at the series of tiny cuts that had appeared. The wheat beneath my hand moved when the blood dripped onto it. Tiny silver filaments rose from miniature spikelets to absorb the small droplets. Each turned black when it touched the blood.

"Oh, that's creepy as hell." I hopped up onto the cu sith, and we rode into the north.

CHAPTER TWELVE

I T WAS HARD to tell how long I'd been riding on the cu sith's back, but by the time she stopped, I was ready to walk. Muscles I didn't know I had ached and my thighs screamed at me before my feet even hit the ground.

"You need a saddle," I said, scratching Bubbles behind her ears.

A thick forest of what looked like deciduous trees stood to the east. The canopy blended into the sky like an autumn forest at sunset, the bark shadowed and black. Everything here reminded me of the skin of a gravemaker, and it was utterly unnerving.

A different mountain range towered in the west now, casting jagged shadows in directions the sun should not have allowed. I wondered how much of what I was seeing was real, and how much was my brain trying to comprehend a different world.

Bubbles lowered her nose to the ground and began sniffing her way to the edge of a nearby cliff. I followed her, and nearly shouted at the sight that waited below us.

An ocean of fire stretched from one edge of the horizon to the other. Rolling tides of flame gently lapped at a black sand beachhead. It was a beautiful, impossible sight. The winds brought a comfortable warmth with them, and I didn't look away until Bubbles barked and bounced on her hind legs. She took off at a sprint toward the mountains. I grumbled and started jogging behind her.

Wheat sprang up behind Bubbles, growing in clumps with her every footfall, leaving a trail of paw-sized vegetation. By the time I reached the odd formations, they had grown up to my waist. The blasted things cut me where my skin was exposed and started lapping at the blood. That only lasted about thirty seconds before I got pissed and raised my arm.

"*Modus Ignatto!*" Raw power—far more concentrated than the ley lines I was accustomed to—lanced through me and I gasped. A sideways cyclone of fire shot forward until I strangled the flow and cut the incantation short, leaving black smoke to curl through the air. "What in the hell?"

The wheat expanded, devouring every last bit of heat and flame, chasing the wisps of smoke into the air. The stalks grew together, twisting as they bound to one another until the thinnest growth was as thick as a tree. The surface hardened into a bark-like substance.

"Son of a bitch," I snarled, glancing behind me at the distant forest. "They're like saplings."

The forest had spread at least a mile to the south. To the north, only a tiny walkway remained, separating the forest from the fiery ocean below and creating a barrier between Bubbles and me. I groaned and made my way toward the narrow path.

I stood at the precipice. I could either inch along the chasm that would surely be the death of me if I fell, or I could put a hand on the trees that liked to drink my blood. The ridged back of some great beast lingered on the surface below before diving back into the sea of flames.

I shivered and looked back to the forest. "Gloves. Next time I'm packing gloves."

A quarter mile down the narrow path, Bubbles waited. She sniffed at the trees and then backed away. I knew how she felt. I kept my eyes on Bubbles and walked forward at a slightly faster pace than I thought sane.

Twice I had to reach out and balance myself on a tree. I didn't feel any cuts or burns or surprising pulls on my aura. Maybe the forest wasn't so bad. Maybe it was just the wheat. Maybe—

The branch came out of nowhere.

I flailed my arms like a windmill, like I was stuck in some ridiculous black and white cartoon world. Panic could make you do stupid and useless things. The thought of landing in that rolling sea of fire cut through the thunder of my heartbeat. I grabbed onto the branch, realizing that was at least a safer gamble than cliff diving into an inferno.

The branch thickened and jerked into the air, pulling me toward the forest. I didn't know why. I didn't know what might be waiting between those black trunks and crimson leaves, but I didn't hold on long enough to find out.

I released the tree and the momentum slammed me into one of the outside trunks. I scrambled up into a run, Bubbles barking at me like some furry, flaming personal trainer. Another branch moved, and it threatened to sweep me off the cliff. A quick hop brought me past it before the next tried to flatten me with a downward strike. I guessed the damn trees weren't picky about getting their blood from a pancake on the ground.

The focus came into my hand. I summoned a blazing golden soulsword and swung it in one awkward movement. The voices crashed through my head for the first time since I'd entered the Burning Lands. A million souls that, until then, I had forgotten were even there. Had they been quiet? Or had I grown accustomed to them? I didn't know, but the sound grew into an overwhelming cacophony until I let the soulsword fade.

Only silence remained, and the nearby huff of a cu sith.

I took the few last steps to meet up with Bubbles as something rumbled and crashed behind me. I turned to watch bloodied branches collapse along a third of the trail, sheared off at a forty-five degree angle that had taken the tops of the trees with them.

It didn't make any sense. The soulsword wasn't long enough to strike like that, but the gash in the tree line was a good twenty-five feet deep, and may have gone further if not for clearing the canopy. I looked down at the hilt that ended in two quatrefoils and frowned before tucking it back into my belt.

In the distance, a rocky mountain vista waited, full of jagged stones and shadows that could hide anything. A few souls ran through the fields, dodging the occasional troll. The giants kept to themselves, which made me question what had motivated them in Gettysburg.

Ahead, a cluster of golden light waited near a dark opening in a cliffside. I squinted, trying to make out more detail, but I could see little more than the humanoid shape of the lights.

My arm burned, and I glanced down to find it bleeding. It wasn't the cuts that burned so badly—they were suspiciously numb—it was the gentle curve of the pack mark on my forearm. It glowed golden, brightening and dimming with my heartbeat.

"Odd …"

Bubbles bumped me with her hip. I looked up just as the branch hit me square in the forehead.

✦   ✦   ✦

THERE ARE HEADACHES, and then there are "a sentient tree smashed my head with a log" headaches. I hoped to never have the latter again.

I knew I was in the Burning Lands when I opened my eyes, so at least my mental faculties hadn't been shaken up too bad. People shouted nearby, and it made my head feel like a ripe melon, ready to split at a moment's notice.

"Quiet," I muttered into the sandy dirt, but the word came out slurred and mangled. It was only then I realized I was lying on my side in the shadow of the mountains I'd seen earlier. Golden lights waited nearby. Maybe that hit *had* jumbled my brain a bit. I touched my forehead.

By the time I had enough self-awareness to roll over, a growling werewolf waited above me, thin and golden and filled with a startling promise of violence.

"Look what decided to join us," the wolf snarled. He punched me, and my head rebounded off the ground, sending my vision into a blur of stars and darkness. I yelped at the pain and almost puked.

I tried to say something over the ringing in my ears, but squinting at the godawful lights was all I could do.

"Jimmy!" someone shouted.

My vision cleared enough to see Vicky leap forward and

kick the werewolf so hard that the stone cliff cracked behind him. "Back off, wolf. You are nothing here."

"Vicky?" I asked. "Bubbles, we found Vicky!" I winced at the sound of my own voice.

A golden arm reached down and picked me up. "How was the journey? You don't sound good."

I recognized the voice as the world tilted and nausea struck again. I blinked and squinted and focused on Carter's golden eyes. Maggie stood behind him, a completely inappropriate grin on her face.

"What has you so happy?" I half slurred, half whispered.

"You can take a punch," she said.

I gave her a snort of a laugh and stretched my back, regretting the movement immediately.

"How did I get here?" I asked, looking back at the distant forest.

"Bubbles dragged you most of the way here," Carter said. "Maggie carried you the rest."

I closed my eyes and raised my eyebrows, testing my headache. "Thank you." I found Bubbles staring up at me when I cracked my eyelids open again. "Thanks, pooch." Her tongue snapped out and ran down her muzzle.

"Welcome to the Ghost Pack," Carter said with a sweeping gesture around the small group.

Some of them looked unimpressed, but Carter and Maggie were the only ones I really knew. Jimmy had died shortly after I'd met him. I hadn't realized he still hated me so thoroughly.

My gaze froze when it came to a bulky wolf with an odd splotchy covering. My bell had definitely been rung. It took a moment to realize it wasn't a wolf at all, but a ghost panda.

"Happy?" My legs wobbled a bit and I decided to sit down before my balance failed me.

The panda snorted and settled onto a grassy patch of dirt. Bubbles trotted over and flopped down beside the bear.

An even stranger creature shuffled up from the shadows. It looked familiar somehow, but it wasn't until its horns caught the unmoving sunlight that I realized why. It flexed a pair of leathery wings, and then took a knee in front of Carter.

It could have been Mike the Demon's little brother—not in his human form, but in the brain-searing incarnation I'd seen only a handful of times.

"What news?" Carter asked.

"The Smith has been sighted outside of the fifth fortress. I have delivered your message."

"Thank you, Vala."

"Free my brother, Great Wolf, and I will serve your allies for all time."

"It will be done," Carter said.

"Then I swear upon the noble Ronwe, the words I have spoken are truth." The demon stood and bowed to Carter before walking into the shadows of the mountain.

I stared after the creature. Ronwe was a name I knew. Could there be more than one? Or could this be the demon that owed Zola?

"Damian?"

I looked at Carter, and he almost flinched.

"Are you well?"

"I've been better," I said, frowning at the slurred speech. "I probably have about fifty concussions after the morning I've had."

"Vicky can tend to that," Maggie said, patting my arm.

"What do you mean?" I asked, honestly wondering what they expected Vicky to do. Something tugged on my shirt and I turned to find Vicky standing beside me. "Hey, kiddo."

"Give me your head."

"What?" I asked, raising my eyebrows. She looked normal here. The black streaks on her face were gone. I wasn't sure if that was good or not.

"Sit down so I can reach your head." I glanced at Carter, and when he didn't protest, I sat down on a somewhat flat boulder.

She laid a hand on my cheek. It felt warm, and then cold, and then intensely hot.

"What are you doing?"

"You're bleeding," she said. "In your head."

"I'm fine. It's just a headache."

Vicky closed her eyes, and yellow light exploded from her hands. I felt a brief, sharp pain, like an icepick cutting through my eye, but by the time I could react, it was gone. And my headache was gone. And so was the odd fuzz around everything.

"The hell?" I said.

"Fairies aren't the only creatures able to heal," Carter said. "I was as surprised as you."

I stood up and stretched. "She's not a creature."

"What?" Carter asked. "No, that's not what I meant." He frowned and turned to the three wolves I didn't know. "Go to the fourth fortress. If Vala has betrayed us, they'll come through the gateway. Summon Vicky if the need arises."

"Thy will is done," said the tallest of the three wolves. He was skinny for a wolf, though I was sure he'd be bulky if he shifted. He placed a hand over his heart and bowed. If I had to guess, he was a very old ghost.

Carter watched them go. "I trust Vala in most things. He's proved useful in the past, but we're not taking any more risks than we have to today."

I still didn't like what Carter had said, calling Vicky a creature.

"It's okay," Vicky said, patting my wrist. "I know what I am. What are we doing now?"

Carter looked to the south. "We make for the fifth fortress."

CHAPTER THIRTEEN

"OKAY," I SAID. "Let me get this right. There's a fortress between each circle? And each circle is like its own country?"

"I thought Mike had already told you these things," Carter said, gravel crunching beneath his boot on the rocky path we'd taken into the mountains. Here, he was as corporeal as I was.

"No, not really. I haven't talked to Mike since Gettysburg."

Something stirred in the mountain cliffs. I looked up, trying to see what crashed and slid along the dark stone above us. Carter and Maggie marched on, their indifference to the sounds reassuring on some level. Happy and Vicky trailed behind us with Bubbles. The cu sith kept staring at Jimmy. He looked uncomfortable, and I kind of liked that.

"Where are we, exactly?" I asked.

"A few miles from the fifth fortress," Maggie said, "in the nameless mountains."

The scuffling sounded above us again. I studied the ridge of the nearest cliff, and then the next, but saw nothing. "What *is* that?"

"What?" Carter asked.

"Don't you hear it? Something's following us from above."

"Something will always be following you in the Burning Lands," Carter said. "It's the nature of this place."

His confidence and lack of concern didn't do a damn thing to reassure me after that statement. He'd spent more time in the Burning Lands than I had, by any measure, but this didn't feel right. Every step we took, the walls felt closer on either side of the path.

I glanced behind us. It wasn't my imagination. We all walked single file. More sounds whispered down the stones. The air wavered and then stabilized again, not fifteen feet above my head.

"Did you see that?" I said.

"Damian's right," Maggie said, squinting at the burning sky. "Something is following us."

Carter's gaze roved across the path. "Not much room to move here. I hope you're wrong, but make ready."

We continued on for another fifteen minutes, until I could see a widening in the path up ahead. Far in the distance stood a great stone wall, its center essentially a castle, but its scale beyond comprehension. The wall rose into the air like a skyscraper. Turrets and parapets shot out in random places, stacked onto rectangular sections of mismatched stone, giving the entire structure a weird presence.

"Carter," a voice hissed on the wind.

The werewolf froze and studied the landscape before him.

More shuffling echoed around us, and whatever had made the noise before had been joined by several more.

"You were banished from this place," the airy voice whispered. "To come here is to break the truce."

"We only need the Smith," Carter said. "We were told he was at the fifth fortress."

Silence was the only response.

"Let us pass, Servant of Berith. Let us take our friend from your lands."

"You expect me to bow?" the voice said. "To give in to your demands because you come with the favor of Hephaestus?"

"No," Carter said. "Stand to the side. There is no need for conflict this day."

"He abandoned us to our fate before the second civilization rose across the Burning Sea." The voice cracked into a savage shout. "He is no idol of Berith! Kill them!"

The pepperbox was already in my hand. I tried to turn, to make sure Vicky was okay, but I only cracked my elbow on the stone cliff.

A nightmare threw itself over the edge of the cliff above us.

Silver fangs flashed crimson in the light of the sun. It had horns like Vala had, but these were not curved. They were long and sleek and gleamed like the tip of a sword. *He's going to impale me with those things.* The demon lowered its head before the thought was complete.

My finger moved from the first trigger to the second. All six barrels of the pepperbox fired at once. The horns shattered like brittle iron, and the demon screamed as it crashed into me. The impact took the breath from my lungs. A sharp rock cut into my back as I bounced off the narrow canyon's wall.

The demon wasted no time. It struck out at me before we'd regained our feet. I barely dodged the blow. It wasn't as fast as a vampire, but it was faster than *I* could move.

Some part of me knew there were more creatures attacking our group, but if I turned away for even a moment, the talons on the thing's hand could gut me. I snapped a precise kick at the demon's head, and it batted my foot away effortlessly.

I raised my left hand. *"Pulsatto!"* The incantation caught the demon in the chest, and he doubled over, wings snapping out only to smash themselves on the stone walls. I flipped the pepperbox and grabbed it by the barrel, bringing it down as hard as I could on the thin bones of the demon's wing.

The thing screamed as its body cracked beneath the blow. The wing's gray membrane slackened, and thick blood leaked from the wound.

It could bleed.

It could die.

"Modus Glaciatto!"

Shards of ice riddled the demon. My aim wasn't perfect, and I saw one of the werewolves flinch when the dagger-like hail cut into its hide. I couldn't focus on the wolves. They remained golden lights in my periphery as I dodged a blow from the wounded demon.

Its leg bent at an impossible angle. I braced for the impact as best I could, but the sweeping blow caught my left arm and part of a rib. Crashing into the side of the canyon didn't soften the blow.

The next attack came on the heels of the first.

"Impadda!" The shield formed slowly—the odd variances in the magic here coming at the worst possible times—but it still allowed me to deflect the second kick. The demon stumbled, and I hit it with another ice incantation before screaming *"Modus Pulsatto!"*

The demon screeched as it dug its talons into the sides of the canyon. Its backward momentum stopped. It launched at me again. For every blow I evaded, it landed two. Even glancing blows sent a world of pain into my limbs. I watched the creature spiral off my shield into a tight, spinning sweep. It caught my ankle and slammed my head into the rocks.

The demon leapt, a wicked-looking blade extended for a killing blow.

Vicky hurdled over me as a soulsword solid enough to be the sun erupted from her fist. She bounced from one wall of the canyon to the next, each movement ending with a severed piece of the demon flopping off in a random direction. Blood sprayed across us both as the creature crashed to the earth beside me, a confused look etched across its face.

I slammed a speed loader home and fired two quick shots into the demon's head. It didn't move again.

I crawled to my knees, wincing at a pain in my wrist that told me it was likely broken. Vicky bounded over the were-wolves, and I could only stare.

Gray bodies split open and spilled their lives upon the stone. Vicky leapt from wall to wall, a spinning ball of death to everything around her. Heads fell to the earth before the creatures so much as knew they were dead.

The demons' bodies tumbled, twitched, and collapsed. The next died before the first fell. Vicky was silent, the click of her boots on rock louder than anything save the Ghost Pack's war cries.

By the time she slipped past Maggie, the rest of the demons were running for their lives. The retreating adversaries cast glances over their shoulders, while the child who would become the Destroyer stood watch. Vicky held up a soulsword and pointed it at the farthest creature.

A blade of light a quarter mile long snapped out of her fist, and the demon exploded in a distant puff of blood and gore.

Vicky calmly repeated the process, annihilating every creature that had dared to attack us one after another.

"Pathetic," she snarled before turning back to us.

It was perhaps that moment when I truly understood what Vicky could become. If we didn't free her, she'd become the Destroyer. She'd have the power of soularts and a well of darkness to draw from, older than history itself.

She stopped at each wolf, asking if they needed any assistance or healing. There I saw the little ghost girl I'd come to care for. A tenderness lived in those tiny golden flashes of healing. Vicky gently lifted Jimmy's arm, turning his palm over before healing a long gash that bled luminescent.

It wasn't long before she got to me.

"Nice work, kiddo."

"That?" she asked as she glanced over her shoulder. "Those are the foolish demons from the third circle. They don't know their place."

"I mean the healing."

"Oh!" She smiled. "It's a neat trick, right?" She poked at my ribs, and I winced at the last touch. "That one's cracked. This is going to hurt."

"Doesn't it always?" I said. The question cut off in a grunt when the cracked bones in my chest regenerated in a burst of healing light. Vicky moved on to my wrist and forearm.

"You did good for such tight quarters," Carter said as he leaned onto the canyon wall beside Vicky.

I rubbed at my wrist and looked up at the wolf. "Is that a common thing?"

"The attack?" Carter asked. "We run into small ambushes fairly often."

Maggie stepped up next to him. "Do you need to rest? This trail will be safe with the demons dispatched."

I didn't much feel like camping out in the small puddles and pools of blood. When I looked for the nearest demon, it was gone. "What?" I said, looking around the canyon. "They're all gone. Are they still alive?"

"In a sense, I suppose," Carter said. "Mike can explain it better."

I took a step forward and my leg cramped. I winced and looked at Maggie. "Maybe just a minute."

She nodded. "Take your time. You'll need to be mobile if we get hit again."

Footsteps sounded behind me and my heart leapt into my throat. A quick glance showed me Happy in his human form. The old samurai rounded the bend in the canyon, trailed closely by Bubbles.

"Who the hell is that?" Jimmy asked.

"It's Happy," Carter said.

"The panda bear?" Jimmy said, his voice rising. "You were serious? He's a shapeshifter?"

"My name is Shiawase." His hand rested on the hilt of his sword. A leather guard—one that did not seem to fit with his samurai armor—graced his upper arm. When he shifted his shoulder, I could see the panda stitched into the black band.

"Nice panda," Vicky said.

I raised my eyebrows at her rather cutting sarcasm. Shiawase laid a finger across his lips and smiled. Vicky quieted, but a wide grin lit her face.

Carter eyed them both and then looked down at the cu sith. "How did she do?"

"Bubbles destroyed their flanking maneuver the instant they entered the canyon," Shiawase said. "She is a beast."

"Good," Carter said. "That's very good."

Bubbles scrunched her face up and sniffed before her tongue rolled out and splatted on the ground.

"Terrifying," I said flatly.

Bubbles sucked in her tongue and chuffed at me, wiggling her way past Shiawase before settling in next to me. I scratched at her ruff.

"The fire doesn't burn you?" Jimmy asked.

I glanced down at the flame-like fur running all around Bubbles. "Doesn't seem to. I actually rode on her back most of the way here."

"Like a panda," Vicky said.

Shiawase sighed.

I flashed the samurai a grin. "Yes, exactly like a panda. So noble a steed was never had before, in legend nor in—"

"Damian," Shiawase said with a put-upon look. "Shut up."

Maggie snorted a laugh. "He's only saying what we all wanted to say."

Vicky crossed her legs and settled onto the rock beside me. "Why didn't you use a sword when the demons attacked?"

I slid my backpack off and rooted through it for some jerky and a Frappuccino. "I did on the other side of the forest. My soulsword was as long as the ones you used to kill those running demons. I didn't want to risk hitting you or one of the wolves in the canyon."

She nodded. "You're pulling too much energy. Pull less, except when you want to stick something at a distance. All magic works differently here."

Carter and the other wolves and the samurai made for the end of the canyon while I rested. Shiawase pointed into the distance, but I couldn't make out what they were saying.

Vicky rearranged herself beside me. "Why did you save me?"

A wind howled in the distance, roaring ever louder as it ripped through the canyon. I waited for the sound to pass while Vicky kicked at the stone with her heels.

"I didn't save you, kiddo."

She frowned. "You took me to Happy. He's the best friend I ever had."

"He's a good bear. Samurai. Whatever."

Vicky smiled and leaned back against the jagged rocks. "You killed the last Destroyer. Why save me?"

"You aren't the Destroyer."

Silence greeted my words and Vicky fell still. "You know that's not true. I can hear her talking sometimes. I don't … I don't think I can win, Damian."

I ground my teeth together. "You don't have to win, kiddo. You just have to hold on while I kill some things."

"You're good at that."

I didn't argue with her as the wolves made their way back to us. I popped a piece of salty beef into my mouth and chewed. It was tender, and then it turned into an inferno that made my eyes water. "That's good."

"Damian," Carter said, "you're crying."

"Spicy," I choked out as I held up the bag.

Carter took a small piece. I thought he was going to sniff at it before he flinched away. "Gods!" He dropped it back into the bag. "What in the hell is on that?"

"Spice." I unscrewed the lid on the Frappuccino and took a deep drink. I flexed my leg and wrist, testing them out after Vicky's healing. I felt almost whole again, normal, except for the crimson sky and eerie shadows of the canyon.

I zipped the jerky closed and stuffed it back into the pack. "Where to now?"

Carter turned and pointed to the massive structure closer to the horizon. "We make for the fifth fortress, and hope Mike is still there."

CHAPTER FOURTEEN

EVEN AT A great distance, I'd known the fifth fortress was huge, but standing in front of it, my jaw dropped.

Stone watchtowers that must have been half a mile high soared into the air and those were in turn dwarfed by spindly black obelisks. It was an unfathomable, impossible structure. Its own weight should have pulled it to the ground, and yet here it stood.

A great black metal gate—a lattice of darkness with a darker promise for any who would face it—blocked our path. Power sparked through the patterns, and I had little doubt of its intent.

"Let me guess," I said. "You touch it and you die."

Carter let out a slow laugh. "You touch it and it paralyzes you so something else can come and claim you."

"Like I said, you touch it and you die." My eyes traced the wall. Carved wards glowed every few feet. The entire structure surged with magic, but each ward lived on its own. One could be severed, leaving the rest intact. "How do we get past that?"

"We wait until Mike comes out."

"I can go," Shiawase said. "The gate will not—"

Vicky's scream cut the samurai off. I spun to face her, in time to see her collapse onto the gravel.

"Vicky!" I slid up next to her shaking form and turned her

over. I almost jumped away. Black streaks marred her face. They followed her veins and arteries like an infection, fracturing off into a web of capillaries.

When she spoke, it was with the voice of a devil. "What now, Anubis-son? What now when the Destroyer lays claim to your own?" Her face curled into a vicious smile, and a bellowing laugh tore through the air.

"No more time," I said, turning to the fortress gate and drawing the focus.

"Damian, no!" Maggie shouted. "Breaking down a gate would be a declaration of war against the inner circles."

I glanced back at Vicky's twitching body. "They already declared war."

I channeled and slashed with the pillar of golden fire that raged from the focus. The gate collapsed, and the wall behind it, and the statue behind that.

"They're coming," that terrible voice said. "You cannot stop them."

I raised my right arm and reached for the deadliest power I could, my fingers curled into a claw for the Hand of Anubis, twisted into my own design. I froze and sucked in a breath. When my power reached out for the dead and the gravemakers, they were everywhere. They were everything. The world was mine.

"Damian?" Maggie whispered, taking a step away. "What is that?"

"Stay behind me." I hooked the focus into my belt and raised my left arm. "We're going through."

The screams came first, guttural, fierce cries that spoke of the deadly things closing on us. I felt the chaff of a gravemaker licking at my fingertips, and I stepped forward. The earth rose in a black wave around me, and I passed through the gate.

Power crackled from the broken latticework, but the shadowy mass around me devoured it. The voices inside my head became one, with one purpose. The demons rose up in black waves, foot soldiers sprinting forward with swords and flaming warhammers, while winged attackers took to the sky as I stepped through the gate. The enclosed stone courtyard grew thick with the enemy.

I smiled and closed my fists. The masonry erupted before the demons, and two of the Hand of Anubis rose to greet them. It was not the decayed bark-like debris I was so used to seeing that burst from the stone floor; it was sleek obsidian darkness. Bodies crunched and collapsed. Sickening little pops echoed through the wide hall as the demons were smashed against the floor.

The dead were in the walls, in the floors, and in the very air around me. I released the Hand of Anubis and swiped laterally with my arm. The fortress bent to my will. Stone became blades, lancing out to impale the airborne demons that had dodged the hands.

It left a tangled web of spikes and bodies hanging in the hall, some five feet above my head, and some so high they were lost in the shadowed recesses above. But I knew they were there. I could feel them with every fiber of my being.

As the stone grew thick with the demons' blood, their charge faltered. They weren't prepared for resistance like this. They weren't prepared for me. The first turned to run, and the rest followed, peeling away from the assault.

I considered killing them, but letting them live would

spread word of the power they witnessed here. What creature would want to engage with a being that could turn their own walls against them?

As the last of the demons escaped, I released the hold I'd kept on the world around me. My mind exploded into the cries of a million lost souls when the power fled. It felt as though my skull would burst, but I could scarcely remember where I was. I knew I'd fallen to my knees, but the cries tore through my thoughts, burying my awareness in a tidal wave of anguish.

The world changed from red to golden to black. Even blinded, unable to see anything but the shadows and stars around me, I heard the screams.

✦   ✦   ✦

A DEEP VOICE scratched at my awareness. I knew that voice, but I didn't think it could be him. We hadn't found him.

"And then he collapsed?"

I pried my eyes open when someone turned my head.

"Good morning, necromancer," Mike the demon said. "You made quite a mess of the gate."

"They didn't want to buy my cookies," I grumbled.

Mike laughed and looked at someone behind me. "I suspect he's fine. He likely didn't know this plane is built from dead things."

I pushed myself into a sitting position and groaned before cradling my head in my hands. Everything smelled like freshly churned earth and burned flesh. I'd apparently passed out on my backpack, and now my spine felt like a pretzel.

"I should have brought pretzels."

Something trilled and chittered nearby.

"He's okay?" Vicky asked. I looked up and found Vicky and Happy, but the wolves were nowhere in sight.

"As fine as he can be, I suppose," Mike said.

"Where are the wolves?" I asked.

"You left them behind," Vicky said. "Happy could barely keep up with you."

"What do you mean? I barely took three steps past the gate."

"No," Mike said. "You should perhaps look back at your path." He pointed to a fortress, far in the distance. I realized I was sitting on grass, and not stone.

"What the hell?"

I looked up at Mike, half expecting to see the terrifying creature I'd once glimpsed in a burst of flame. He still looked like himself, bulky and thick, as though he could crush stone in his bare hands. The hammer hung at his waist, suspended by the braided leather of his belt.

The chittering sounded again, and I glanced at the ground. "Jasper?" I said, eyeing the rolling ball of gray fluff around Mike's feet.

Jasper trilled and swelled before flowing toward me, flashing his silver dagger-like teeth in the crimson light of the plain. He spiraled around my bent leg before shooting up my back and settling on my shoulder with a puff.

I reached up and scratched him between his solid black eyes. "I thought you were keeping watch over Sam."

A vision of Gettysburg flashed through my mind. A tentacle wrapped around Sam, threatening to crush her. Jasper carried the Leviathan away, shredding it and burning it so it could never harm anyone again. I shivered as the vision faded.

"Welcome to the Burning Lands," Mike said. "What in the hell is in your backpack, Damian?"

I winced as I pulled my arm out of the strap and swung the pack around. Jasper chittered and hopped over the quickly moving strap. "Beef jerky. You want some?" I unzipped the pouch on the front and pulled out some of Frank's beef jerky.

Mike slowly raised one of his eyebrows.

"Oh," I said, stuffing the jerky back into the pack. I opened the largest compartment and slid out the Book that Bleeds. "It could help." My eyes flicked to Vicky and back.

Mike frowned. "That is the Book of the Dead. Lost for millennia. Not seen since the fall of Atlantis, and even then, it was only a rumor. How do you have this?"

There were few people I trusted more than Mike the Demon, but I still hesitated to tell him where it had come from. "Koda," I said quietly, after a time. "It was hidden within the Black Book. It only needed the key to open it."

Mike looked back at the trail behind us. "That's where I've seen your attack before. Long ago it was called the Blades of Ares, wielded by gods and madmen."

I sighed. "I guess I'm a little bit of both."

"Vicky," Mike said, turning to face the ghost. "Go back to Carter and lead him to us."

She nodded and hopped up on Happy's back, glancing back at me once before the bear trundled off through the plains.

Mike settled onto the ground beside me once Vicky and the ghost panda vanished against the shadows of the distant fortress. "Her time grows short, Damian. Once the Destroyer has risen, our mission will change."

Jasper trilled and his gray fluff flashed blood red.

I eyed the dragon before turning back to Mike. "I found some passages on Timewalkers that are promising."

"Hmm." Mike drummed his fingers on the head of the Smith's Hammer. "Timewalkers are not bound to any particular plane. It is an interesting thought, but we've lost months already."

"We just unlocked the Book that Bleeds, Mike. Every time I look at it I find something new. It's like the words didn't exist before."

"I've heard much the same from the Old Man and Homer."

Knowing the Old Man had some knowledge of the book didn't surprise me. He'd been to Atlantis and wandered the halls of the library at Alexandria. "Homer?"

"The old Greek poet," Mike said as he spun a blade of grass between his thumb and forefinger.

I threw my hands up in the air. "Sure, why the fuck not? You knew Homer. Of course you did."

Mike didn't so much as twitch. He held my gaze until I looked away. Maybe I was being a tad bit dramatic.

"Did Koda tell you of the Demon's Sacrifice?"

"The what?"

A sad smile crossed Mike's face, and a black shadow flickered to life beside him. The little necromancer coalesced.

"No! That is not for his ears."

"It is not our decision, my love." Mike reached out and the ghost took his hand.

"You aren't corporeal here? But the werewolves …"

"The werewolves are bonded to you, and the Pack feeds them power through your bonds." The little necromancer wrung her hands together. "Damian, Hugh asked me not to tell you, but you're weakening the River Pack."

"What?" I looked from Mike to the little necromancer and back. *"What?"*

Jasper's dust-bunny-like texture expanded and contracted as he rolled around my backpack. He finally settled onto my knee, and I absently scratched his back.

"Not now," Mike said with a brief shake of his head. "Your Timewalker idea is a noble one, but I fear we don't have the time to perfect it."

"Vicky will die without a Timewalker bond if her devil dies," I said.

"How do you know that?" The little necromancer asked. "Most of what we know about demons is theory."

"It's in the book." I ran my fingers over the gory cover. The blood didn't flow freely here in the Burning Lands, but its blood was still slick and visible.

I let my aura expand until it brushed against the little necromancer's aura. She flared into golden light, and Mike stared.

"You'll need Ward," she said, running her fingers over her forearm. "He may be the only one left who remembers how to make the knot."

Mike stood up and wrapped his arms around her.

"I know," I said. "Nixie is already looking for him. If she doesn't have any luck, we may have to go to Falias. But if that's not the answer … what's the Demon's Sacrifice?"

"It is an old magic," Mike said. "It is death and soularts and all the things one usually thinks of when discussing necromancers."

"Dark necromancers," I muttered. But what necromancer was darker than me now? I had a million souls bound to me. I ran my hand over the short blades of grass, half expecting them to wither and die at my touch. It didn't matter now. All that mattered was stopping Prosperine.

"Stop," the little necromancer said. "You've done more good in this world than most people could do in ten lifetimes. Listen to Mike if you want to save that girl."

I frowned and then nodded, turning my attention back to Mike.

"Even should you succeed in killing her devil, in bringing an end to the tyranny of Prosperine, another devil can take her."

His words hit me like I'd been stabbed in the heart. "What?"

"The Seal is broken, and that changes the rules of what can and cannot be severed in this place. You cannot kill all of the devils, so you need to change the very fabric of their existence."

"You mean we need to fix the Seal?"

Mike narrowed his eyes before shaking his head. "I don't believe that would be enough. It may be, for a time, but Philip managed to bring Propserine onto your plane through the Seal."

Mike was right, and I knew it. "What can I do then? You're saying I could kill Prosperine, but Vicky could still become the Destroyer?"

"No, if you kill Prosperine, the Destroyer will be no more. That does not mean one of the other devils would not jump at a free vessel. There are worse things in the Burning Lands than the Destroyer."

"You know the dark-touched have already fled this place," the little necromancer said. "There are some left behind, certainly, but most are already on your plane. Their master dwells in the Burning Lands, and she is a slumbering devil. She could possess Vicky, or one of the Summoners, or even the fire demons."

I ground my teeth together. "Why didn't you tell me this before?" I snapped.

"We didn't know," Mike said. "It's taken months of … of research in the Burning Lands."

I frowned at Mike the Demon. "Research?"

"We've been threatening the people who would know," the little necromancer said. "Sometimes it's the only way in this place."

"In this hell?" I said.

Mike slowly shook his head. "This is not the Hell of human religions. I think you know that. The demons here draw power from emotion, and they are empowered by suffering."

"Fuck, Mike. That pretty much sounds like a hell to me."

"It is not so unlike your government, Damian. Men horde power and goods and lord over the people they see as less than themselves. It may be a different kind of power here, but the principle is the same."

"That's … I don't know what to say to that."

"You'll see more of it as we move through the circles, and you'll see the worst the Burning Lands has to offer when we reach the tenth at the center of the realm."

"Tell him about the Demon's Sacrifice."

Mike glanced at the little necromancer and held her gaze. She didn't look away until he sighed and said, "So be it. This plane is built on rules, not unlike your own, but those rules were forged by ancient creatures. Changing them would be much like altering the ley lines in your own realm so no fairy could use them."

"That's impossible."

Mike gave me a half smile. "Damian, this plane was designed by one of the first dead gods, a predecessor even to the creature you know as Hades. Your powers can affect anything here. It's how you tore through the fortress and destroyed half a regiment of demons."

"How many?" I said, raising my eyebrows. "I remember the wave, and the spikes, but how many demons were there?"

"Our best guess is five hundred," Mike said.

"Maybe a bit less," the little necromancer said, "but not by much."

"How do I not remember that?"

Mike ignored me. "To answer the more pressing question, the Demon's Sacrifice is a soulart performed using willing souls. It only works with those who volunteer, and the belief is that an unwilling soul cannot be destroyed entirely."

I stared at Mike, expecting some ominous drumbeat to sound a march around his words. "What do you mean? I have to destroy a willing soul to even try the incantation?"

"Yes."

"And where do I find a willing soul?"

"You ask them," Mike said quietly. He turned his gaze back toward the fortress.

I followed his line of sight. Vicky led Carter and Maggie and Jimmy toward us in the distance. A fiery Bubbles pranced beside them. I cursed under my breath. "No."

"It is hidden within the cover of the Book that Bleeds, or so it was some three thousand years past. No one has had the complete book in their possession since, so it should still be locked away. You need not decide this moment, Damian, but in the end it may be your only choice."

CHAPTER FIFTEEN

"**W**E NEED TO make camp," Mike said. "The hour grows late, and the Burning Lands will soon earn their name in kind."

"Where should we go?" Maggie asked. "Our favorite necromancer turned the fifth fortress into a burial ground." She jabbed me in the ribs.

"Ha," I said.

"Then we travel to the sixth," Mike said.

"What do you mean the Burning Lands will earn their name?" I asked. "And the sun is still in the same spot. How do you know it's late?"

Mike pointed toward the disc in the crimson sky. "The light dims, and soon the black sun will be upon us."

I glanced up and my neck twitched involuntarily. Half the bloody sun was covered in darkness. "What happens?"

Carter started forward at a quick marching pace. "You meet the dark-touched, and you understand how the breaking of the Seal was so bad a thing."

Bubbles chuffed and head-butted my lower back, propelling me forward to match Carter's pace.

"I thought the dark-touched had already crossed over onto our plane," I said, stumbling as Jasper swirled around my legs before coming to a stop on my shoulder. He made a series of clicking sounds before stilling.

"Several of them did," Carter said. "We've still found a few here. They mostly stay inside the tenth circle with the would-be rulers of the Burning Lands."

"I thought there were only nine circles in Hell," I said.

Mike cast me a thin smile over his shoulder. "I already told you this isn't the metaphorical Hell of any human religion."

A trio of golden souls flashed into being before vanishing over a hill with shouts and whoops.

"Who are they?" I asked.

"*What* they are is more important," Maggie said. "They are free souls, sent hunting those who suffer."

"They don't hunt them," Jimmy said, breaking his silence. "They track them and free them."

"And they're corporeal? They weren't part of the Pack, were they?"

"That was me," said a firm voice.

I looked up at Vicky as she swayed on Happy's back. "You did that?"

She nodded. "We needed allies."

It sounded so simple, coming from Vicky. We needed allies, so we what? Created them? Made the freed souls corporeal? Her powers had developed in ways I could never have imagined. It shouldn't have surprised me. She'd been thriving in this place, a realm I could scarcely understand, even with a fire demon at my side.

We walked in silence for a while, Jasper hopping from my shoulder to Mike's and back again. I never saw him take to the wolves. If Mike or I weren't close, he'd roll along the ground beside Happy and Vicky.

"How far is the next fortress?" I asked, looking up at the thin disc of the red sun that remained.

"It is farther than we can walk before darkness reaches us. We make for the Jaws."

"That doesn't really answer my question," I muttered. "And what are the Jaws?"

"A great jagged chasm," Mike said. "There are fingers of earth that stretch out above the cliffs. They are easily defended, which makes them a prime choice for our camp."

We still didn't have much in the way of food, or water, for that matter. I didn't know if camping without those things was such a great idea. "Mike, what about water? I didn't bring any."

"I am quite sure I told you the story of water in the Burning Lands," the demon said. "When the sun darkens, the storms will begin. It may be harder to find food if your body rejects the fruit of this plane. I suppose we will know soon enough."

I wasn't sure if I wanted to know what he meant by rejecting the fruit of any plane. I held up my pace, carrying Jasper and the backpack with me as a great darkness grew in the distance.

Someone matched my pace after a time, and I was surprised to find Jimmy there when I glanced away from the horizon. We were both silent, until the shadows grew longer and the werewolf spoke.

"Why did you come here, Vesik? Why now?"

I glanced over at Vicky. She and Happy were a good distance away, on the far side of Carter and Maggie. "For her."

Jimmy looked at the girl riding the ghost panda, and then back to me. "You came here just for her? Not even the draw of the Pack bonds was strong enough to bring you here? But you came for her?"

I nodded. Maybe Jimmy would understand if he knew the whole story. Maybe he already knew and he was baiting me into something else. Either way, telling him why I was here wasn't going to hurt anything, and it might bolster my own resolve. My words were quiet, little more than whispers. "We couldn't save her. Foster and I couldn't save her."

"You slaughtered the men that killed her."

So he knew the story. "Yes."

"Rumors in the Pack say you put the souls of her killers into a dark bottle, and Philip used them to raise Prosperine. You gave him the very tools to curse her in this life."

His words stung. I knew he wasn't wrong, but it still kindled a fire in my gut. "Sometimes things go bad, and we have to make do with what we can."

Jimmy blew out a breath through his nose. "So now you've come to the Burning Lands to die? That's selfish, and it doesn't help anyone."

"I don't intend to die."

"That little girl doesn't deserve to become the Destroyer, Vesik. She's been through enough."

"That's why I'm here."

He eyed me for a moment before turning his head away. "You get people killed and damned to existences they don't want. I'll help if I can, because I understand Vicky needs to be freed, but it still seems like killing you before Stones River ever happened would have been best for everyone."

His words weren't angry. They were matter of fact, like he'd thought about them for a very long time. I pondered that, thinking how Carter and Maggie would still be alive. Philip wouldn't have gotten his souls, Cassie never would have faced Gurges. My pace slowed, and Jimmy pulled ahead of me. The young wolf's broad shoulders left his back in shadows in the rising darkness. He clenched his jaw and gave a violent shake of his head before walking away. I think he meant well underneath the venom and hate.

Jasper chittered on my shoulder and started bouncing. I reached up to scratch him, and as my fingers met the soft dust-bunny-like clumps of fur, a series of visions flashed through my mind. Sam saved from Devon, Zola freed from Philip's grasp, my parents saved from a madman, and Nixie ... the water witches might never have tried to change if not for Nixie and me.

"Thanks, Jasper."

He trilled and purred and settled against my neck.

It didn't take away all the doubts, though. War was coming between Nixie's faction and the Queen's. More people would die, and it would be on my head again. I guess I wouldn't have to worry about that if we didn't survive the night.

That dark thought kept me company while the sun turned black and the shadows came to life.

✦　✦　✦

"I'M A LITTLE confused," I said as I looked out across the plain. What had been short, innocuous-looking grasses had grown and changed into a rolling field of fire. Not much more than ankle high in most places, but still, walking through fire didn't seem like a great idea.

"Think of it like a tide," Mike said. "Only, instead of an ocean of water, the fire seas move through stone and rise through the ancient roots. There are deeper places of the world where the fires reach higher than the fortresses themselves."

I frowned at that thought, remembering the imposing mass of the fortress that vanished into the skies above. "If it's a tide, does that mean these small flames are going to grow throughout the night?"

Mike nodded. "It's one of the reasons we're camping here."

I glanced down at the embers beneath my feet. "This doesn't seem like a very good place to sit down."

Mike gestured to the north. "See the darkness ahead?"

I did, and it was close; maybe one hundred yards, maybe less. "What is it?"

"The Jaws."

We'd closed most of the distance when I came to understand why they called it the Jaws. Sharp, teeth-like protrusions of earth and stone jutted out from the side of a cliff. Far below, deeper than I imagined a canyon could be, a dim orange light filled the blackness.

My boots thumped onto white stone. There were no grasses here, no channel for the flames to rise up and scorch us. Farther onto one of the wider fingers waited a half-dome of rock, like some ancient amphitheater dropped into the middle of the Burning Lands. It looked natural, which made it even more odd.

"Camp," Mike said as he led us forward. The fire demon raised his hand and snapped his wrist forward. An orb of floating, burning light zipped into the cavern, revealing how large the dome was.

We were farther away than I'd thought. It took a good minute to cross the rest of the rocky earth that led up to our

ERIC R. ASHER

campground. A gentle downward slope led to the dome. I ducked as my head neared the floating ball of fire. It was mesmerizing, a constant roll of fire and shadow that licked up from the bottom of the orb and crackled as it turned to ash.

"How far are we from the sixth fortress?" I asked.

"Two hours at most, but there is no need to risk the journey," Mike said.

I glanced at Vicky as Happy paced the depressed inner circle of the dome. She stood silently near the entrance to our little camp.

"That is not what I meant," Mike whispered as he crouched beside me. "The black sun will last but three hours, and then we will have twelve hours until darkfall."

"Darkfall?" I said.

Mike raised his thick eyebrows slightly. "You do not know the word?"

I shook my head. "Should I?"

"It is the hour that demons ascend, and devils are born."

"Vicky," I hissed as I turned to look at the girl standing at the other end of our shelter.

"Yes. Time grows short, but being in the open during the black sun will do nothing but get us killed."

"You lived here for years," I said.

"Centuries," Mike said. "I survived by not being an idiot."

"I guess being a demon didn't hurt either."

Mike offered a weak smile. "No, it didn't. I will stand guard. Try to rest, or do what you must."

The fire demon walked to the base of the finger. He started talking to Carter and the other wolves while I pulled the Book that Bleeds out of my backpack, and tried to get comfortable on the stones.

112

CHAPTER SIXTEEN

M IKE SUMMONED A webwork of fire that arced up from the earth and met the dome's edge above. Bright white flashes of power shot through the thinnest parts of the pattern, revealing that the barrier wasn't merely fire. Mike talked to Carter while I flipped through the Book that Bleeds.

"It will keep out the majority of things during the black sun, and most importantly the dark-touched."

"I've seen them walk through fire," Carter said.

"In this plane, perhaps," Mike said. "This fire is different, as I think you know."

Happy wandered over and nudged me in the back. I leaned forward and he wiggled himself between me and the wall. I leaned back into the furry ghost bear, grateful for the cushion. Jasper swirled around my arm before settling in the crook of my elbow.

I flipped to the back cover, looking for any indication of something hidden within it. The front was just as bare, save for the sticky blood and rough leather. I ran my fingertips across the spine, feeling the raised bands beneath the surface.

It waited on the bottom edge of the book, in the center of the back cover. A thin bump, much like the tiny bands on the spine. I couldn't see it when I looked at it, but it was raised beneath my index finger. The leather was thicker than it looked and I finally looked up when a knife blade entered my field of view.

"Thanks," I said, taking the knife and cutting the leather before handing the blade back to Mike.

A sliver of gray metal waited within, and I pulled on it with my fingernails. The book resisted at first, grasping at the metal as though refusing to give up another secret. When the sliver of matte gray Magrasnetto finally slid out, there were enough runes carved into its surface to make my head spin. I could have sworn it was the same pattern as the metal Cara had formed into a dark bottle, the plates we'd found in the lost city of Pilot Knob.

Jasper's growl vibrated my entire body.

I flipped the metal over, and it was not runes that greeted my eyes. An incantation waited there, so long and complex I thought it might have been a speech. I traced the etched letters with a finger, and came away bleeding for my trouble. The letters themselves were jagged and razor sharp.

I rubbed the bleeding pad of my index finger against my thumb. The blood stopped almost immediately, and I raised my eyebrows as the wound closed on its own. I looked back to the incantation and read.

By the time I finished translating half the text, I realized it wasn't just an incantation. It was a document citing the abilities and bloodlines needed to perform the Demon's Sacrifice. There were names on that tablet that I knew as gods, Hephaestus, Hades, and a slew of others. Toward the bottom, I found what I feared I might.

Anubis.

The last line was the incantation itself; five little words, a simple chant that could destroy a soul utterly and turn its power into a weapon beyond comprehension. If ever I had feared that the arts I controlled were those of a dark necromancer, I knew that this would cross the line. This was the blackest of arts.

I let the sliver of metal slide out of my hands and thunk against the cover of the old tome. Vicky stood at the edge of the dome, her arms crossed, looking out through the blazing wall Mike the Demon had raised.

There weren't any guarantees. I might use the most powerful art inside the Book that Bleeds, and we could still lose Vicky to the Destroyer. And then what? Then I would use the Demon's Sacrifice to strike down the very girl I'd sworn to protect?

"You look troubled," Mike said as he sat down in front of me, crossing his legs.

I held up the etched plate.

Mike frowned. "I have not seen that in a very long time."

"It's one of the most awful things I've ever read, Mike."

"It is a weapon of the gods, Damian. Most of the great arts are as terrible as they are powerful."

I ran my fingers over the book, my voice quiet. "There has to be another way."

He nodded slowly. "Perhaps, but if the Destroyer possesses Vicky's body, she'll gain the ability to walk between the planes. Prosperine is one of the last wanderers, much like Gaia.

"The Destroyer will be able to come into our realm at will?"

"Yes," Mike said. "That is the way of these things."

"If she would be free to move between realms … I understand why you said it could be our only chance, but what if I'm wrong? What if coming here was wrong?"

Mike raised an eyebrow. "I am surprised to see such doubt in you. It doesn't suit you."

"It's Vicky, Mike. I *can't* be wrong about this."

"I understand your concern, but what if you wait? If now is not the time, when?"

I didn't answer.

"One thing I can tell you that the centuries have taught me: now is the only time we have, Damian. The world is set to tear itself apart in upheaval, in a war no one can win. If Glenn or Hern moves to strike humanity, commoners will face weapons beyond their understanding. That scale of death alone could bring forth the Destroyer."

"She didn't rise in Gettysburg," I said quietly.

"No, but I cannot tell you why. Luck, perhaps? I don't have all the answers." Mike stared at me for a moment before looking away. "This is our chance, or when next you quest to help the child, it will be to kill her."

His words rang true, and they were like a blade in my chest. What wouldn't I do at this point? Everything that girl had been through: the kidnapping, the murder, the possession. My fingernails cut into my palms as my hands curled into fists.

The wolves surrounded us before settling onto the stones that formed a rough bench to my right.

"The black sun will be gone soon," Carter said. "We'll have to be quick if you mean to reach the tenth circle before darkfall."

Vicky seized up in my peripheral vision. She shivered and trembled before she started to fall.

"Vicky!"

The panda sprang into motion, dropping me back against the stone as he sprinted toward her falling form. We were all too far away to prevent the crack of her head on the stone floor, but Happy got a paw beneath her before violent seizures wracked her body.

The girl released a stuttering scream, and tears leaked from her eyes. Happy howled, shaking the cavern when Vicky's tears hit his fur. Smoke rose wherever the droplets struck. I pushed the bear's paw out of the way and cradled Vicky's head.

Her skull slammed against my hands hard enough to break bone. I didn't move.

"Damian," Carter hissed. "We don't know what this is. Get away."

Vicky slammed her head into my palms again, and the sharp sting told me something had cracked in my palm. Her tears found my skin, and I ground my teeth as my flesh boiled and smoked.

"You cannot save her, necromancer." That awful, cold laugh filled the cavern and I raised my right hand above Vicky's chest.

"Excutio Daemonium!"

Golden light slammed her against the ground and the bones in my left hand crumbled. I was past caring. If it took the Demon's Sacrifice to rid her of this beast, I'd pay it gladly. Smoke rose from my already blistered skin.

Vicky's eyes shot open, revealing a thicker covering of the black flecks I'd seen in them before. Her gaze rolled up to meet mine and held it. Tears rolled down her face as she curled up into a ball. "You have to kill me."

It was the single worst sentence I'd ever heard. I didn't fight the tears in the corners of my eyes. I gathered the girl up in my arms and let her sob into my shoulder. I hadn't felt anything like the awful knot of hopelessness in my chest since I'd watched Sam get her throat ripped out.

"You are not wrong about Vicky, Damian," Mike said. "This is the time, and we cannot fail."

The laughter came first. Low and slow, just outside the gate of fire. It sounded like someone laughing through gritted teeth. The voice was deeper than the Old Man's, and just as gravelly.

"The allies of Camazotz are weaker than I imagined."

"Be gone," Mike growled at the hunched shadow outside the flame.

"Do you know what I am, little demon?"

"A messenger, soon to be dead." Mike drew the hammer from his belt, and it burst into fiery life. He held out his left hand, and closed his fingers into a fist. The grid of flame vanished, leaving an afterimage burned into my retinas.

"Brave," the shadow said, "or foolish. Do you treat?"

Mike hesitated. "I treat."

I wondered if Mike thought he could glean some bit of information from the shadowed figure, if that's what had stayed his hand.

The messenger stepped forward, and its gray skin stretched in the light of the Smith's Hammer. I almost flinched when I realized the leathery mouth was smiling. Fangs as long as my fingers curled out from the thing's mouth.

"The word of the Fallen Smith. A powerful thing indeed."

"Do not attack it," Mike said.

The form stood up straighter and cocked its head to the side. "You would only break our treat. I would not be so disappointed to devour your friends."

Happy placed himself between the shadow and Vicky. I lowered her to the ground and slowly stood up, taking the few steps to stand beside Mike.

The creature turned to face me, and the mockery of its almost-human face glowed in the hammer's light. It smiled, baring a row of sharp fangs, dwarfed only by the two curved teeth that looked more like those of a saber-toothed tiger.

"Welcome, Anubis-son," the thing said as it straightened its posture. It towered over us, at least eight feet tall, and fluttered the tattered cloak around its shoulder. "Forgive my appearance. I have been here long."

"What do you want?"

The thing's face curled up in a brief smile. It rolled its neck. "So direct. My, how the formalities change."

"The only formality is deciding whether or not to kill you," I said as I crossed my arms. Vicky whimpered behind me, and my rage mixed with hopelessness.

"You would kill your friend by betraying his word," the creature hissed. "Such a sad fate to befall the noble Hephaestus."

"Creatures from the Abyss are not bound by Mike's word," I said. He wasn't from their plane, but did that really give him an out?

"It matters not. While you speak with me, my people begin to consume your realm."

"You speak for the dark-touched," Mike said, his eyes tracing every movement the thing made.

"I *am* the dark-touched."

"Jasper," I said flatly.

The innocuous ball of fluff exploded, filling the cavern with his reptilian form until his head snaked out over our guest.

The creature glanced up at the blazing eyes of the dragon and bowed. "I stand corrected, Anubis-son." It raised an arm, and the tattered cloak fell away to reveal an emaciated gray body. Thin straps of leather wrapped around its torso, holding enough blades against its chest to arm an entire company.

"The dark-touched are mindless killing machines," Carter said, taking up a position on my left while Maggie and Jimmy flanked Happy.

"Oh," the thing said with a laugh as its sleek forehead wrinkled. "And dead wolves stay dead."

Jasper leapt out of the cave, soaring past the creature and landing on the fiery plain with a thump.

The gray-skinned creature spread its arms, revealing a thin membrane, laced with more bones than I could count. "Imagine ten thousand of my kind, starved for millennia, unleashed on your hapless realm. You will not find them so talkative."

"Begone," Mike said. "You have made your point."

"I have not even begun to make my point, demon." The dark-touched vampire crouched down, curling into a hunched form once more. "Too long we have spent locked behind the Seal of Anubis, trapped in this fiery wasteland. We will take our vengeance in blood."

Bubbles growled, and the sound shook the earth.

"Not today, dog," the creature said. "I take my leave, in peace." Its face curled up again, exposing those curved fangs. It moved like a shadow, slithering and shifting around Jasper before launching itself into the air. The thin wings on its back expanded, catching the heat rising from the flames below and propelling it forward. When they swept forward and flexed, the vampire shot forward like a rocket through the night sky.

Jasper shrank and collapsed onto himself before flowing across the earth and back into the dome.

"We should have killed it," I said.

The dragon chittered his agreement as he took up his position on my shoulder.

"No." Mike let the hammer fade before raising the gate of fire again. "Unless you wish to find the tenth circle without me."

The little necromancer faded into view. "A parlay with a creature as old as the dark-touched is binding. Had Mike not kept his word, it may well have killed him."

"What?" I asked. "I know he's bound to the hammer by his oath, but how could an agreement like that hurt him?"

The little necromancer stared off at the black sun before turning back to me. "Magic, as much as it is the same in our realm, is different in the Burning Lands. I don't know if it's because of the devils that live here, or if the devils came to live here because of it, but agreements are binding to both parties, regardless of the plane."

"Shit," I snapped. "It might have been good to know that ahead of time."

"I never dreamed we would encounter a speaking dark-touched," Mike said.

"That was really one of them?" I asked.

Mike nodded.

"And there's an army of them now, somewhere in our world?"

"Yes."

"How many of them are as smart as that one?"

"Not many," Carter said. "The ones we've fought have been silent beasts that would sooner grunt and utter that terrible screech than speak. Even fewer would take the time to treat. It is concerning."

"So what was this one, then?" I asked. "Was it a leader of some sort?"

Mike shook his head and sat down beside Vicky. "They don't have leaders. They are more like a Pack without an Alpha—chaotic, destructive, and hungry."

I lowered myself to the ground near Vicky and picked up the Book that Bleeds. I knew it wouldn't sound good, but I said it anyway. "We have bigger things to worry about than some chatty-ass vampire."

"For once we agree on something," Jimmy said from behind Maggie.

CHAPTER SEVENTEEN

I SPENT THE last hour of the black sun reading through the Book that Bleeds. It wasn't until Mike let the gate of fire fade and the black disc above us turned crimson again that the idea struck me. I turned the book over and ran my fingers around the front cover.

Nothing.

It was perfectly smooth, outside of the ribs beneath the binding. I flipped the cover open and studied the end papers. There were faded runes at each corner—ehwaz and uruz—repeated and alternated. They were the same runes used to summon Aeros at Elephant Rocks. One corner had a tiny slit at the front of the book. I'd almost missed it until the light caught.

I ran my fingernail over it and frowned. It was flush with the cover. That seemed wrong. I could clearly see the cut in the paper, but I couldn't feel it. This book was as frustrating as it was helpful. I jammed my fingers into the cover hard enough for my nails to tear the paper. The slit bulged and started bleeding.

I tried not to gag when ancient rotten blood oozed out, stinking of decay. I peeled enough of the end paper back to see inside. Fibers like striated muscles waited below and I barely handled the smell. Etched inside of that gory thing was one simple sentence.

The Book of Souls lies hidden in the history of the Flame.

"Gee, that's helpful." I gingerly tucked the edges back into place and closed the book.

"It is almost time to go," Mike said. "What did you find?"

"Just some cryptic note about a Book of Souls being hidden in a flame or some shit. Nothing that would actually help us."

"The Demon's Sacrifice could still accomplish the task."

He was right, of course, but that meant losing friends, again. I ran my fingers through my hair and ground my teeth. "There has to be another way."

"If there is, I do not know of it."

I glanced at Vicky, curled up at Happy's side. "And if it doesn't free her? What then? Find more friends to strike her down?"

"Yes."

I slammed my fist onto the stone, and was surprised when it shattered beneath the blow. I expected pain and blood across my knuckles when I turned my hand over, but there was none. Bits of stone floated around me for a moment before pattering onto the earth.

"This place weirds me out," I said, brushing the crushed stone away from the divot I'd made. "Almost as much as this damn book." I slid the Book that Bleeds back into the pack and threw it over my shoulder.

"We need to move faster," Mike said. "You are slowing us down too much, Damian."

"What the hell? I've been moving just as fast as you. Sometimes faster."

"Yes," Mike said, "well, let's not do that again. Ride on

Jasper's back. The wolves can run indefinitely, as can the bear."

"I'm sorry?" I said, raising my eyebrows. "You want me to do what?"

Jasper's tree-trunk like legs whumped into the earth as his gray scaly body erupted all around me. Claws long enough to impale Aeros scratched at the stone around us. His wings swept back, adding a fleshy canopy above our heads.

Bubbles thought this was *fantastic*. She chuffed and bounded up the dragon's back, settling into the crook of his neck. Her massive tongue waggled in the air before Jasper's chest.

The dragon raised his head, curling his neck back until it was upside down. Bubbles sucked her tongue in and sniffed at the inverted dragon snout. Jasper slowly uncurled his neck before turning the black eyes in his broad head to me. The dragon shuffled his butt backwards and lowered his tail, making a perfect ramp up to the cu sith.

"What am I doing?" I asked as I stepped onto the tail, and made my way up to Bubbles. Jasper stood up, and I yelped as I slipped backwards. I managed to lock my legs onto the dragon's shoulders before I fell to the earth.

I peeked over the edge of the dragon at the ground far below. "It looks higher than I expected."

Mike flashed me an entirely inappropriate smile.

"We'll meet you at the sixth fortress," Carter said. "Try not to fall. He's ... fast."

"Have you seen him—"

My question cut off with a squeal when the dragon lunged forward. I would have fallen off if not for the cu sith's quick thinking. She used her tongue as a pink seatbelt, and I did my best not to judge her godawful doggy breath.

Bubbles pulled me down and I grabbed onto her ruff as her tongue released its somewhat abrasive hold. I glanced behind us once I grew familiar with Jasper's bounding movements. The Jaws were nowhere to be seen. A gentle slope replaced the sudden drop of the canyon, and another forest rose off to our left. I wasn't sure which way was north or east or anything. The bone-jarring pace of the dragon left little time for anything but remembering to hold on.

In a matter of minutes, my thighs ached. I figured I'd look like a bow-legged cartoon cowboy by the time I stepped off the dragon.

✦　　✦　　✦

I SQUINTED INTO the distance, unsure of what I was seeing. It looked like a black mountain range stretching from one horizon to the other. I wondered how we'd cross it, and how I'd be able to hold on to the dragon any longer.

Carter and Maggie and the rest of the Ghost Pack had been fighting the devils of this place for over a year now, or was it two? They'd freed trapped pack members and recruited others, apparently at the cost of the River Pack's strength. I wondered if that was why I hadn't seen Hugh as much. Was that why so much of the River Pack stayed away from Gettysburg in the fight against Hern and Ezekiel?

Jasper slowed as we reached the towering black mountains. Now that we were close, I could see they weren't mountains at all. Massive obsidian cones stretched from the earth up into the sky. Entirely unnatural towers rose from the cones' surfaces in various spots.

Another minute and I could make out a humanoid shape

standing outside another gate. I wondered if Carter or Mike had beaten us here, but that seemed unlikely when broad wings stretched from the figure's back. Power flashed through the gated cones behind him.

I'd expected an army to be waiting for us at the sixth fortress, just like the fifth. Instead, a lone demon stood outside that towering gate. A few souls flickered into being outside the fortress before they sighted the demon and dashed away.

"Go no farther," the demon said.

At first, I'd been concerned that the figure was the dark-touched vampire we'd encountered earlier, but he was not. This creature stood like any other man, set apart only by the fleshy wings on his back and the deep burgundy skin that glowed dimly with its own light.

"Return from whence you came," the demon said.

I patted Jasper's neck and the dragon came to a halt. Bubbles hopped to the earth first and I slid down Jasper's neck beside her, landing on a soft bed of clover-like flowers.

I wondered if being polite to this apparent gatekeeper was the best strategy, or if I should attack him outright.

"That would be unwise."

I raised an eyebrow.

"Your thoughts are a simple thing for me to pluck from your mind. Your necromancy leaves you exposed in this realm."

"Try this," I said, narrowing my eyes and letting the ocean of souls inside me rise up uninhibited. The voices were still quiet here. Perhaps the Burning Lands provided some kind of inherent barrier to the utter chaos in my head.

It was plenty to throw the demon off. At first he frowned.

His jet black eyes shot wide open a moment later and his clawed hands slammed over his slightly pointed ears. I let the whispering voices overwhelm my thoughts, losing my own self to the tide.

Only when the demon stumbled and fell to a knee did I lock the souls away once more. Ten steps carried me to his side.

"Let us pass." I gestured with my hand for him to move aside, somewhat surprised to see golden wisps of power tracing my arm through the air.

His eyes rolled up to meet mine and he spoke through gritted teeth. "What are you?"

"I'm not hunting you today, demon," I said.

His eyes narrowed. "A Harrower, one of the Ghost Pack, come to slay Prosperine."

I reached for my focus. "Now I have to kill you." We didn't need Prosperine to know we were coming. We especially didn't need her to know our plans. This demon had likely plucked them from my head already, if he was half as good as he thought he was.

The demon slowly stood up. "You are right, and I will be rewarded." He crouched and flexed his wings.

"Jasper," I said.

I couldn't be sure exactly what the dragon would do, but he didn't disappoint. The demon launched himself into the air, only to scream a second later. The gust from Jasper's wings almost knocked me over as the dragon rocketed into the sky, locking his jaws around the demon before slamming the bastard back to earth.

Bones shattered at my feet and thick black blood oozed from the broken body.

"You shouldn't have been such an asshole." I slowly curled my hand into a fist, feeling the familiar pull of the gravemakers all around me. The Hand of Anubis rose up, a gleaming obsidian thing in the light of the Burning Lands. The demon screamed once more as the fingers crushed him and dragged him beneath the flowers.

Jasper huffed and a curl of smoke rose from his scaly nostrils. I patted his snout and glanced over my shoulder. The Ghost Pack stood there with Mike the Demon.

"Christ," Jimmy said. "Remind me not to sucker punch him ever again."

Carter shot him a cockeyed smile. "You're getting smart in your old age."

Vicky wandered up around Bubbles, leaving Happy to stare at the dragon. She wrapped her fingers into my left hand and pulled me forward. "We have to go through the gate. Try not to blow everything up this time."

"I'll try," I said.

"I think Sam would say not to believe you."

Someone snorted a laugh behind me. I turned to find Maggie walking nearby. "At least I didn't threaten to kill anyone the first time I met them," I said.

Maggie frowned slightly. "I promised to maim you, at worst."

"Actually," Carter started.

"Shut up, wolf," Maggie snapped. "Now, as I recall, you just met that demon, and he is quite dead."

I looked back at the disturbed ground and pursed my lips. "Touché."

CHAPTER EIGHTEEN

T HE BLACK OBSIDIAN carried over into the gateway, changing from a smooth exterior to what felt like brick. I ran my fingers across it, half expecting the power-laced lattice that had waited for us at the last fortress. But it was only stone.

"What made this?" I asked, tracing the intricate lines and patterns that repeated, ever expanding, until they peaked in a sweeping gothic arch.

"Stone demons," Mike said. "They were once the most populous of the demon races. Only a few survived the wars, obsessed with art and beauty as they were."

"Are they all gone now?" I asked, stopping near the center of a pitch black rotunda. A statue that would have been at home in Faerie's Royal Court adorned a pedestal. A beautiful cloaked woman stood with one hand behind her back and the other outstretched, welcoming all who came through the doors. Her face stayed in shadow, no matter the angle we approached from.

I paused when we reached the statue's back. A blade with a rounded pommel glistened in the hidden hand. I frowned and stepped closer, having to look almost straight up. The detail was incredible, every inch of her looked like flesh or cloth, but my focus stayed on the blade itself. Runes circled the pommel. I'd seen it before.

I turned to Mike. "That's a Key of the Dead."

"Of course," he said with a nod. "She is death."

My skin crawled, knowing it was death who greeted us so humbly.

"Come," Mike said, passing me by and starting toward one of the four hallways at the back of the room.

Vicky grabbed my hand again and dragged me away. I looked back from the mouth of the hall. I could have sworn death watched us, and her gaze knew no limit.

"Where is everyone?" I asked.

Mike's bulky form didn't turn around. His voice bounced through the corridor. "This was the house of the dark-touched after they destroyed most of the stone demons."

My steps stuttered before resuming their normal pace. "How many are here?"

"Were," Mike said. "Were here."

He sounded very sure of the fact, but recent events led me to think otherwise. "What about the one at the Jaws?"

"An outlier, I assume."

"They are not all mindless aggressors," Maggie said. "We have seen sound strategy."

Mike started to shake his head and then hesitated. "I will say it is unlikely, but not impossible. I expect the dark-touched to become a plague in your realm as much as they were here."

"Some of the stone demons survived, didn't they?" Carter asked.

Mike nodded and led us around a corner, his footsteps echoing in the narrowing hallway. "Yes, a few."

The hall thinned enough that Jasper condensed into the black-eyed ball of gray fur. He perched on my shoulder and vibrated. I didn't think he liked the close quarters any more than I did.

Bubbles stayed close to Jimmy and growled when we passed a rounded hall.

"What's that?" I asked, looking into the shadows.

"We are not alone." I jumped at the voice right beside me. Shiawase walked effortlessly at my side, as silent as he could be.

Mike studied the shadows and then picked up his pace. "They may leave us alone if we traverse the fortress quickly."

Something creaked in the darkness, like steel dragged across a stone floor. My heart rate accelerated. "What's in there?"

"I don't know," Mike said. "It could be anything if the dark-touched are gone."

"Or it could be a trap filled with dark-touched," Maggie muttered.

Mike gave one sharp nod. "If it is, they won't be quick to engage with a dragon."

I glanced at the furball. "He's … not very imposing at the moment."

Jasper squashed himself up against my neck. If I didn't know better, I'd think something out in the shadows scared him. The thought alone curled my toes. I'd seen Jasper lift a Leviathan into the air before slamming it into the earth and flaying it. Maybe he was just afraid of the dark.

Mike's pace slowed when we rounded the next curve. I could see another rotunda up ahead. A second statue waited there. This one held one hand up in warning while the other held the raised dagger.

Something screeched behind us and I shivered. Bubbles

growled and it shook the air around us. The screeching grew
louder. Mike glanced over his shoulder. His breathing was
quicker than normal. He either didn't know what was in here
with us, or he did know and he was worried.

"Quickly," Mike hissed.

Carter sprinted around me and matched Mike's pace.
"What are they?"

"Servants of the Tenth," Mike whispered. "They should not
be here."

"Famous last words," I muttered between breaths. We were
almost jogging now. Bubbles raised her ears straight up and
swiveled them. Vicky kept up effortlessly, and even the bear
raced on with an odd, trundling stride.

We passed the second statue and entered the waiting
mouth of the next corridor. Something laughed, the sound
echoing up and down the halls around us. At first I thought the
voices were in my head, that the souls inside me had picked the
least opportune time to break my tentative hold on them. Then
the things spoke.

The mighty Hephaestus, come home to die.

The voices grated together, dissonant, beautiful, and horrible all at once. One voice soothed in dulcet tones while another
rang off key, sounding more like squealing metal on a black-
board. The last meshed with them both, sometimes
complementing, sometimes clashing, and always disturbing.

"Ignore them," Mike said. "They will speak your fears.
Avoid their fangs as best you can. The hallucinations are the
stuff of nightmares."

Prosperine has already claimed victory.

The words were stuttering hisses and pops that barely

sounded like a human tongue. The passage narrowed again.

"It sounds like they're right on top of us," I said. My legs burned, pounding the stone floor at a near sprint. The ghosts didn't seem winded. The fact Mike's breathing had grown heavy gave me some hope that the things chasing us might be fatigued as well.

Abandon all hope, mortals.

Hearing that voice as we flooded into the next rotunda almost made me stop before the towering statue. Gone was the patient look. The pedestal was now a body, and the cloaked figure's dagger glistened like blood.

"Fucking hell, this is the same room, isn't it? Mike! The corridors are taking us in circles!"

The Destroyer has risen.

"It is their design," Mike said between breaths. "We have one layer left before we reach the other side."

Darkness wrapped around us again as we entered yet another hallway. Or was it truly the same corridor? I hadn't paid close enough attention to recognize the turns Mike took.

Light waited at the end of the narrow path. We burst out of it as a creepy, slithering voice echoed around us.

The fates have spoken.

The last statue was Nixie. Her body was stone, shattered across the floor.

"It's not her!" Mike shouted, as though he knew exactly what I was seeing.

In the fragments, I saw Sam and my parents and friends I hadn't seen in a decade. A dark specter rose in the center. I stared at the hooded form, the mirror image of myself, standing upon a kingdom of death.

"Don't!"

Mike's words were lost to the rage.

The Servants had miscalculated. They thought the vision would break me, that I'd somehow abandon my quest to save Vicky. The only thing broken that day would be them.

The scream that echoed from my chest wasn't mortal. It wasn't human. It was the death throes of a million souls, the fear of the lost, and rage of the hopeless. The room exploded into a bath of golden light.

I could hear nothing above the voices inside my head. Opening myself allowed me to siphon away every ounce of power that fueled the Servants' illusions. Three of them huddled behind the rubble of an actual statue.

Their faces moved and twisted as though each was made from a tangle of vines. Vacant holes met my eyes and I let a deathly smile curl up over my clenched teeth.

"Stay back," I hissed, and my voice echoed through the room, whispering my words back to me.

"No!" Someone shouted before they yanked on my arm. "Stop!" A small girl stood before me, pushing on my chest. "Damian, stop!"

"Vicky, move."

"You'll bring the fortress down and kill us all. *Stop!*"

Her words cut through the bone-rattling cascade of voices in my head. I stepped backwards, slowly releasing the mass of power that I'd gathered. But what if she was an illusion too? What if it was all a ploy?

It was too much to risk, either way, so I released the power and watched the Servants. One of the creature's faces slithered where a mouth should have been, and the voices sounded through the chamber once more.

He is no mortal!

"Leave this place," Mike growled.

Fire demon, you have no power over us.

"This house was abandoned by the stone demons." Mike raised the hammer and it burst into fiery life. "Abandoned by the dark-touched." His body grew and distorted, his voice reaching the depths of Aeros's. "You are welcome to challenge my right, but it will become my prerogative to destroy you."

A loose reading of the laws. We know of your oath. You cannot harm us.

The trio stepped out from behind the statue. The broken stone peppering the floor flickered and levitated before the cloaked woman reappeared with the dagger in her hand.

Mike laughed through his teeth. He opened his jaws and his entire body burst into flame. "I swore never to harm the innocent, Servant. You have misjudged."

Wings burst from Mike the Demon's back as he leapt into the air. The first of the wriggling creatures exploded beneath an overhand blow from the Smith's Hammer. Flaming bits of serpent-like flesh splashed onto the far wall.

It was then that I noticed the terrible burn in my own hands. I held my palm up and marveled at the cracks appearing in the flesh, leaking golden light. I'd siphoned off too much power, and it had to be released.

A shadow formed at the corner of my eye, the Little Necromancer. She could help. She knew a great deal about the darker arts, and if I gave her just a little … The mere thought was enough to cause an arc of golden light to leap into the ghost. She screamed at the sudden shock and her eyes went wide, locking onto me.

After a moment she whispered, "More."

I didn't know the why, or the how, really. The knowledge just bubbled up. I let some of the fragmented souls loose, bits of power without enough sense of self to ever remember who or what they were. The ghostly light flowed and seeped into the Little Necromancer. Her body grew brighter, and the light faded as she became more than a ghost, as she stepped back into a world not meant for the dead.

It would be temporary—I knew, though I don't know how I knew—unless I tied everything together. I pinched the flesh at the back of her neck and sent a needle of necromancy through it. It anchored the souls to her throat chakra and color returned to her aura.

I expected a flash of knowing, something, anything, but nothing came. The cracks in my arm closed and hissed, leaving only thin tracers of burnt flesh behind.

"Sarah?" Mike's voice shook. He held one of the Servants by the throat. The distraction left an opening for the last. It threw its arms wide, and snake-like *things* erupted from his chest. They burned and twirled and hissed as they closed on Mike's face.

The Little Necromancer held up her hands and chanted three words before pushing at the air in front of her. An impossible gust of wind blasted the snakes out of the air and smashed them against the black stone wall.

Mike squeezed, and the second Servant's neck collapsed with a gurgling crunch. The body writhed when it hit the floor, only to still a moment later.

"Sarah?" The flames around Mike dimmed.

She smiled and made a quick gesture with her hand. A brand appeared on the last Servant, a tangled web of lines and runes that was nothing I'd seen before. The Servant screamed and clawed at his chest, tearing away his cloak and the flesh beneath.

In the time it took for Sarah to wrap her arms around Mike, the Servant was ash.

"What the fuck just happened?" Jimmy said, stepping toward me, and then veering off toward Carter.

"I'm not sure," Carter said.

Mike fell to his knees. Sarah ran her fingers delicately over the thick, twisted horns on his head.

"It's Anubis," Mike whispered, his voice shaking. "You have the power of Anubis, Damian. Lord and master of the dead."

My knuckles cracked as I clench them into fists. "Ezekiel. Goddammit."

"Can you do that for us?" Jimmy asked. "Make us real again?"

The hope in his voice made the words feel so much worse on my tongue. "No, it's different. You're all bound to the River Pack. I can't … it's like some of the parts are missing. I don't think I can do it with any ghost. Sarah has a gift in necromancy, and we're inside Mike's realm. It felt like I was just restoring a bond that was already there."

Jimmy looked away and frowned.

"You're still real," Vicky said. "We're all still real."

Jasper hopped back up onto my shoulder. I wasn't sure when he'd climbed off. He rolled down my arm until his eyes were level with my wrist. The furball studied it for a time before returning to my shoulder.

I reached a shaky hand up to scratch him. Vicky leaned on Happy and held her stomach.

"You okay?" I asked.

She nodded. "I just feel a little funny. I'll be fine."

"We need to move," Maggie said. "Time is short, and we cannot fail."

"Come on kid," Jimmy said, putting his arm around Vicky's shoulders. Happy bumped the werewolf with his hips and trundled over to Mike.

Sarah pulled on the demon's hands until he stood over her once again. "Come on. We have to help Vicky. Happy's right." Quietly, I heard her mutter, "So is Maggie."

CHAPTER NINETEEN

OUR PACE QUICKENED as we made our way through the sixth fortress. It felt like we walked in constant loops until we finally turned a corner and a gate waited for us. Mike pulled it open with one hand. There was no visible lock or mechanism on the black obsidian latticework, but it slid smoothly to the side.

I followed the wolves out, Bubbles walking at my side. The gateway slammed closed behind us, leaving our group beneath the crimson sun once more. Pockets of that awful forest waited here. The only path around led to a cliff.

Mike waited at the edge with Sarah, the little necromancer, and I stopped behind them both, my heart dropping to my feet.

"What is this?" I asked.

"Burning Sea," Mike said. "Barrier between the sixth circle and the rest of the Burning Lands."

"Ugh, it's like the street that cuts between the bad neighborhood and the good neighborhood," Jimmy said.

I agreed wholeheartedly, and as much as I wanted to smack the kid sometimes, I kind of liked him.

"Except it's demons instead of minorities in the bad neighborhoods," Jimmy said.

And in one sentence I was back to not liking him. Some people were just born to be assholes. "How do we get across?"

"I thought this would be low tide," Carter said. "We don't have time to wait for the seas to recede. Look at the sun."

"He's right," Sarah said. "We don't have enough time. We'll never make it to the tenth circle before darkfall."

"Damian can get us there," Mike said.

"What?"

"Anything you can imagine, you can create in this place. This is the calmest part of the sea," Mike said. "We can sail across, or you can build us a bridge."

"I can what?" I tilted my head and stared at the demon. "What do you mean?"

He studied the earth beneath our feet. "I did not mention it before as I hoped your time here would temper your magic. Accidentally destroying the world with us on it would be unwelcome."

I slowly arched an eyebrow.

"You have the powers of any god that has ever walked within this realm." Mike raised his eyes to mine. "Use them. If you can't help us all across, get yourself to the last fortress. Find Prosperine, and destroy her."

He was telling me to leave them behind. "I can't do it alone."

"When you raise the Demon's Sacrifice, the souls will come to you," Mike said in a quiet voice. "They need not be beside you."

A shadow moved, leaping up from within the Burning Sea. It struck fast, launching a trident at Mike. The fire demon deflected it. The tines clattered against the rock as Mike's hand stretched out and snatched another from the air.

Happy struck like a jackhammer, his paw flashing out to

smash the demon into the stone cliff. It didn't look like the wriggling masses that formed the Servants we'd encountered. His red flesh looked almost normal compared to that.

I unholstered the pepperbox and leveled it at his head.

He leaned forward, hissing, before Happy smashed his face with a quick paw strike.

"Strike me down, Anubis-son. It matters not."

"It's going to matter to you," I said.

Happy cracked the demon's head again, and I winced. Parts of the demon's face weren't where they had been a moment before.

"Prosperine controls the gathering of souls," the mangled face whispered. "You can't stop her."

I glanced at Carter and grimaced before turning back to our captive. "You're wrong, demon. I am not bound to the rules of my realm in this place." I flexed my hand, and the ground exploded around him. The fingers of the Hand of Anubis wrapped around the demon and ignited, pulling the burning creature into the earth. His screams grew muffled before they vanished entirely.

"There goes another one," Jimmy said.

"Damian …" Carter said. "It seems you wield enough power here to kill any creature foolish enough to strike at you, and yet your confidence seems thin. What aren't you telling me?"

I holstered the pepperbox and ran my fingers through my hair. "I know how to kill Prosperine in this realm, to bring an end to the terror she showers on the world."

"That's fantastic!"

"No. It requires a soulart, Carter, and half a dozen willing souls."

Carter glanced back at the Ghost Pack. He sighed and looked to the sea.

Maggie stepped up beside him, her eyes blazing with golden light. "Will it free the girl?"

I gave one sharp nod. "It should."

"Then there is no choice to make," Carter said. He turned back to me. The crimson light glinted on his golden eyes and caught fire.

I frowned. "Yes, there is. You'll die. We have to find another way."

"We're already dead, Damian," Maggie said. "We told you once we were thankful for the time we had together. If we can help destroy a demon and bring about peace for that child, you won't stand in our way."

"I *can't* do that," I said, clenching my fists. "The pack needs you."

Carter's mouth lifted in a small smile. "Damian, the pack has Hugh—a rightful Alpha for hundreds of years now. Vicky needs us. When the time comes, when you can strike down the Destroyer once and for all, that will be our purpose. That will be our legacy."

"Let us help," Jimmy said, biting off the words.

I was taken aback at the young ghost's heated words.

"No."

I turned to look at the speaker.

Vicky frowned and eyed the wolves. "No one is dying for me."

"You are our strength, little one," Carter said. "When your curse is broken, there will be no need for the Ghost Pack."

Vicky's lips trembled. "You're my friends. My best friends

other than maybe that stupid bear."

Happy chuffed and flopped onto the smooth stone ground.

"That is the end of this conversation," Carter said.

"This is not a decision to be made lightly," Mike said. "I would consult with Hugh before enacting something so severe."

The demon was right. "How?" I asked.

Mike turned to Carter. "You can contact the Alpha at will, yes?"

"At times," the ghost wolf said. "There are other times he seems blocked, for lack of a better term."

"It is the bond with Damian that allows it," Mike said, and his certainty surprised me.

"How can you know that?" I asked.

"It is the only thing that makes sense. No one can communicate across the Abyss, except for Hugh and the Ghost Pack. The only thing unique about them—"

"Is me."

The demon nodded. "If you channel through the Pack Marks, you should be able to reach Hugh."

I looked around the Burning Lands. There were no ley lines here. "Channel what?"

"Souls."

The thought made me shiver. Intentionally channel a soulart through my pack marks? I cursed and crossed my arms.

"It is the fastest way," Mike said. "We have ten hours at most before darkfall."

Ten hours. It sounded like a lifetime. I looked at Vicky as she ran her hands through Happy's fur. Ten hours until that girl might vanish into the creature known as the Destroyer.

I raised a fist to my chest. "Then we have to try."

"Use us," Maggie said. "We can lead the others if Carter's connection is strong. Take my hand."

I wanted to say no. I wanted to say no fucking way in hell would I ever do anything to hurt them again, but if we failed … if the Destroyer claimed Vicky …

I slammed my palm onto Maggie's. She took one of Carter's hands and Jimmy took the other.

"Ready?" I asked.

The three wolves nodded in an eerie unison. I laid my fingers on the curved line of pack marks on my left forearm. All I had to do was *think,* and the scars glowed. Knowledge I shouldn't have had flowed into my consciousness, and I understood exactly what to do.

I pulled on Carter's soul first, and his body stiffened. I wrapped a thread of that golden light around my arm until it touched every scar Hugh had left on me. Maggie's came next, and then a small piece of Jimmy's. Only small pieces, so small that no one would be hurt.

My mind opened to the roar of souls trapped within me, but instead of bringing me to my knees, they flowed freely into the pack marks. I felt the Seal as my consciousness passed through, trailing into the Abyss until it locked onto a golden star in that black infinity.

The world collapsed onto itself, and Hugh was suddenly there, looking as if he were a brilliant golden member of the Ghost Pack. He stared at me, his eyes wide.

"Damian? You are supposed to be inside the Burning Lands."

"I am." I heard the words echo as though we huddled inside

a cavern. I concentrated on the ghostly shadows behind Hugh, and the werewolf den on Howell Island came into focus. Hugh stood before the square sectional couch, a monstrous shadow waiting behind him.

"Is Alan there?" I asked.

He glanced over his shoulder and nodded. "You cannot see him?"

I shook my head. "Can you see Carter, or Maggie or Jimmy?"

"Barely," Hugh said. "I cannot hear them. How can this be?"

"We don't have time." I rambled at the wolf, crashing through the theory of the Timewalkers, what we needed to bind Vicky to one, how we needed a volunteer, why we needed Ward, and how close the Destroyer was to taking everything away.

"How long?" Hugh asked.

"Ten hours until darkfall. I still have to find the tenth circle, and Prosperine herself."

Hugh sighed, and a wave of emotion hit me like a truck. A wave of despair rolled over me before acceptance became determination. "Carter and Maggie and the others … they have already agreed to this?"

"Yes."

"I will not dishonor him by contradicting his decision, but his loss will be immeasurable."

My heart sank. I knew it would, but we were out of time, out of options.

Hugh flinched and held out a hand. "Damian, I can feel your thoughts. It is … you are blinded by anger."

I took a deep breath. "I don't want to lose them, Hugh. I don't want to lose anyone. I'm not blinded. I'm focused."

Hugh shook his head. "How you can live balanced upon such turmoil inside your mind … you need calm."

"Once Prosperine is dead, we can talk about that."

"So be it. You hunt a devil in its own realm, Damian. Beware the world around you." Hugh frowned and leaned on the couch. "We will find a volunteer. I know what saving the girl means to you, and I know what failing means for the rest of the world. How will you return here for them?"

"I will take you to them when the time is right," Mike said. I couldn't see the fire demon, but his voice filled the void.

I nodded. "Mike will bring me over." Mike had once offered to send me into the Burning Lands. I had little doubt he could walk me out of them.

"How long do I have to gather everyone?"

"No more than four hours," Mike said. "The journey may take as long."

"Four hours," I said, watching Hugh's golden spirit before me. "You have four hours at most."

"We will be ready."

CHAPTER TWENTY

THE CONNECTION VANISHED. Had Hugh broken it? My consciousness spilled back through the Abyss, crashing through the damaged Seal, and finally smashing into my skull on the stones of the Burning Lands. I cracked an eye open and sat down hard.

The Burning Sea churned and spun below me. It felt as though I had an icepick lodged in my eye.

"That was … unsettling," Carter said, rolling his neck and flexing his arm.

"I couldn't move," Jimmy said. "What was that?"

"That wasn't normal?" I asked, holding one eye closed against the brutal headache. "I could feel emotions coming off of you, and Hugh."

"Then you know our determination," Maggie said. The pain began to subside as she patted my shoulder. "And no, this was not the same. We couldn't move, or speak."

"You've all returned," Mike said. The surprise in his voice told me this might not have been the safest way to go about things. Bubbles nestled in beside me, her black snout sniffing at my arm.

When the pain in my eye receded, I noticed the burning sensation beneath her nose. I held up my arm and stared at the smoldering pack marks. "What the hell?"

A warm puff of air blew my hair back. I glanced up to find Jasper in his full dragon form, looming over me.

"Uh, hi."

He leaned down and sniffed at the scars. Shiawase stood beside him with his hand on his sword, having abandoned the form of the panda.

"I told you he'd be fine," Vicky said.

"We could not be sure, little one," the samurai said.

"What happened?" I asked.

No one answered.

"What?" I snapped. "Tell me."

Sarah stepped forward, leaving Mike's side to crouch down beside me. "It looked like you were becoming a gravemaker, only instead of looking like a dead tree, your skin turned to black obsidian."

"What?" My voice shrank. "What do you mean?"

"I mean what I said. It started at your fingers." She traced a line, just above my skin, from my fingertips up my arms. "I could see it inching up your neck before the souls poured back into you."

Mike and Vicky nodded at Sarah's description. I looked up at Jasper. "You were going to eat me if went crazy, huh?"

The dragon sniffed and cocked his head to the side. Bubbles growled. Jasper collapsed in on himself until only the gray furball remained. He took up residence on my shoulder once more, staring down the cu sith.

"Stop it, you two," I said, putting a hand on the cu sith's snout. I scratched her ruff and she laid her head on my leg, almost burying me beneath her floppy ears.

"Then it is agreed?" Shiawase asked. "Our goal is the tenth

circle?"

"We don't have time to get all the way there before darkfall," I said. "I'll be taking a shortcut later with Mike. For now, we need to get you across the Burning Sea."

"Quickly," Mike said, "for darkfall is upon us."

I followed his gaze up to the crimson sun. A ring of black outlined it, a shadow over the world's light.

Shiawase offered me his hand and pulled me to my feet. "What now?"

The Burning Sea didn't look lower. If anything it appeared to be higher on the cliff side now. "I guess I try my hand at bridge building."

"You're in no condition for that," Mike said. "If you disable yourself, the battle is already lost."

"If I don't have my friends at my side, the battle is already lost."

The demon said more, but I didn't hear him. The roar of the seas below and the hum of the land around me drowned his words as my necromancy crawled forward and spread out across the cliff. A world full of the dead, a world at my beck and call. Ezekiel should have moved here instead of trying to kill off humanity.

I thought of the old bridge that crossed the Missouri River by the shop. I held that image in my mind. I'd walked by it more times than I could count, and I'd stood beside it. I'd buried bodies beneath it with Foster.

Earth flowed forward and a golden trickle of souls flowed with it. The bridge arced out several feet before a pylon shot down into the Burning Sea. It continued like that, chaff and earth oozing across the bridge, the unfinished edge rolling

150

slowly forward. Pylons and roadways and framework shot up all around us until the earth stopped moving.

I blinked, and the bridge was there. It was a dark, black, ominous thing, wider than we could possibly need. I stared at my hands. I wasn't channeling anything. The bridge still stood. The fiery waves below us lapped at the structure without effect.

"The Old Man taught you well," Mike said.

"He didn't teach me that," I whispered. "No one taught me that."

"Aren't you supposed to be a god now?" Vicky asked. "It seems like building a bridge shouldn't be such a big deal. Come on, let's go."

I watched her run past Sarah at the edge of the bridge, and step out on it. The expanse dwarfed her to an almost comical degree, but there was nothing funny in my mind. This was insanity. The bridge had to be miles long.

"Are you going to make me walk?" Vicky asked as Shiawase stepped up beside me.

"It is times like this I am reminded why I did not have children." His hands widened and bloated before his body shimmered. The bear trundled forward, chasing the giggling little girl, the demon destined to become the Destroyer.

I clenched my fists and followed them.

✦   ✦   ✦

"THIS IS AMAZING," Carter said, touching the bridge as we walked. "You even made hand railings."

I didn't understand how I'd done it, and that fact unnerved me. Jasper stayed on my shoulder, and I wasn't sure if he wanted to be close, or if he was planning on eating me if things went south.

Bubbles stayed beside Carter. Apparently all it took for her to like werewolves was for them to be ghosts. I'd have to tell Alan the good news.

Something is following us. Happy's Guardian voice boomed out across the bridge, rattling through my head. *It is distant, but it is there.*

Mike looked at the sky. "We've been walking close to an hour. We need to move faster. I don't think we're more than halfway yet."

The thought of jogging was brutal. The heat rising from the Burning Sea was intense, humid, and threatened to sap our energy in a heartbeat. I took a deep breath and lifted my legs a little higher, stretching them out into a slow jog.

I managed maybe fifteen minutes before the sweat and heat bogged me down. I stumbled to a slower walk and cursed.

Sarah matched my pace. "Are you okay?"

I glanced at her. It was still jarring to see the dark brown hair and green eyes instead of the ghostly shadow I'd grown used to. "I'm fine. Just hot."

She pulled at her cloak and blew out a breath. "You're telling me. I didn't have to worry about that before. Now I'm a puddle." She stayed silent for a moment and then whispered, "It's nice to feel again. Thank you."

I gave her a weak smile. "I don't know exactly what I did."

"Some part of you did at the time. I think you're tapped into an ancient Nexus."

I frowned. "Like a ley line Nexus?"

"A bit, but not really. One of the old witches I knew before Mike found me used to talk about it. He said there was a vast mind wrapped around all that was. We only needed the door to find it."

I groaned. "Sounds like he would have gotten along fabulously with Zola."

Her steps hesitated before she shook her head. "He was fond of slavery. He would have fought for the South in the war." She looked behind us, and then turned her gaze to the road ahead. "I knew good people who fought for the Confederacy, Damian. He was not a good man."

"Are they still behind us?" Carter asked, drawing me out of the conversation with Sarah.

Yes. Happy slowed ahead of us, Vicky straightening from a deep crouch on his back.

"Should we hunt it down?" Jimmy asked.

"No," Mike said. "We have no time."

"Jasper," I said.

The furball on my neck perked up and chittered.

"Go see what's chasing us." I held my hands out and he jumped into my palms. A vision flashed into my mind, of me throwing him off the bridge so he could swoop down below us without being seen.

I doubted he would be concealed entirely, but I followed the vision he'd shown me anyway. A trail of loose gray fluff followed him over the side until his form exploded into the monstrous reptile and he swooped toward the Burning Sea.

"What's he doing?" Maggie asked.

"Recon," I said. "I want to know what's following us. He can catch up easily enough."

We stayed at a brisk walk for another fifteen minutes. I kept looking for Jasper, but I saw nothing. Bubbles walked the bridge in front of me, growling and sniffing at every little bump in the bridge. It was unnerving, at best.

"We are at the seventh fortress," Mike said. "The trials here are unique."

"Should we just climb up on Jasper and fly over?" I asked. "Seems easier."

Mike shook his head. "There are terrible spells above the walls to prevent that. Everything from the Burning Sea on is no place for reckless speed. You will see, inside here."

"Where?" I asked, and then I saw the dip in the earth. We walked forward, and where the bridge ended, high up on a cliff, a steady decline fell away. At the bottom waited another of the impossibly long castle-like structures.

"Be wary. We will not be left alone."

I turned back to the bridge. "Should I drop it into the fire?"

"It is tempting," Mike said. "Should some of us need a path back, it would not be advisable."

Mike said a lot without actually speaking his fears. If he died, or if I died, everyone else would be trapped. Some part of me wondered if that was really true. The Ghost Pack could come and go as they wished, but would that change after darkfall? Or would the rise of Prosperine change the Burning Lands forever?

A dark shadow zipped over the Burning Sea and vanished beneath the cliff we stood upon. A massive claw hooked over the edge of the rock, and Jasper's long neck followed it up. He folded in on himself until nothing remained but the furball rolling up to my feet.

I held my hands out and he jumped into them again. This time, the vision showed me the dark-touched we'd met before, walking across the bridge behind us, but something was following him, as well.

"It's the same bastard from before," I said as the vision faded. "Something's behind him, though, moving in the shadows."

"Strange," Mike said. "I do not understand his motivation. He doesn't have the power to challenge us on his own."

"Intel perhaps," Carter said.

"Let us hope you are wrong," Mike said with a long look over his shoulder. "Perhaps whatever follows him is no more an ally to the dark-touched as to us. Enough delay. Come, we make our way into the land of thieves. Be wary of anyone we meet. Things are not what they seem."

With that, he stepped onto the steep slope and began a long slide down the rocky face.

I watched him until he came to a halt before a stone bridge. "I guess this is one way to die," I muttered, and followed him down.

CHAPTER TWENTY-ONE

W E MADE IT down without any broken ankles or gravel-marred faces, though there was one casualty. I dusted off my jeans and frowned at the hole in the knee.

"Damn. I liked these jeans."

Mike waited on the other side of the quaint stone bridge. I looked over the edge and groaned. What appeared to be a never-ending chasm vanished into absolute darkness far below.

I walked the rest of the way across the bridge without looking down. Instead, I focused on the turrets and giant stones of the castle wall before us.

"Damian."

I looked up at Mike the Demon.

"Look again into the chasm."

I glanced down, surprised to find I'd crossed the bridge already. When I looked back at the chasm, something slithered. A grating series of clicks echoed up from the darkness. It wasn't nearly as deep as I'd thought, which meant whatever was clicking at us was far closer than I wanted it to be. "What the hell?"

"This place is filled with things best not disturbed. We make for the gate, and beyond that we will encounter the next chasm. There are many chasms here in the seventh fortress."

The earth shook beneath us, and I followed closer to Mike.

We moved quickly to the gate. This one sparked like the first, but Mike did not slow his approach. He walked into it, and vanished.

"It's not physically there," Sarah said. "He should have explained that, but he's in a hurry." She followed the demon through.

"Oh," I said. "Sure, now everything makes sense."

"Come on," Maggie said, dragging me by the sleeve of my T-shirt. "You can grumble later."

Vicky and Happy stepped through next. I walked beside Maggie. Lightning and power licked at us, and I could have sworn I felt a jolt of shock, and then nothing. We were through, and the others waited in a modest stone corridor.

It looked familiar. Too familiar. "This is the Royal Court of Faerie," I said.

"An approximation of it, yes," Mike said.

The massive statues here were black obsidian instead of the cold marble of those in Faerie. Souls wandered freely in the halls, golden life given purpose in the hollow fortress.

I looked to either side when we reached the center. It was a perfect copy of the Royal Court. It felt like the center of an empty stadium, circled in stone benches and evenly spaced, ornately carved thrones. Only Glenn's throne was different here. It bore the head of a dragon and not the horns I remembered.

"You've done well."

I spun to face the speaker. The dark-touched stood at the entrance we'd come through moments before.

"I'm afraid I can't let you go farther." His wings unfurled, stretching toward the roof of the fortress. His fangs grew longer and thicker as we watched.

"Let's kill him," Jimmy snarled. The wolf shifted in a heartbeat, and pounded across the stones.

"Jimmy!" Maggie shouted. "Stop!"

The dark-touched barely moved. A quick swipe of his wing talon tore a hole through the ghost's side.

Jimmy screamed and fell to the stone floor.

I ground my teeth and unholstered the pepperbox, taking aim as the vampire leaned down to the werewolf. Two quick shots drew his focus, and he glanced at the holes in his chest.

Clearly bullets weren't much good against the dark-touched.

"You're a fool, as is your master."

It may not have damaged him as much as I'd hoped, but at least I had his attention. I let my aura flow out, calling to any dead thing I could find. I smiled when the whole world responded.

The dark-touched stretched his wings and crouched down. "Come, let me relieve you of your—guck—"

His words cut off into a gargled mess. A blade appeared in his face, wide enough to have cut through his throat at the same time it split his nose. The bloody silver vanished, only to be used as a scythe, sending the dark-touched's head bouncing across the floor.

A reptilian form stepped into the light, grabbing a section of the dark-touched's wing to wipe her blade. I'd seen her before. I knew her face.

"Utukku?" I asked.

She raised her scaly hand in greeting. Her yellow eyes glistened in the light of the crimson sun.

"What are you doing here? Shouldn't you be in the courts?"

She walked closer, her thin reptilian lips barely raised in a smile. I glanced at Mike. He didn't move. Neither did the wolves, nor Jasper.

Utukku was close enough now for us to see the subtle break in the color around her eyes. Nothing else in the room moved. This was wrong. She wouldn't be here without her glamour. She'd remain hidden, she'd ...

The strike came fast, a quick lunge that almost skewered me. She missed and turned the blow into a slicing attack, aimed at my leg.

"*Impadda!*" I didn't know what would happen, but when the option is risking an art without a ley line or getting your leg cut off without protest, you take chances.

Instead of the electric blue crackle I expected, a dome as black as the night flashed up from my hands. Utukku's blade shattered on the stone-like surface. I released the incantation and drew the pepperbox in one motion.

No more chances. I pulled the second trigger. Utukku's head split open with the boom of the pistol. No smoke rose here, only the echoing blast and my throbbing palm told me the gun had fired.

Utukku collapsed, and her body changed. Something smooth and red and squishy replaced her on the floor of the fortress.

My allies began moving again. Maggie ran to Jimmy's side, helping him up and inspecting the hole in his stomach. The gap looked translucent.

"Vicky," Maggie said. "Can you please help him?"

She nodded quickly and knelt beside Jimmy, holding her

hands up to form a small circle. The wound closed as I watched her work. How much had the kid seen as a Harrower in the Burning Lands? I couldn't stop the frown that crossed my face.

"Fuck," Mike spat. "How did you kill it? It had us all."

"I shot it."

Mike frowned. "Unlikely. Gunpowder doesn't work here."

I dumped the shells out and reloaded, taking aim at the body and firing again. The pistol jumped, and the boom echoed throughout the hall. The body jiggled from the impact. I started to break open the pepperbox when Mike put his hand on my arm.

"Don't. Just aim and shoot again."

"I don't have any rounds left."

"Just … try."

I slowly pulled the trigger until it clicked, and the gun boomed again, tearing flesh from the gelatinous body before us. "Oh."

"So what's it shooting?" Vicky asked as she leaned over the corpse. "It definitely shot something."

Mike nodded. "This entire realm is at Damian's command. It is firing what it can, even if it is the very air around us, condensed and mixed with fragments of stone."

I stared at the pepperbox for a moment before holstering it. "That wasn't Utukku."

"It was a Geryon," Mike said. "An imposter."

A small knot of angst untied itself in my chest. I remembered Utukku's story about her people's genocide by necromancers. A small part of me feared I'd added to the toll.

"What the hell is a Geryon?" I asked.

"A shapeshifter," Sarah said. "An imposter that can take

any form."

"They are not usually so bold as to attack a group," Mike said. "They are subtle and vicious and terrible."

"Enough," Carter said, toeing the body with his foot. "We need to move on. Darkfall is almost upon us."

We fell into a quiet march, following the one-time Alpha of the River Pack. The werewolves led us into the next corridor, leaving the Geryon's body behind. Bubbles took up a steady trot beside me, her fiery ears rotating at every sound and breeze.

✦ ✦ ✦

THE STATUES DIMINISHED in the next hall, perhaps only a foot taller than I was. The details lessened, breaking down into abstract forms and bulges, where the giants before had been intricately made.

"Why are these so different?" I asked, studying the smooth lines of the nearest sculpture.

"You slew the Geryon before it completed this room," Mike said. "Come, keep up with the wolves."

I looked ahead and realized how far out Carter and Maggie were. Jimmy and the others trailed behind them while Mike and I took up the rear. My pace quickened. I felt like I was nearly running, but Mike still had an easy stride. It was unnerving and a blatant reminder we were entirely different beings.

"That creeps me out," I said, watching his feet take smaller steps, yet cover more ground than me.

He glanced down and smiled. "It's an old trick. I can only do it here, at the inner circles."

"Why?"

Mike shrugged. "I don't know, honestly." He nodded and pointed ahead. "We're at the next chasm."

Carter and the others had stopped before what looked like an old bridge made of wooden planks and rope.

"Will it hold?" Carter asked when we wandered closer.

Mike frowned. "Yes, it has held for thousands of years, but I don't understand this."

"What do you mean?" Carter asked.

"This is the natural state of the chasm. There should be a Geryon here, an imposter of some sort, but I see nothing."

I looked out over the chasm. It was a short walk across the pit, maybe twenty yards at most, but infinite darkness waited below. I shivered and looked away. My fingers flexed on my pepperbox. I wanted to shoot anything that so much as blinked.

"We should go while we have the chance," Maggie said. "We don't have time to bicker about this." She struck off across the bridge.

"Maggie, wait!" Carter hissed and reached for his wife. "We don't know if it's safe." By the time he'd finished talking, Maggie was across the chasm and gesturing for the rest of us to follow.

Maggie gave Carter a sharp wave and he sighed. "She's usually right," he said. The werewolf walked forward with long strides, crossing the bridge in a matter of seconds. Bubbles followed with Jimmy, sniffing at the ropes as she closed the distance to the wolves.

"It's not even shifting a little bit," I said. The ropes and boards didn't move an inch. I expected to see some kind of sway or give or an indication of motion.

Vicky and Happy went next.

"It won't move," Mike said. "Each bridge over the chasms is carved from the flesh of an ancient titan. There are few beings that can manipulate it."

"Like an Old God? The bridge is made from an Old God?"

Mike nodded. "That is the simplest answer, though there is more to it. Let's join the others."

I stepped onto the bridge behind Mike, still expecting to feel some sort of movement, but the planks beneath my feet felt solid as stone.

At the other side, we moved forward across a rocky plain. It wasn't long before another chasm appeared, but this crossing wouldn't be so simple.

CHAPTER TWENTY-TWO

"I DON'T SEE anything," Maggie said. She gestured at the endless plain before turning back to Mike.

"This is the next chasm," Mike said, his voice growing quiet. "How I wish it were not."

"What's wrong?" Sarah asked.

Mike flickered and wavered in front of us.

"Mike?" I said.

"We must pass through Nightmare," Mike said, casting a shaky look back at the seventh fortress.

I followed his line of sight to the distant shadow that cut into the horizon. It didn't feel like we'd walked that far. This place screwed with my perceptions at almost every moment, and that made it more dangerous that I could imagine.

By the time I turned back to Mike, the smooth plain was no more. Darkness closed in around us before it exploded into violent life.

The world shook. Cannon fire. I wouldn't have known it if I hadn't heard the guns at Gettysburg. We stood on a plain, and suddenly the rocks and small clumps of grasses were gone. We were in sparse woods. Men ran past in worn dark blue military uniforms, chased by men in gray.

The sky changed to a fiery dawn, turning a smoldering pillar to a shadow, riddled with light. Bursts of smoke and the distant pops of black powder rifles sounded all around us. A tree branch shattered above, sending splinters across the party. Vicky dove to the side, pulling Sarah with her before the limb snapped and crashed to the earth.

"No," Mike hissed as he raised a hand to his forehead. "No. Sarah? Sarah!" The demon ran over the hill, and we followed, weaving through the trees faster than any sane person should. One twisted ankle, one broken arm, and that could be all it took to die in this place.

"Mike," Sarah said. "Mike, I'm here!"

I heard her voice, but I didn't see her. She'd just been with Vicky, right behind us. I knew damn well she was right beside her. A shadow formed beside Vicky, and then vanished again. We crested the hill. I froze.

"No," Mike said. "This cannot be!"

I knew the place. I'd seen it in history books. The tree line stopped dead before a tangle of muddy trenches and makeshift bridges leading away from a gaping hole in the earth. It was almost exactly as I'd imagined it, as Aeros had described it.

Blood from a blanket of corpses ran into the earth, and the humid air mixed with released bowels and burned flesh. I gagged, but I couldn't turn away.

This is where Sarah had died. Whatever this illusion was, it had Mike the Demon by the throat. He dashed out into the trenches, and jerked when a bullet grazed his arm.

It was then I realized I couldn't move. I was trapped, like my friends had been with the Utukku imposter. My eyes could still move, and I hunted for the Geryon. With so much chaos and so many bodies, which one would it be?

Down below, huddled in one of the trenches, was a young

girl. She held a bloody bayonet. Four men lay dead around her. None of them showed the trauma of a bullet or even a deep wound.

Sarah. Mike's little necromancer.

The demon's bayonet must have done its job. She squeezed her eyes shut and stood to run. I saw her collapse when the bullet took her. I heard the roar of the demon. The Smith's Hammer burst into life. I couldn't remember if he'd had it at the Battle of the Crater. What had Aeros said?

Soldiers closed on him, but sides were forgotten. Union men and Confederates alike emptied their rifles at the demon. Mike turned his back on Sarah to face the attackers.

But Sarah stood frozen beside Vicky.

Fucking hell.

The Sarah by Mike wasn't real. It had to be the Geryon. I couldn't so much as gesture. A savage grin split Sarah's face as she raised the cursed bayonet. Was it really Mike's bayonet? Would it kill him?

There was one thing the Geryon couldn't take from me, and that was the souls. I opened my mind and let them flood my consciousness. The visions weren't defined in chaos like this. There were only brief flashes of pain and joy and terror and love. I saw the dead while they still lived, felt their loss as they died, until all I could see was blinding golden light. The sheer force of a million wills shattered the black web of power the Geryon had restrained us with.

I wrapped my fingers around the pepperbox and drew it, choking back the cacophony of those visions, firing without hesitation. The first shot missed, but it got the Geryon's attention. Did the thing know that gunshot wasn't one of its own? What kind of power must it have to pick that out of the screaming, booming chaos?

A cannon shot split a tree in half beside me and I felt the splinters cut into my leg.

"It's the Geryon!" I screamed and fired again. I caught the imposter Sarah in the shoulder, and she fell.

Mike moved to help her, and she lunged.

My heart stopped. The demon grabbed the Geryon's forearm and snarled. His eyes traced our party and settled on the flickering form of Sarah beside Vicky. She flashed from shadow to flesh and back again. The Geryon was still trying to hide her, even as Mike gained the advantage.

He turned to the imposter and snarled, pulling the Geryon up to his face. "You dare? "You *dare!*"

Mike slammed the imposter into the mud while soldiers fired their rifles into the demon. Mike stood on the Geryon's chest and raised his arms. The Smith's Hammer splattered the Geryon's head like a rotten tomato. The battle around us faded. Soldiers collapsed and vanished until only the terrain was left beneath the splattered body.

Sarah stumbled forward, almost flying down the hill to Mike. She threw her arms around him. "I thought it had you."

"It nearly did," Mike whispered into her hair.

Sarah pulled back and ran her fingers over Mike's wounds. "You're bleeding." Trails of black blood wept from the bullet holes across his side. Mike didn't even seem distracted by them.

The demon held a hand over the wounds and hellfire flashed up around him. When he lowered his arm, even the holes in the leather armor he wore had vanished. "I am fine, Sarah. The Geryons have no power over me."

From what I'd seen, that wasn't exactly true, but I sure as hell wasn't going to say anything about it.

"Come," Mike said, sliding the hammer back into his belt. "We make for the eighth circle."

✦   ✦   ✦

WE CROSSED TWO more chasms bridged by the stuff of the Old Gods before Mike spoke again.

"This is the final chasm. Beyond it waits the Sea of Souls and the eighth fortress." He turned and looked at the rest of us. "They won't come for me again. It will be one of you."

"They already tried me," I said. "So I'm off the hook, right?"

My mom used to say that. "Take the phone off the hook." We'd be on the old green couch and she'd shoo Sam or me to do it. Why was I remembering that now? We'd sit down to watch a movie and she'd tell us to take the phone off the hook.

A sudden pain felt like a dagger in my eye.

Take the phone off the hook.

The world shook again, and we stood on a suburban street beside a quaint home. The vision was a part of me this time, the house where my parents raised Sam and me. A shadow stalked through the yard before casting a glance over its shoulder.

Silver fangs flashed in the moonlight. Even though I knew it wasn't real, it wasn't really happening, I moved forward.

The earth rumbled and split, and what had been a distance of only a neighbor's yard became a chasm of fire. It rose up to become a mountain, spouting ash and flame into the air. A memory flashed through my mind. Sam and I had watched footage of a volcano burning a city to cinders.

This nightmare was born of it.

Take the phone off the hook.

I had to cross the mountain. If I didn't, everyone would die. My parents would burn in their beds and Sam would join them when she tried to help. I'd seen it happen a hundred times.

"Forward!" A distant voice shouted.

I turned my gaze to the left and saw another shadow. This one was small and scared and glowed with a golden light. "Damian! Don't leave me!"

The voice pulled on me, and my mind reeled. Something was wrong here. Something was unhinged. I needed my parents. I needed my sister. I'd never feed her toys to Jasper again.

I ran toward the mountain. It was easy climbing, especially for a seven-year-old who was practically a monkey. Mom liked to call me her monkey, too. I scrambled across a loose gravel slope and paused at an outcropping of rock.

Strange animals came up through the fiery vents, rabbits with fangs and snakes with fur. A gray cloud with teeth the size of my hand swallowed them all. It didn't make sense, but they didn't matter. I ran past them, focusing on my house. I could see the roof in the distance.

Take the phone off the hook.

The phone rang.

The world boomed and the mountain cracked open. Heat from molten lava seared my face as it flowed past. My arm blistered in the passing steam. This wasn't right. There should be rocks here to jump across. I knew this place. I turned away, and when I turned back, the rocks were there, jutting up over the river of fire.

I climbed up it. My hands fit into tiny cracks as small as I was. The red rock—Dad called it granite—lay fractured and split, forming large rounded swells. I hopped from one to the next. When I reached the top, the house was already in flames. I crouched down, ready to jump, ready to save Sam and my parents.

It was a wide gap, but I could make it. I'd made the jump before. I could do it.

Something hit me. Something hit me hard enough to knock the wind out of my lungs and send the world spiraling around me. My thoughts cleared, but the nightmare held fast. A blonde child's face stared down at me, her forehead scrunched up like a worried mother. My mom would help her. I had to get her to Mom. The nightmare broke when I remembered her name.

CHAPTER TWENTY-THREE

"**V**ICKY?" I WHISPERED. "What ... what happened?"

She glanced over her shoulder, looking away. "You almost jumped into the Sea of Souls."

I leaned up and a chill wracked my spine. It looked like the Sea of Flames at first glance, but then a head would pop up, or a limb, or other less-whole bits of souls. Golden wisps of ether hovered over the flames and churned inside them.

"What the fuck?"

Vicky maneuvered herself under my arm and helped me up. My brain still felt split between the visions and where we stood. Neither seemed real now.

"They're here!" someone shouted behind us. I turned, shaking, with one arm around Vicky.

"Mike the Demon," I said as the bulky man came sprinting down the hill.

"You remember me?" Mike asked, narrowing his eyes. "What did I forge for you and deliver in the presence of the Old Man?"

"A ... weapon." I frowned, remembering the scene. I remembered him attacking me with the Smith's Hammer.

"What was its name?" Mike said, reaching out to pull Vicky away from me. The girl slapped his hand away.

"The splendorum mortem."

The demon blew out a breath. "I thought we'd lost you. Was it the souls? I did not consider the impact the Sea of Souls might have on you. Was it their nightmares that tried to drag you down?"

"Their nightmares?" I frowned and shook my head. "It was mine. An old one of Sam and my parents." I turned to look out at the fiery sea. "It felt so real. I was … I was just a kid again."

"No sign of the Geryon," a strange-looking man said, dressed in old armor.

"Shiawase," I said, and something felt sharp inside my brain. "Happy. What … why can't I think straight?"

"The Geryon is still alive," Mike said. "It has taken its leave, but there is still some damage inside your head."

I winced at another cutting pain behind my eye. "Really? No one's going to take the easy shot?"

"Can you make another bridge?" Vicky asked as she put her hand on the side of my face. "Look at me." She frowned when I looked up. "You're bleeding, behind your eye."

"How bad?" Maggie asked.

"It's not good. I can try to heal it. Don't move." Vicky squinted at me, meeting my gaze with the darkness in her eyes. I ground my teeth. She may have thought I was bracing against the pain, but I was having a much harder time containing my rage at that moment.

Vicky's arms glowed, and I grunted as her healing threatened to set me on fire.

"Done," she said.

"Thanks, kid." The sudden absence of pain was dizzying.

"So?" Vicky said. "Can you make another bridge?"

"It's too far, and the sea is too deep here." I paused and

frowned. "Isn't it?"

"Yes," Mike said, narrowing his eyes. "But it's not necessary. We can ride the ship of bones from here. I still have some influence."

Before I could so much as ask what he was talking about, Mike formed a circle of fire in the air before him and pushed it forward. It expanded and rose until it became a beacon as large as the sun. A series of symbols flashed through the center, and then it was gone.

"What was that?" I asked.

A drum crashed in the distance, deep and booming. A second beat sounded close by before the drums echoed each other in a steady march.

Mike crossed his arm and watched the Sea of Souls. "It is already time for us to return to Hugh. Once everyone has boarded the ship, I will take you to him."

The drums grew louder, and the Sea of Souls roiled with the damned and the fires. Hell or not, this was as close as I ever wanted to be. The thick flames parted like water, giving way to a main mast like something out of a child's nightmare. A skeleton manned the crow's nest, and I didn't think it was there for decoration.

It raised a bony arm and signaled Mike. The demon returned the gesture. I watched that sack of bones lean over the pale white round of his perch, drumming a sharp staccato on the ship that sent the crew scrambling across the sinewy lines below.

The ship rose in earnest, rocketing through the souls and fires until a mighty bone hull breached the surface. It curved like the skull of some great beast, turned upside down and set to float across the fires. More of the skeletons began moving across the ship, pushing screaming souls off the sides, back into the fires, like grisly sailors swabbing the deck.

"It is not designed to carry souls," Mike said, somewhat answering my unspoken question.

As the ship grew closer, clicks and grinding sounds echoed up from the vessel. Each came with a gesture or nod from one of the skeletons, and it wasn't long before I realized they were communicating.

"They don't speak?" I said.

Mike shook his head. "It's all clicks and beats. They don't really hear, from what I understand. They feel the vibrations in the air, or in the bones."

The deep, hollow drums sounded again. I traced the echo to the back of the boat where two bulky skeletons beat on the rounded skulls of some unknown giants. The march was steady and perfectly timed, regardless of the rolling waves of fire.

A wheel formed of human bones stood before a cabin made of the same. Another skeleton stood behind the wheel, an ancient black captain's hat upon his head, and a skeletal parrot resting on his shoulder.

I stared. It couldn't be.

"Will we be safe on that?" Carter asked. "If they can't transport souls … I don't want Maggie to be left in that sea."

Maggie wrapped her hand around Carter's bicep. "Wherever we go, it will be together."

Mike crossed his arms and didn't take his eyes from the ship of bones. "You are not like other souls. The Ghost Pack is known to this crew, and you will be safe. All of you."

"Graybeard," I whispered.

Mike jerked back like I'd struck him. "What did you say?"

The ship came closer, and rose into the air.

"Oh, Christ," Jimmy hissed, stepping back from the cliff's edge.

Shiawase stood beside me, his panda form abandoned as he gawked at the spectacle below. "What madness is this?"

I didn't see it at first, until my gaze swept low on the starboard side. The hand of an enormous skeleton, impossible in every way, lifted the ship from the sea. Fire dripped from the bow like water, splashing and running like thin lava.

"What in the hell is that?" I asked, turning my gaze on Mike.

He was staring at me. "What did you *say?*"

"Graybeard?" I said with a frown. "What's wrong?"

A monstrous breath sounded above me. I glanced up to find Jasper's reptilian head a foot above my own.

"Is it him?" I asked the dragon.

He chuffed at me, and it was all the answer I needed.

"That's my parrot," I said to Mike.

Sarah burst into laughter despite the look of utter disbelief on her face. "Of course it is. Of course it's your bloody parrot."

Then I remembered what that parrot was. I'd stitched him together when I was a kid. I'd pieced him back together with what I thought was a random ghost with delusions of grandeur.

My eyes shifted to Mike. "Umm, is he mad about getting turned into a bird?"

"By the gods, Damian. I don't know."

In the length of time it took me to consider how badly this reunion could go, the ship docked at the edge of the cliff, held aloft by the giant skeletal hand. Graybeard made his way to the railing. The hollow eyes of the human skeleton stared at me before the golden glow of the parrot's eye sockets burst into life.

"Vesik," the parrot squawked and released a grating laughter. Graybeard's perch kicked a bony plank down to smack against the rocky earth. Dust rose and the sound echoed in the silence. Every skeleton on the ship had stopped moving. They stood as still as old vampires. Only the faint screams and lapping of waves below dared to make a sound.

Graybeard cocked his head to the side before turning to Mike. "I have come to your aid, fire demon. Our debt is done."

"Once you transport my friends safely across the Sea of Souls, our debt is done."

"So be it." Graybeard's perch stepped onto the plank and made his way down to the cliff's edge. He rested his hand on the hilt of a gleaming saber. "You have aged, young necromancer."

I rubbed my hands together and flashed an awkward smile. "You aren't upset about getting turned into a parrot, are you?"

Laughter escaped the parrot, and the man's skeleton shook like it was in hysterics. He spoke again when the skeleton settled. "No. I am the only member of this crew with a voice. I need not click my jaws together in some tedious semblance of speech."

"Oh, good."

"What brings you to the Sea of Souls? You appear to have more than enough locked up inside yourself already."

I narrowed my eyes. "You can see them?"

"Of course. I am the captain of this ship, am I not? I see much."

"We need only a crossing," Mike said.

"Why not fly upon your dragon, fire demon?"

Mike glanced at Jasper. "He is not my dragon. He is Damian's. And you know we cannot fly into the tenth circle."

The golden light in Graybeard's eyes dimmed before it bloomed again. I thought it looked a lot like a blink of sorts. "He's always been a temperamental beast."

Jasper chuffed.

The parrot turned its focus to me. "You are full of surprises, necromancer. You are not truly a necromancer, though, are you?" Graybeard walked closer, standing between Vicky and me. "You have become something far more than that. What purpose do you have in the Burning Lands?"

Carter and the wolves shifted closer, two in back one in front. It was a pattern of attack I'd seen more than once. I glanced at Mike.

"It is safe to answer," the fire demon said.

Graybeard looked at the demon before returning his gaze to me. "I mean you no ill will. Except, perhaps, the fire demon. What brings you here, Damian?"

I still remembered hiding the barely feathered parrot corpse in a shoebox under my bed. He had told great tales of his adventures in the Caribbean, and occasionally got into fights with Jasper. I smiled remembering the flying feathers and chomping teeth.

"She brings us here," I said, gesturing to Vicky with an open palm. Bubbles snorted and bumped up against her. Vicky ran her fingers through the cu sith's bristly fur.

Graybeard studied Vicky for a time. "She is bound to a devil." His voice was low. "You truly make for the tenth circle?"

He turned to face the ship and look out across the fiery sea. "It makes sense now. I have seen them flocking around the tenth. There are a great many adversaries in your way, Damian Vesik."

"Not enough," I said quietly.

The parrot hopped and turned around on the skeleton's shoulder. "Have you found a weapon to slay a devil? Has the mighty Hephaestus forged another immortal blade? For you know the splendorum mortem cannot kill the lords and ladies of the Burning Lands."

I don't know how Graybeard knew about that, but this didn't seem the time to ask. Maybe the breaking of the Seal tipped people off after Ezekiel died? Of course it did. "I know," I said.

"That theory has never been tested," Mike said. "But considering the power tied to the dagger, I suspect you are right."

"Who do you hunt?" Graybeard asked. "You bring the ghost pack and a cu sith and a dragon, while the two of you are already gods. Why endanger the others?"

"They couldn't keep us away if they tried," Carter said.

Graybeard watched the werewolves for a moment. "I mean you no harm, wolves, but I will strike you down if you attack me or mine." It wasn't a hostile threat; it was a simple statement of fact. "Who do you hunt?"

"Prosperine," I said. "She is bound to Prosperine."

Graybeard looked up at the sky. "You mean to slay the Destroyer?" The parrot laughed again. "Save yourself the effort and jump into the Sea of Souls. Let the fires do their work. It will be quicker. Like a hangman's noose."

I crossed my arms and stared at the old pirate. "This is

worth any price, Graybeard, and I am willing to pay it. Vicky will be free and Prosperine will be dead, or we'll all die trying."

The lights in Graybeard's eyes dimmed. He looked at Vicky before nodding and turning back to me. "It is a man's own prerogative to choose where he dies. Darkfall is not long away. We must move if you are to prevent the rise of the Destroyer."

"How long has it been?" I asked Mike.

He glanced at the sun. "Four hours. It is time to return to Hugh."

"Do you not travel with us?" Graybeard asked.

"The others do," Mike said. "I must return Damian to his realm. There are ... *tools* we need for the battle ahead."

"So be it," Graybeard said. "Send him from the Sea of Souls. It will carve a new path through the Burning Lands, and make it easier for him to return."

I looked down into the roiling sea of fire. "I don't think that sounds like a great idea."

Graybeard laughed quietly. "No, Vesik. I mean from the deck of my ship. There are laws, natures, that govern the Burning Lands, but there are ways around them. You have to know the right demons."

"We have safe passage then?" I asked. "For all of my allies here?"

"I will treat them as though they were my own crew."

"Just keep their skin on, yeah?"

The parrot cackled as the skeleton turned away. "I missed your nonsense, Damian Vesik. I will protect you and yours so long as they are under my watch. Come, board the ship so you may tell people of the glories of the Bone Sails."

"Do you trust him?" Maggie asked as Graybeard vanished

over the railing.

"As far as I can throw him," Mike said. "That's actually pretty far."

I grinned at the demon. "I feel like I'm rubbing off on you."

"Gods help us," Sarah muttered.

CHAPTER TWENTY-FOUR

THE DECK OF the Bone Sails was solid beneath my feet. I'd expected it to have some give or flexibility to it when I saw the leather ties holding the ship together. When I reached the top of the stairs leading to the wheelhouse, I stomped on it again to see if it was any different.

Several of the skeletons looked up at the sudden tap, and I swore the nearest one frowned at me. It made a shooing motion with its bony fingers and I slowly backed away toward Graybeard.

"You make too much noise," the parrot said as the ship tilted slightly.

"Sorry?"

"I'm sure they'll get over it." Graybeard watched skeletons move across the deck, tightening the leather and bone sails. "You have loyal friends, Damian Vesik."

I looked at my motley group of allies as Jasper settled onto Bubbles's back. The wolves were spread out between Mike and Sarah, while Jimmy pointed at something in the distance and started shouting.

"Not the most patient of wolves, that one," Graybeard said.

"No shit," I muttered.

"How is Samantha?"

I glanced at Graybeard before grabbing the smooth railing,

almost flinching away from the polished femur. "She's good."

"You always were a terrible liar. Is she well?"

"She's a vampire," I said, remembering the late nights I used to spend talking to this parrot. He'd tell me tales of dark things not fit for a child, and they were some of my favorite bedtime stories. I took a deep breath. "It's my fault."

"She is one of the beings you stretched your soul out for."

"What?" I asked, turning around and leaning on the railing.

"I can see the stretches and ties that are not the substance of nature, Damian Vesik. Perhaps an unintended consequence of my ..." The parrot looked down at the pirate's chest and up to his hat, before he finished. "... altered state."

"Maybe."

"I am sure you did not intend to make her one of the un-dead."

"Mostly not. Only when I realized she was going to die."

Graybeard stayed silent for a time, until the ship grew nearer to the fiery waves. "A nobler effort than bonding a man to a parrot, I think, if no less forbidden."

"How do you know that? How did you know that was forbidden?"

"Your master told me much before she sent me into the Burning Lands with Ronwe."

"Zola," I said with a laugh that trailed off as I considered the rest of his words. Graybeard knew Ronwe?

"Brace yourselves!" Graybeard shouted.

I looked around for some kind of imminent threat, but that wasn't what he'd been warning us about at all.

The hull of the ship slammed into the Sea of Souls, sending up arcs of flame and screaming souls alike. I watched the skeletons sweep the clinging souls away, and cringed at the contorted faces and cries for help.

"Do not pity the monsters," Graybeard said. "Those are the demons who would have destroyed the Burning Lands. Betrayal and murder are all the imposters know."

"They're Geryon?"

"Once," Graybeard said. His bones clicked as he gave a sideways nod. "You encountered them in the sixth circle?"

"Three of them, yes."

"And you're alive. Impressive. What of the imposters?"

I turned back to face the bow, watching the waves of fire crest and crash and swell as a hot dry wind whipped across the deck. "They're dead."

"Truly?" He remained silent until I turned around.

"Yes, why?"

"It is a rare thing for the imposters to die. They are notoriously difficult to kill."

"We aren't so easy to kill either, although they didn't exactly go down without a fight."

"We are nearly at the midway point," Graybeard said. "Fetch your demon and make ready."

"I don't think Mike would like you calling him mine," I said, smiling.

"I mean the child. Her soul is wandering."

My gaze snapped to where I'd last seen Vicky. She wasn't there.

"Where's Vicky!" I shouted as I hurdled the railing and cracked onto the deck below, running to the others.

"She was just here…" Shiawase looked around and frowned deeply. He drew his sword and turned in a slow circle.

"Graybeard!" I said. "Ask the crew!"

He nodded and began rapping out a stuttering pattern on the bone wheel. The skeleton closest to us pulled on my sleeve and gestured to the shadowed hold at the bow. I followed the fleshless creature to the front of the ship, the others trailing behind us.

The skeleton clicked and rattled and pointed to shaking form by a coil of rope that was anything but rope. It looked fleshy, and I didn't want to know what the thing was. I bent down and scooped Vicky up.

The world exploded into a booming laughter and Prosperine's decayed voice shattered the peace of the Bone Sails. "I can taste her, Vesik. She is a vessel of legend! I can feel what she feels and see what she sees." Vicky turned her eyes on me, and only infinite darkness greeted me.

"I can send you into the black," I hissed. "You won't have her."

"Your pathetic edicts mean nothing, Anubis-son. My time has come, and you have failed once—"

Excutio Daemonium!" The light was not golden here, it was black and red and smashed into Vicky's body like a battering ram. Her voice, the voice of a child, screamed in pain as the incantation ripped the demon from her.

My arm ached and throbbed. It was covered in blood. I ground my teeth and blocked out the pain as best I could.

"Vicky," I prodded at her shoulder gently.

"She's out," Mike said.

"It will be a while before she awakens," Shiawase said. "Remember how long it took for her to recover before."

I pushed her eyelid back and cringed. Almost everything

was black now. A few flecks of color remained, and the rest was shadow.

"We must go to Hugh," Mike said. "The time is right."

A golden hand settled on my forearm. "Do you want to say goodbye to her? In case you don't make it back?"

I stared at Carter and almost snarled, "Never."

"Mike, let's go." Something jerked me to my feet by my backpack. "Alright, I'm ready."

Mike turned to Graybeard. "Keep them safe, or you will deal with me, and Adannaya."

"How will you get the boy back to his realm?" Graybeard asked.

"On a river of hellfire?" I muttered. "I guess I can't be choosy now."

Mike shook his head. "When I planned to send you here unaided, yes, that would have been my vehicle of choice. From here, I can return you to the Abyss."

I perked up at the thought of not having to get set on fire. "Gaia can take me the rest of the way?"

"Yes. Once you're through the gate, the hand should be able to call her."

"That's risky," Carter said, eyeing us both. "What if she doesn't respond at first? What if she doesn't recognize the call from inside the Abyss?"

"Then Damian could be lost to the void," Mike said quietly.

I shook my head. "It doesn't matter. It's this or we lose Vicky. Neither option is without its risks."

"I won't argue that," Carter said.

"Do you have the hand ready?" Mike asked.

My backpack shifted, and I could have sworn someone

pushed me again, but there was no one standing behind me. I pulled the backpack off one shoulder and opened the flap. Gaia's hand waited on top. I didn't remember putting it there. It must have shifted when I was moving.

I lifted the hand out and closed the pack.

"I'm afraid I still need to set you on fire," Mike said.

"Why?" I asked. "I thought—"

"Don't let go of the hand!"

I screamed as the demon picked me up and hurled me overboard in one quick motion. The fires of the Sea of Souls rose up to greet me, and the army of souls inside my head screamed back.

CHAPTER TWENTY-FIVE

HEAT. I REMEMBERED heat as I plunged toward the sea, and expected the bite of the flame to cut into my flesh. How long had I been falling? I knew I should have hit the fires by then. Gaia's hand was still clenched in my own. Would it be ash by now? My eyes snapped open, embracing whatever fate awaited me in the Sea of Souls.

Light circled me, black and crimson and golden all at once, spinning around me in a sphere of fire and blood. The pattern thinned at times, giving me a glimpse beyond, a peek at the crushing weight of souls saturating the sea around me. They clawed and screamed and moaned, smashing into the sphere before being hurled deeper into the flames once more.

I trusted Mike. I trusted him more than I trusted most people, but for a moment—while I sank deeper into that awful place—I worried there was more darkness to him than I'd thought.

Slowly, the sphere of light and fire started flickering. Symbols and runes expanded and contracted like a lightning strike in the roiling rhythm of flame. The pattern was black, but as bright as the sun. I couldn't stare at it without pain, but I couldn't look away.

The pattern swelled again, and this time it did not fade. A wall of runes rose before me, but I recognized none of them.

"Now!" Mike's voice barked from nowhere and everywhere. "Grab the hand!"

He sounded pained, and I wondered how much this had cost him. I slammed my palm into Gaia's and the world went white.

✦ ✦ ✦

WHEN I OPENED my eyes, I saw nothing but darkness. The stars of the Abyss did not wait for me. The road to nowhere did not feel solid beneath my feet, and when I looked down, I floated in blackness.

"Shit," I muttered. My voice echoed back to me a hundred times, and then a thousand, and then the echoes grew into a cacophony that threatened madness. Gaia's hand spasmed and locked onto mine with the force of a vice.

Slowly, in that cursing hell, the hand began to glow. The golden motes congealed, and the more of Gaia that formed beside me, the lesser the noise became.

I breathed a sigh of relief when the stars appeared around me, and Gaia offered me a smile.

"I nearly lost you, Damian. How did you come to be here?"

"Mike the Demon threw me into the Sea of Souls and shot me here with some weird mojo."

"Mojo?" she asked. "I am not familiar with this term."

We took a step forward, and the infinite road appeared beneath our feet.

"Magic," I said. "It's a, uh, slang term."

Gaia eyed me briefly, but didn't question it further. "You have a noble goal, Damian, but there is much that is uncertain. You may slay the devil, only to have it reborn inside the child.

You must bind her to a Timewalker, or even in victory you will find defeat."

"How long do we have after the demon dies?"

Gaia shrugged slightly. "You may have seconds, or you may have a year. The ancient things within the universe are not so concerned with time."

"Can you take me to the tenth circle?"

Gaia looked pained. "I fear I cannot, and I am sorry for that."

"It's okay. I figured it couldn't hurt to ask."

"There is a way, perhaps, to get you to the ninth circle, but you will need the dragon to pull you from the Seal."

"Jasper?" I glanced over my shoulder, half expecting to see back into the Burning Lands. Only the road and darkness waited behind us. "I can't risk going back."

"You will not need to."

"What do you mean?"

"He is in your backpack."

"What?" I swatted at my pack and heard something chitter. "Son of a bitch. Sneaky little bastard."

"Have you acquired a key to Prosperine's enclave?"

"What?" I said, frowning at Gaia.

"You cannot enter a devil's enclave without it, not by force and not without invitation."

"Gaia, we don't have time. We only have a couple hours until darkfall. We have to get into the tenth circle before then. And for all I know, the dark-touched could be overrunning my home right now.

I curled my free hand into a fist. "I need more time."

"You can defeat the dark-touched, Damian. Your strength

is enough."

"I can't. I can't be everywhere at once, and if they were dumb enough to gather in one spot, they'd overwhelm me."

"That is true, but there may be a way for you to be in many places very quickly."

"How?"

"Take my power and use it as your own."

I stared at the spirit beside me. What the hell did she mean by that? Take her power? Gain her abilities? Or get myself locked into some half life where I spent eternity wandering the Abyss?

"Say I was insane enough to try that," I said, keeping all my questions locked away. "What would I need to do?"

"You would need to awaken me."

"Awaken you?" I said. "Awaken the slumbering Guardian beneath Rivercene that everyone avoids so much as setting a toe near?"

"Yes."

"Can you survive that?" I asked. "If you lose your power, will you die?"

"You cannot take all my power, Damian. I can give you much in return for your help. I believe it is the right thing to do, for the king's spell still makes me feel happy when I say these things to you."

I sighed and looked out into the darkness. "How do we know that crazy old bastard didn't program a self-destruct switch in you? Made to destroy anyone that could do that very thing."

"We cannot," Gaia said.

"Do you know how?" I asked. "What kind of ritual would

be required? I don't want to kill anyone else."

"There is one who would know, and she would have a key to Prosperine's enclave. Her name is Tessrian."

That name. It hit me hard enough that I stumbled, tripping over my own feet.

"Are you well?" Gaia asked, slowing enough to allow me to regain my footing.

"Tessrian."

"You know of this demon?"

Know of her? I remembered retrieving her bloodstone prison from the graveyard at Mount Zion Church. I remembered the awful smile on Zola's face—warm as a knife's edge—and the blood coursing over her teeth when she beheaded Agnes. I remembered Zola allowing Philip to escape. I remembered hiding the bloodstone in Death's Door …

"I have her bloodstone," I said quietly.

"That will make it easier to find her, though you will still need a gateway to enter the stone. There are old spells and dark weapons that would allow your entrance."

Was this Glenn's plan all along? Is that why he left it in my possession? I frowned and glanced at Gaia. "I have a key."

"There is only one key I know of that can open a blood-stone, Damian. It is a dangerous thing that should not be trifled with."

"It was a gift of sorts from Gwynn Ap Nudd."

Gaia cocked her head to the side slightly and a small smile turned up her lips. "A gift from the Fae royalty should serve you well."

I didn't say anything else about the Key of the Dead. Gaia's suddenly blank expression was a stark reminder of the spell the

Mad King had imprisoned her with before the Wandering War. I wondered who she had been before that conflict. An Old God? She seemed too human for that, or at the least too Fae-like.

I squeezed her hand a little tighter as we weaved through the stars in the darkness, and the monsters frozen within.

CHAPTER TWENTY-SIX

I TUMBLED OUT of the Abyss and fell, shouting before my fall stopped abruptly on something that was slightly soft, slightly bony, and very angry.

"Get off!"

"Sam?" I asked, perplexed as my sister picked me up and slammed me into an empty chair. My stomach lurched at the violent shift. I was in the reading nook on the second floor of Death's Door. My head hadn't stopped spinning by the time I realized Ward and Hugh were staring at me.

Reality bent and wavered as a thin orange line appeared near the stairs. It widened and rounded, smoking like a wet campfire until Mike the Demon stepped through, and the portal vanished. He eyed the room with one hand on his hammer. The demon was ready for a fight, which was somewhat unsettling. I wondered how I'd beaten him here, but I had other things on my mind.

"What are you doing here?" I said, turning to Sam. I knew the answer as soon as I'd asked the question, and my face hardened. "No."

"Time is short," Hugh said, apparently unfazed by my sudden appearance.

I only half heard him. I was still staring at Sam.

She brushed her raven-black hair with her fingers and narrowed her eyes. "There's no one else, okay? I wouldn't let anyone else do it, even if they could. I'll do anything to help her, Demon, just like you."

I sagged into the chair and squeezed my forehead. "We don't know what will happen. What if it's different because of what I did to you?"

"You mean how you saved my life?"

I slammed my arm down on the chair. "Dammit, Sam. That's not what I mean."

"The fragment of your soul that held Sam together should only strengthen the Timewalker bond," Ward said quietly.

I turned to shout at him, to let him know he wasn't helping, but I didn't even get to open my mouth. He shut me up with one tiny phrase.

"It's our best chance to save Vicky."

Every protest died away. I leaned forward and stared at the carpet. My backpack started chittering and vibrating. I glanced at the white knuckles of my clenched fist and slid it off. "I didn't want to risk anyone else."

"We are all here of our own accord," Hugh said. He wore a patient smile. "Ward has agreed to help, regardless of his oath."

Ward frowned when he looked at Hugh. "There are some things worth breaking an oath for. If my art can help you prevent the Destroyer from taking over Vicky ... that is why you have it."

"I have it?" I asked.

Jasper exploded out of my backpack and flowed across the chair, leaping onto Sam.

"Jasper!" she said as she gathered the loose ball of fluff into her hands.

Mike studied Ward. "It is done? You have already applied the knot?"

Ward nodded.

Applied the knot? Did that mean he'd already attached it to Vicky somehow? But she'd been with us the whole time. The obvious answer hit me like a truck and my heart sank. I turned my gaze to my sister. "Sam?"

She ran her fingers over Jasper's head before tucking him into the chair beside her. She turned, back to the rest of us, and lifted her shirt. It was subtle and thin, but the lines carved into her flesh were unmistakable. The pattern I'd seen in the Book that Bleeds was now carved into my sister's back. Ward had branded her with a Devil's Knot.

"You can't keep me away from this, Damian. Don't even try."

The look on her face reminded me of better times. She used to get that look right before she kicked my ass, generally right after I fed her toys to Jasper. I smiled slightly and the fierce lines of her scowl softened.

"Then we go together," I said.

"Always together."

Jasper purred beside her.

I nodded and turned toward Mike. "What do we need to do?"

"Take the Key of the Dead and carve the center rune into her back," Ward said.

My gaze slowly turned to Ward. "What?"

"It is the rune mannaz. A symbol of your intertwined destinies that lies at the center of the knot."

Something crashed downstairs. "Foster!" I shouted. When

no one responded, I said "Frank?"

"The store's closed," Hugh said.

"Frank's at the Pit," Sam said. "The fairies left for Falias, as far as I know."

Rapid footsteps beat their way up the stairs. A bristly green head with a black snout popped up over the top step. I exhaled and patted my knee. Peanut wandered down the aisle and stopped by Mike.

The demon scratched the cu sith's ears, and Peanut purred like a pony-sized cat.

The footsteps on the stairs didn't stop. "Who's there?" I snapped.

"Peace," Hugh said. "It is Elizabeth, Cornelius's apprentice.

I glanced at the werewolf as the blood mage reached the end of the aisle. She held up a hand in greeting.

"Why are you here?" I asked.

"Wow, you *can* be an ass," Elizabeth said, stopping beside Mike and Peanut.

"Told you," Sam said.

"Cornelius could not help me bind the knot," Ward said. "Elizabeth volunteered."

"What the hell goes into one of these things?"

"That should be obvious by now," Elizabeth said.

I frowned.

"Wards, blood, and souls. That's what it's always been. You'd think the guy would be a little more appreciative of my help. I can never bind another Devil's Knot, you know that? This is it. One and done."

"You should probably apologize now," Sam said.

I blew a breath out and glanced at the ceiling. "I'm sorry.

I'm a little stressed right now."

"Get the dagger," Sam said. "Quit stalling."

Her words jarred me. She was right. I had been stalling. I didn't want to touch anyone with the Key of the Dead, much less use it to carve something into my sister. I grimaced and pulled the chest out of the wall.

I picked up the velvet pouch that held the dagger. I looked up at my friends, and Sam. No one was looking at me, no one except Jasper. I could have sworn his black eyes were fixed directly onto me. The others couldn't look at me, not really, not so long as I had my hands on the trunk. I lifted the small stone—decorated with whorls of green and red waves—and slid it into my pocket before closing the trunk and setting it back into the wall.

"That is … disturbing," Hugh said. "I know you did not leave this room, but I could not focus on you."

"Blame Zola," I said with a weak smile. I looked at Hugh and then Ward. "What if this doesn't work?"

"What if you fail to perform the ritual correctly?" Hugh asked.

I nodded.

"Vicky could become the Destroyer and inherit the power of the Ghost Pack."

"Shit," I said. "Seriously Ward?"

"Yes," he said as he ran his hand over his bald head. His cloak sleeve slipped enough to reveal the farthest edge of the tangled wards tattooed on his flesh. "The answer is clear."

"It is?"

Elizabeth laughed quietly. "Don't fuck it up."

I sighed and pulled the Key of the Dead out of the pouch,

tracing the circle of runes around the pommel. I tested the edge of the dagger with my thumb and raised an eyebrow. "This thing isn't sharp enough to cut a banana."

"It won't need to be," Ward said.

"Do it," Sam said as she lifted her shirt up over her head.

I blew out a breath and kneeled on the floor beside her. She lifted her hair, exposing the tip of the knot at her hairline with one hand while she squeezed Jasper to her chest with the other. I laid one hand on her back in an effort to steady myself. Her skin was cold. It may not have been as pale as some of the other vampires, but it certainly wasn't as dark as it had been when we were kids.

"You're sure?" I said.

She nodded.

I was afraid I'd have to push hard to cut her, but blood ran freely the instant the blade touched her flesh. The blade moved like it had a mind of its own, and my hand was only an extension of it. The x formed first before the blade traced a line down either side, extending past the base of the first cuts.

The Devil's Knot flared into life.

I leaned back and watched the golden fire ignite across my sister's back. The Devil's Knot spun, and the arm of the design that had peaked at Sam's neck became the arm that aimed at the floor.

"Are we done?" Sam whispered.

I nodded. I realized she couldn't see me so I said, "Yes." A steady light throbbed inside the knot. I didn't need to ask Ward if it was done. The spell was plain to see.

"You must carve the rune into Vicky's neck," Ward said while Sam rearranged her shirt. "It is likely she will fight you if Prosperine has already begun her rise."

"Super."

"Do not worry," Hugh said. "It gets much worse."

I frowned at the wolf. "What do you mean?"

Ward brushed a green dust bunny off his cloak. Peanut sniffed at the floating bit of fur and then huffed at it.

Ward took a deep breath. "Once the key has tasted the blood of those who would be bound, you must plunge it into your heart."

"What!" Sam and I both snapped. Jasper echoed our outcry with a high-pitched whine.

"So long as the ritual is performed correctly, and the carving of mannaz is complete, you should survive."

"Oh," I said. "I *should* survive. Super."

"As Elizabeth said, perform the act precisely and you'll be fine."

I ran my hand over my hair and sighed. "Okay. I can do that. Sam doesn't need to be in the Burning Lands? We're sure about that?"

Ward nodded. "Timewalkers are not bound to any realm. Their bonds can be forged at the greatest of lengths. Even through the Abyss."

"How much time do you have left?" Sam asked.

I closed my eyes and frowned. "Not much. Mike?"

"We should return."

Jasper chittered and whined as he hopped out of Sam's arms and flowed into my backpack.

"Take care of him," Sam said.

"I will."

Jasper released a low stuttering chuff from inside the pack.

"At least the furball understands."

I frowned at Sam. "Harsh." I winked at her. "No sense in

long goodbyes. I'll see you all soon enough." I walked down the aisle. Ward tapped my arm as I passed him and I offered a nod.

I paused by Elizabeth. "Thank you. For bringing the book, and for this."

"Just … just save the girl, yeah?"

I nodded.

Mike tore a hole in the world and stepped through, vanishing into the hellfire gate.

"Why did he even come?" I asked.

"Probably to make sure he hadn't killed you in the transition," Ward said.

I adjusted the backpack. "Strange demon, that."

"Damian," Hugh said as I reached the stairs.

I turned to face the werewolf.

"The Demon's Sacrifice … from what Koda and Ward have said, I believe it is a variation on an art known as the Army of Souls."

That tickled something in my memory. "I've heard the name before."

"See if you can find the reference. It may be wise to consult Zola. She knows much of the darker arts."

"It won't change my mind."

Hugh shook his head. "I have no intention of changing your mind."

I eyed the wolf for a moment and nodded. "Sam is risking just as much as me Hugh. You already know what I'll do to keep her safe."

"I do."

I turned and started down the stairs. I heard Hugh whisper.

"This will be worse."

CHAPTER TWENTY-SEVEN

WHY DIDN'T I tell them? Was I afraid they'd stop me? I frowned at the Key of the Dead in my palm as I walked to the 1932 Ford Victoria in the back lot. They wouldn't think I was doing anything out here. No one would try to stop me. I settled in and closed the door before pulling the bloodstone out of my pocket.

It didn't look like anything more than a pretty rock. I leaned forward and set it on the narrow dashboard.

I laid Gaia's arm across the seat beside me. Jasper's black eyes peeked out of the backpack.

"You ready to go for a ride?"

He purred and it shook the car.

"I shouldn't do this without Zola." I reached for my phone, and then hesitated, remembering her last words to me.

We'll meet again boy, be it in this life or the next.

I needed to do this alone, or as alone as I could be. Sam was already in danger, and the wolves of the Ghost Pack had basically agreed to lay down their lives to kill a devil. I cursed and slammed my palm against the steering wheel.

Jasper let out a whining purr.

"Hold on," I said. "Guard the stone, okay?" I pointed to the bloodstone on the dashboard. Jasper stared at me. "I'll be back as soon as I can. I need to talk to Gaia."

I wrapped my fingers into Gaia's before I really considered what a bad idea this was. I felt Jasper climb back into the backpack and wanted to curse at the furball. The light dimmed as the vortex swallowed me and wrapped me in darkness. I stepped into the Abyss with the Key of the Dead gripped tightly in one hand and Gaia in the other.

Gaia recoiled when she saw the weapon in my hand. "You should not have brought that here," she hissed. A confused look crossed her face before the placid smile returned.

"I aim to speak to a demon, and free another from her fate."

Her eyes didn't leave the Key of the Dead. "You move to break the bond with the Destroyer?"

"I do."

She leaned away from the dagger. "I do not wish to be close to that blade, though I am compelled to be near you. The conflict is … confusing."

"I will not burden you with its presence. Send me to the stone. I have to talk to Tessrian."

"You need only cut the air and step through. A key such as that will always take you into the nearest bloodstone when stepping from the Abyss. Wound the air twice inside the bloodstone to return to me. I will wait here."

"Will I need your hand?"

She shook her head. "It cannot travel into the stone. Be well."

"Thank you." I held the blade up and slashed at the air. Reality screamed and bent and a red gash opened in the Abyss. I released Gaia's hand, and stepped through.

✦　✦　✦

THE BLACKNESS OF the Abyss vanished in a burst of blinding red light. The souls inside my head screamed, only to fall silent moments later. I was on a cold, faceted floor. Darkness wrapped itself around me, and what little light there was bounced off flat planes of crystal, or vanished into deeper shadow.

"Long have I waited," said a low, grinding voice. "Come at last, Adannaya?" A foot paused just inside a circle of light and a tattered gown swept forward. I heard something inhale as my eyes adjusted to the dim light of Tessrian's prison. "You are no necromancer. The scent is wrong. The magic is wrong. Gaia. The Betrayer. Titan of old, come to see the enslaved?"

"I am no Titan," I said, climbing to my feet. I held the Key of the Dead firmly in my grasp. I felt for the backpack, relieved to find it still there. "And I am not my master."

Tessrian stepped into the light. My heart hammered a frantic staccato and I had only a fraction of a second to compose myself. She looked like Prosperine, smooth red skin marred by black canyons of flesh.

"I can hear your heart, boy. You fear me. You are a fool to come here, where I have power and you have none."

She didn't attack. Did that mean she was curious? Did she know something I didn't? Dammit, I should have called Zola. I stood up straighter and joined her in the light. Tessrian's eyes flashed to the Key of the Dead, and then she locked her gaze with mine.

"You meddle in dangerous things."

"I need a key into Prosperine's enclave."

Tessrian turned away from me. She settled on a squared-off outcropping of stone. "I should kill you now."

"You'll never be free of this stone if you do."

"You would grant my freedom?" She released an inhuman laugh, the sound grating like shattered crystal. "You must think me a fool."

I needed to crack Tessrian's resolve, and I didn't think I could do it by force. Not here, not without access to the ley lines. I wasn't even sure if a soulart would work in the confines of a bloodstone. I had one card to play, a card that I didn't know to be fact. I gambled. "Zola freed Ronwe."

Tessrian narrowed the black pits that passed for eyes. "I have no love for Ronwe."

"She knows how to free you. I know how to destroy you. Which would you prefer?"

Tessrian paused. Her gaze lowered, and I wondered if she was listening to my heartbeat. She'd find no hint of a lie. I did know how to destroy the bloodstone, and Mike would help me do it.

"We're going to kill the Destroyer," I said. "There will be a power vacuum in the Burning Lands. You could return there."

Tessrian slowly raised her eyes to mine. "You will fail."

"What if we don't? Can you pass up the chance?"

Tessrian looked away for a time. When enough minutes passed, I worried she'd stopped speaking to me at all.

"I have to leave for the Burning Lands. What's your answer?"

"You have no guarantees. No proof of your power other than that key. I cannot help you against Prosperine with so little evidence."

I tapped my backpack and said, "Jasper."

The gray furball shot out of the pack and took up residence

on my shoulder. Tessrian stared at him, wide-eyed.

"Impossible," she whispered.

"This is my friend," I said. "I have known him since I was a child. He fought with me at Gettysburg. He fought at Falias, and saved my sister. I owe him my life several times over, and yet he is loyal to me."

Tessrian's gaze never left Jasper. When she finally spoke, she enunciated every syllable. "You do not need a key from one of the devils. Nudd's key will cut through any barrier in that place."

I squeezed the Key of the Dead so hard I thought it might leave indentions in the metal. Another of Glenn's manipulations? Did I dare to use the key inside the Burning Lands? What choice did I have? Let Vicky become the Destroyer? I ground my teeth.

"Carve the rune hagalaz upon the doorway to the enclaves, and it will crumble." Tessrian lowered her focus to the crystalline floor. "You have my word that these things are true."

Hagalaz. I knew the rune, drawn like a capital H, but the center line was left at a sharp angle meeting neither the tops of the bars in their center, but that wasn't what concerned me.

"That rune has many meanings," I said, watching Tessrian closely.

She made a deep throaty grunt. "Perhaps in your realm, but not in the Burning Lands. In the Burning Lands, it means only destruction."

I held my backpack open and let Jasper climb back inside. "I'll come back for you."

Tessrian watched me for a moment. "I will be surprised if you survive this foolish quest. I will be equally surprised if you keep your word."

I nodded at the demon before striking the wall of the bloodstone twice, forming a red X. I glanced at her one last time before stepping through. A demon who had fought against Zola, imprisoned here for centuries, and potentially freed by Zola's apprentice. An odd existence, to be sure.

Red light strobed around me and the Abyss bloomed into existence a moment later. Gaia snatched my hand before I could make heads or tails of the starry darkness.

"It is done?" she asked, deliberately keeping her eyes away from the Key of the Dead.

I nodded. "I need to return to my realm and secure the bloodstone."

"Be quick."

The Abyss faded, and the sudden appearance of sunlight almost blinded me as my butt slammed into the driver's seat of my car. I blinked. Jasper squeaked in the backpack.

"Nice aim," I said to the severed arm in the passenger seat. I scooped up the bloodstone and buckled it into my backpack along with the Key of the Dead. There was no reason to subject Gaia to that thing any more than I had to.

I took a deep breath. "Ready, Jasper?"

He chittered back at me from the backpack.

I laced my fingers with Gaia's and returned to the Abyss.

CHAPTER TWENTY-EIGHT

I GROANED AND braced my hands on my knees. "Fuck."

"I did warn you this time," Gaia said, standing before the Seal of Anubis.

"Yeah," I muttered. "That's like warning a drunk they should stop drinking because of hangovers. If you're already drunk, you're probably getting a hangover."

Gaia looked up at the Seal. "You mean to make for the tenth circle, but there is no pathway to it."

"How close can we get?" I squinted and looked up.

"I can only see the seventh. The path to the inner circles shattered when the Seal broke. From there, it will be up to your dragon."

I opened the backpack and let Jasper flow out onto my shoulder. "You ready for this?" I asked the furball.

He purred like an oversized cat.

Gaia looked at Jasper and then back to the immeasurably large Seal. "We must reach the center. It will be an unpleasant journey."

"Do it," I said, wrapping my arms around Jasper and closing my eyes. Gaia didn't hesitate. My stomach lurched as we shot into the air. I clenched my teeth when Gaia suddenly jerked us to the side. The change of inertia felt like a car wreck, and then it happened again, and again. "I thought we just needed to go up." I groaned and put a hand on my stomach.

Vertigo almost brought me to my knees when I opened my eyes. The endless stretch of gray stone reached out in every direction, spinning in my vision even though it did not move.

"Up?" Gaia said. "You have much to learn about the Abyss, young one."

We stood before a fracture in the stone the size of a skyscraper. Massive bolts of power cascaded through the break, meeting in the center to form a core of white and blue. It swelled and receded and crackled like lightning, racing through the broken Seal.

"That is your path," Gaia said. "The center pathway is broken, but it will reach the inner circle if your dragon can navigate the old ways. Jasper must maintain his speed when you exit the Seal, or you will never breach the barriers. Are you prepared?"

I took a deep breath. "More than I was last time."

Yellow light exploded around me. Even prepared, it was a blinding thing. I cracked my eye open. Oh yeah, we were on a direct collision course with the Seal.

I waited for the lightning to serve up one order of crispy fried necromancer, clamping my arms down on Jasper, wrapping him up in my forearms as the first bolts of power tore through us. I expected fire and shocks and stabbing pain, but here it was more like passing through frigid ice water … with shocks and stabbing pain.

Jasper expanded in my grip. My eyes were closed, but I still felt his fur become scales, and my floating body suddenly had support beneath it. I kept a choke hold on the dragon even as my skin froze solid and began chipping away. I didn't watch the exposed muscle and bone this time. I didn't need to see that ever again.

The world became a frozen crystal at the heart of the Seal. I couldn't look away once my eyelids grew translucent in the freezing power. I had a horrible thought of my arms shattering and of losing Jasper, of being trapped inside this frozen hell.

Jasper spiraled through the darkness and roared. His wings spread out to either side, and then he dove. The dragon's head smashed through a crystalline wall that looked like the opposite of Tessrian's prison, and then we were out. The overwhelming power left, and my body became my own once more.

It was only then that my face fractured into a smile. The warm wind of the Burning Lands whipped at my head while I rocketed through the air on the back of a dragon. Below us, the Sea of Flames boiled, and we shot past it, soaring toward the inner circle.

I ran my fingertips over the scales on his throat, and the dragon purred like a giant flying cat. Images flashed through my mind. I'd come to realize it was how Jasper spoke, in images and clips and symbols.

Three things became obvious in his little slideshow. We were about to pass one of the fortresses. We were about to crash through a barrier to catch up with the others. Darkfall was upon us.

My heart slammed against my chest and I stared at the sun. The disc was nearly black. Only a pinpoint of light remained. A dark stone edifice blurred by beneath us, and Jasper tightened his body, hurling us forward at a terrifying velocity. Lightning sparked around the dragon's head, and I saw the golden barrier a split second before we hit it.

Golden bolts of power lanced into the sky and tore into the earth as Jasper plowed through, hurtling over the Sea of Souls. He swooped toward the fiery body, and the heat rising from it threatened to flay my skin.

Ahead were the opposite cliffs and the outline of the Bone Sails. Graybeard raised a fist to us and pointed toward a blood red fortress. Jasper threw out his wings and slowed.

"No," I said, patting the dragon's neck. "Take us to the tenth."

Jasper closed his wings and shot forward once more, catching the heat from the Sea of Souls and streaking forward. I watched the earth below us for any sign of the others. There was nothing. They were already inside the ninth fortress. Without knowing what waited inside, it was better to take Jasper to the tenth. If Gaia thought he could do it, I had to believe.

Turrets soared into the air around us. It would have been impossible to pass this maze of stone without slowing. But was Gaia wrong? Jasper evaded the jagged towers by taking sharp turns and swooping below impossibly tall bridges. Any time I slipped, the dragon righted himself, or nudged me with a wing.

Darkness loomed ahead. I looked back to the sun. Time, we still had time. Jasper didn't have to show me the black grid of power we had to break through. It was plain to see, intertwined with a sickly black and red. It figured that a demon's aura would guard the devils' sanctuary.

Jasper slowed. An image of a golden dragon flashed into my mind, wrapped in power, wrapped in a soulart.

I didn't hesitate. Maybe I should have, but we'd come this far. I unleashed the souls locked up inside me and let them flow around the dragon. They cried out as they filled the crevices between his scales so completely that he looked like a golden screaming sun.

Jasper hurtled forward, falling into a steep dive before pulling up at the last second and smashing into the wall of darkness.

I would have screamed if I hadn't been concentrating on the soulart. A flash of the devils tore into my mind, a legacy of blood and pain and horror. Flayed bodies scoured my vision, but I didn't so much as try to look away. I held the web over Jasper. This was out last chance. We broke through, or Vicky became our greatest nightmare. The dragon roared as though he'd heard my thoughts, clawing at the darkness, stretching the barrier further and further until, finally, it shattered.

A hail of darkness fell below us, peppering the grass and dirt. The sky crumbled above, and for a moment I feared it we were done for. The giant tumbling sections of the barrier caught fire in the next second, and then they were gone.

"Damian!" someone shouted from far below.

"Take us down Jasper. Fast."

The dragon dove, hitting the earth hard enough to crack stone. I grunted as my face smashed into Jasper's neck. "Oww."

I slid off his back and patted his bulky leg. "Where's Vicky?"

Carter and Maggie carried her forward. Her wrists were bound in a hellish light. She struggled, throwing herself against the bonds. Her eyes met mine and she bared her teeth. My heart fell into my gut.

Darkness was all that remained.

"There is still a chance," Mike said. "Turn her over. Carve

the rune."

I drew the Key of the Dead.

"Come now, Vesik," Vicky said, and the voice was all wrong. It wasn't Vicky at all. "Let us discuss your options." The words fractured and the voice put emphasis on all the wrong syllables. "Surely you do not wish for the child to perish here."

Maggie strong-armed Vicky and flipped her over. "She won't shut up." Maggie's face looked hollowed out, haunted. "The things she's said. If we can't stop this, we have to kill her."

I placed a hand on Vicky's back. She bucked and writhed and screamed into Carter's hand. "Vicky help me," I whispered. "Please, if you're in there."

The child's body froze. I didn't wait. Two quick slashes formed the X and two more drew out the legs. I recoiled at the sight of the Devil's Knot. It bloomed across her neck, vanishing beneath her shirt and crawling up into her hairline.

Vicky stilled.

I raised the dagger and aimed for my heart. One deep breath, and then—

"No!" Mike said, grabbing my wrist.

"You heard them," I snarled. "It has to be done!"

"After you kill Prosperine. Do not make the bond until then. You could bond the devil to your sister if you do not wait."

I almost dropped the Key of the Dead at that thought. "Fuck. Fuck! Why didn't anyone say that?"

"Touching," said a cold, familiar voice.

Vicky bucked and shifted in Carter's grasp. "Get off!"

"Vicky?" Carter said.

She looked up and the blackness of her eyes was shot

through with a sickly red. "Mostly."

Her answer sent a frisson of terror down my spine.

"It's her," Maggie said, releasing her grip on Vicky's upper arm.

"So touching," the cold voice said again.

I looked toward the modest wall standing between us and the devils' enclaves. It was there, outside the tenth fortress, that the dark-touched returned.

"You have come far, Vesik. Some of our kind assumed you would. I did not."

"Who are you?" I asked as Jasper paced behind me.

The dark-touched vampire's mouth turned up at the corner. It was almost a smile, but the elongated face made it one of the most horrible things I'd ever seen. "Who? You are a curious being. To most, I am a thing. A thing to be feared. A thing to be battled. But to me, I am a leader set to destroy the last of the necromancers."

I did plan to destroy the dark-touched, but he couldn't possibly know that. A quick glance showed me how close darkfall was. We didn't have time. I played the fool, and asked him. "Why? What have I done to the dark-touched?"

His smile shifted to a flash of silvery gray fangs. "You bear the name of necromancer, but you have no concept of the power of a true lord of the dead."

"You speak in riddles," I said. "Why shouldn't I kill you where you stand?"

"You could not, even if you tried. I am many, and as a whole, we are immortal."

Mike's voice hissed in my ear. "We smash through their lines, and you find Prosperine," Mike said. "Let Jasper carve you a path."

Lines? What did he mean by … the thought trailed off as I realized that the hunched gray stones behind the vampire were made up of at least twelve more dark-touched.

"We can fly over them."

Mike shook his head. "They will shoot you down. Trust me in this."

"Oh, the demon is right," the dark-touched said. "Stand with me my family. Show the doomed to their end."

Each of the hunched forms stood, stretching long legs and longer wings. They looked like bat wings, but each was armed with a trio of wicked-looking talons. The membrane stretched from a slightly too long, human-like arm to the bones at the top of each wing.

They looked delicate. I was certain they were anything but.

Shiawase walked to the front of the line with Vicky at his side. He adjusted his sheath and crouched with one foot far in front of the other. "Leave us or die," the samurai said. "It is your only choice."

Mike's hammer burst into brilliant life and Sarah's hands glowed red. She wore a smirk that made my skin crawl. Jimmy crouched beside me, and his body exploded into a hulking golden werewolf. When he breathed, it sounded like a roar.

"Through the middle," Mike hissed. *"Now!"*

The Burning Lands were lost to chaos. Mike charged across the field, his hammer drawn to the upper right. Red lightning stormed from Sarah's hands, and her voice turned into an unrelenting chant of the damned.

A dark-touched vampire landed a glancing blow on Mike's shoulder. It cost the vampire a leg. Shiawase drew his sword and black light shot out in a wave, slicing through the fallen vampire. The next time the creature moved, its head fell to the rocky earth.

I watched in awe and horror as the body picked up the severed head and reapplied it to the stump of its neck. The wolves barreled into the dark-touched behind Mike, tearing the vampire to pieces before it could finish reassembling itself.

Another of the vampires arced over Mike. It was a feint. The strike was never meant for the demon. The claw tore into Maggie's back and she howled. Vicky hit the vampire like a train. Light exploded around her. Traces of black and red power wound into her aura as bits of the vampire splattered across the field. Carter downed the next as he moved closer to his wife and Jimmy tackled another vampire.

Jasper bucked as I leapt onto him and grabbed his neck. He shot forward, slicing through a dark-touched as he dodged one of Sarah's crackling lightning strikes. I didn't want to leave them behind, but this was our chance. While the others kept the dark-touched occupied, we could breach the tenth fortress. Our allies were more capable of taking care of themselves in the Burning Lands than I was.

"Get us to the wall," I shouted into the wind. I screamed as something sharp and jagged ripped into my leg. I glanced back and found one of the vampires attached to Jasper, his claws in my calf. My first instinct was to grab the pepperbox, but the angle was all wrong. I wrapped my fingers around the cold metal of the focus and channeled. I was expecting the storm of power this time. The golden beam shattered the vampire's arm, and removed a large piece of his head.

I cut off the power flowing to the blade. The body fell slowly until Jasper whipped his tail, sending the dark-touched barreling into one of its own.

Jasper curled his head down and barked out a dense blue fireball. I reveled in the vampire's screams, though I couldn't see the carnage below. The dragon pulled up, spreading its wings and dropping me right in front of another gate.

I shouted as my injured leg took the brunt of the impact. It didn't matter. It was time to find out if Tessrian had set us up. I slid the focus back into its loop and unsheathed the Key of the Dead. I heard the battle raging behind me, smelled the seared flesh and the sharp scent of sulfur that meant someone had called hellfire. My gaze stayed locked on the gate.

This latticework of metal was modest compared to the power-laced gateways of the previous fortresses, but it still stood some fifteen feet high. A solid diamond-shaped pattern ran the length of the gateway's center. It left plenty of space for the rune. I moved quickly, the Key of the Dead offering little resistance as it sliced into the barrier. I cut the two upright legs of hagalaz into the metal first and quickly joined them on the diagonal.

Something screamed and groaned inside the metal, and I stepped backwards. A sizzling blue light traced the rune before shooting out across the lattice. The gateway steamed and hissed and finally collapsed in on itself, slowly dissolving into the stones below.

My fingers flexed around the Key of the Dead. "What the hell is this thing?" I stared at the dagger and sheathed it.

I turned back to the battle behind me. The werewolves tore one of the dark-touched to ribbons, their fangs and claws flashing in the fading light. I turned away when Mike crushed another with his war hammer. It started pulling itself back together immediately.

The things just didn't die.

A shadow caught my attention. The dark-touched I'd hit with the soulsword. It wasn't moving. I stepped forward and ground my teeth against the pain in my leg.

"Vicky!" I screamed. "Soulswords!"

I couldn't be sure she'd heard me until I saw the golden blades lash out. Two of the dark-touched fell to pieces before they understood what was happening. It was the best I could do, for now. I limped into the hall behind the fallen gate, hunting the devil.

CHAPTER TWENTY-NINE

P AST THE GATE, within the tenth fortress, waited a structure that reminded me more of the Royal Courts of Faerie than any other structure. A series of four towering statues, each more hideous and deformed than the last, flanked the pathway to a short set of stairs.

I hurried forward, blocking out the pain of my wounded leg as best I could. The screams and explosions of the battle outside echoed through the dim chamber. I moved through the shadows of tentacle-laden statues, past the ruptured humans carved into their stony grasp.

The last stared down at me, and I half expected the thing to move. Fangs like those of the dark-touched curved out over its jaw, and spiral horns grew from its head. Nothing moved. I pushed on. Darkfall was upon us.

The doors at the top of the short staircase looked like wood. Large rivets stood out around the frame. Something moved behind them. I drew the focus from my belt and channeled, slashing through the door at an angle before kicking it in.

A slow creak filled the hollow space. Beyond waited a throne, one of several positioned around the room. Something breathed and huffed behind me. Small footsteps sounded in the hall. A quick glance showed me Vicky and my hand tightened around the focus.

"Damian Vesik." The voice growled and screeched and filled the air around me with unease.

The light in the room turned, like the corona of a sun flashing in surges and waves to reveal the creature upon the center throne.

"You bring me my vessel? I am surprised."

She didn't look like the red-skinned monstrosity that Philip had pulled into our world at Stones River, but this was Prosperine. Of that, I had no doubt.

"Do you not speak, mortal?"

I looked up at the view through the ceiling: the sun, nearly centered, nearly covered in black. Runes and knots wound their way around the dome, circle after circle leading down into the floor.

Part of a ritual? Part of some Burning Lands religion? It didn't matter.

Prosperine narrowed her eyes and leaned forward on her throne. "I will use the body of the child to kill you. It will be a sweetness unlike any I have imagined. Your suffering will become a legend in this hall, necromancer." Her voice rose until it screeched with madness. "Witness the Darkfall!"

I held up my right hand and closed my eyes. This world was mine. Everything about this world was mine.

The chaff of a gravemaker sliced through my forearm in a dozen places. The golden glow of the souls inside me lined the wounds as my arm became a cracked, blackened mockery of itself. I could *hear* the power rushing through my ears, like a tidal force set destroy a continent.

"Damian."

It was Vicky. The panic in her voice stabbed at my heart.

"Don't leave me."

I focused on pushing the art down, keeping it from consuming me, trying to find a symbiosis with it that I'd never seen the Old Man achieve. It came with the thoughts of my sister and my family. If I failed here, this battle would become theirs, and they weren't strong enough to face the Destroyer.

I turned to Vicky and opened my eyes as the gravemaker chaff rose up to cover my neck. "I won't, kiddo." My voice was rough, tortured by the bark-like debris cutting into me.

Prosperine charged at us, covering more ground than physically possible in such a short time.

Terror drained the color from Vicky's face. The child who had lived through hell and died, only to be brought back into a new hell.

The burn of the gravemaker art crawled up my face, surrounded my eyes and invaded my senses, but I held it in check. "I just have to give the devil her due."

The devil's eyes widened as I spoke, as she must have realized I was still me. She tried to backpedal, but I wasn't giving her an option. I stepped forward, oblivious to the pain that should have been crippling my leg, and raised my arm. The world bent to my will, and my arm shot forward, extended and bloated into a charcoal nightmare.

"No! You cannot defeat—"

Prosperine's protest cut off as her body slammed into the throne so hard its back shattered. She pried at the bark-like fingers throttling her body, finally snapping one of them off.

"You are not Anubis!"

I blinked slowly, forcing a new finger to grow across her face. I raised my chin slightly, lifted the new finger and split it into two. My arm continued to grow and expand as the stuff of gravemakers, the essence of the Burning Lands, swelled to meet me.

I forced the split fingers through Prosperine's eyes, feeling the warmth of her substance around me. I closed the fist until the fingers met my thumb.

"Damian," Vicky whispered. "Don't leave me."

I wanted to. I wanted to become this thing, this force of destruction. I could break nations with my every whim and strike every evil from the earth, but that girl's voice …

We'd failed. I'd failed her before. I'd never fail her again.

"Hellfire," I snarled in a voice that was not my own.

Vicky didn't pause. She fell to her knees.

"On me," I growled. "Light me."

I saw the tears on the child's face, but she did as I asked. I felt the fires rise up beneath me. I felt the burn as the hellfire slid into the cracked flesh of a gravemaker, and I laughed as it flowed down my arm.

Prosperine struggled and screamed in my grip.

The orange blaze of hellfire merged with the gravemaker flesh, and became something new. A part of me knew what it was, knew what it could consume. The white spiral of flame was soulfire. Forged of the lost soul of a gravemaker, ignited by hellfire, it was all-consuming.

I felt it bite into Prosperine's flesh, and I pulled my arm back. Her face tore off in my hand, her charred flesh and skull cracking against the floor. I used my arm as a conveyance, pulling myself to her burning body, pieces of my arm peeling off and falling away where they became unnecessary.

Still she was reborn. New flesh grew over her wounds as fast as I could destroy it. Not even the soulfire was enough. But what if Prosperine wasn't with her body any longer, even for a split second?

My face twisted and I raised my chin to a series of clicks and cracks. Vicky screamed with the channeled hellfire. It was now or never. She couldn't keep this up, and neither could I.

"Excutio Daemonium."

I could see the shock on Prosperine's face as her spirit was torn away from her flesh. The empty husk of her body fell to ash in moments, flayed by the blazing white soulfire.

"Stop," I hissed at Vicky. She let the soulfire fade before falling to the stone floor. The gravemaker body around me sizzled and dripped and fell to pieces as I cut my ties to it. I stepped from the muck and grime as it flowed away from me, vanishing into the cracks of the floor once more.

The focus was ready by the time the last of the chaff fell away. Blood coursed down my arms, but I paid it no mind. I kept my gaze locked on Prosperine. She floated in space with a silent, eternal scream etched across her lips.

I raised the focus, and opened the cavern of souls hidden away inside my head. The beam of golden rage tore through the structure behind the devil's spirit. When it was done, only a ghostly eye remained, floating toward the ground.

I held out a hand. I stared into that golden eye—and perhaps imagined it—but I like to think it was terror I saw there. I channeled a soulart through my hand and closed it around Prosperine's spirit. It hissed and popped until it vanished in a streamer of smoke.

"Damian …"

I turned back to the tiny voice. Vicky cried and shook as a

violent seizure wracked her body. A shadow crossed above us. Darkfall was here.

I drew the Key of the Dead as visions of Sam and Nixie and my family flashed through my head. I held it there for one deep breath.

Vicky screamed, and I plunged the blade into my heart.

CHAPTER THIRTY

M Y PACK MARKS ignited into a ferocious burn and pulled on the Ghost Pack, the spell surging through me. Carter and Maggie and Jimmy graced my mind and smiled as they passed. It was much more peaceful than the time Prosperine had killed them. I caught flashes and snippets of their lives, their alliance with Edgar, their love for each other, and Jimmy's love for crispy rice squares.

The spell turned on me. The power changed from an exhilarating surge in my core to a pain that should have rendered me senseless. Every fiber of my being caught fire, and the city of souls inside my head screamed with me.

The very earth rose up, filtering through my aura and taking little pieces of me with it. I could feel them fly away. I knew what they hunted. They travelled to the Seal.

Beware the gifts of the Fae.

I screamed again, but no sound escaped my throat. I tried to summon a shield, a soulsword, anything, but the incantation was already consuming me. It locked down my aura as surely as it had destroyed Vicky's bond to Prosperine.

Mike shouted somewhere nearby. Was he here too? "That wasn't the Demon's Sacrifice!"

The fires did their work, and it wasn't long before I couldn't feel anything. The world became a numb and vague impression to my blistering eyes.

Dying didn't hurt like I expected it to. I knew something was wrong. Perhaps it was the blood of Anubis that flowed through my veins, the same sense that told me things I could not possibly know as I walked through the Burning Lands.

"Damian!"

I saw the flash of red when they appeared in the vision. Foster. Cara. Brought here by an exhausted-looking Elizabeth.

Tears of fire ran down my cheeks as the Key of the Dead brightened into a golden sun. This was the Demon's Sacrifice. I knew it with all my being. Mike was wrong. There could be no life without death.

I slowly turned my gaze back to Vicky. A stream of golden soul flowed into her, while another line of gold vanished into the ether above me. I could see Sam there, ghostly and pale. This was the right thing to do.

"Damian!" I felt the hands on my cheeks. Things felt thick and heavy there in the Darkfall. I wasn't sure what was real anymore, and what was simply my mind shutting down, giving in to the darkness.

"Vicky will live," I whispered.

I smiled at Cara's face. I saw her turn and scream at a black shadow behind her. It looked like it had antlers. How odd.

Consciousness crashed back into my body, and I felt nothing but pain in the horrid white light, the light come to punish me. An angel's wings spread out before me. Black and white and … and …

I screamed as the sword cut through me.

"It is done!"

Foster? I knew that voice. Foster wasn't here, though, was

he? My memory fractured, and I began losing track of who was with me, who was alive, who we'd already lost. Vicky was all I could remember as the burning intensified, and the world turned golden.

"No no no, he's too far gone."

"I have to try," Foster said. "I have to try."

The healing hit me like a truck. Some part of me came back together and my vision cleared for a moment. It felt like seconds, but it could have been hours. My mind was in ruins.

"I can't let him die," I heard someone whisper. "This is my fault. I didn't know."

A beautiful face appeared over me, hidden within magnificent golden armor.

"Mom?"

Cara smiled. "I'm sorry, Damian. I only just learned of his plan for you. I tried to get here. I tried." She held my face and the tears flowed down her cheeks. "You have to grow stronger. Don't face him now. He knows not what he's done.

"When it begins, draw your sword from his chest."

Sword? I tried to ask, but I couldn't speak anything more. My eyes wouldn't move to look at my chest.

"I don't want to lose you." Foster, that was Foster. My vision faded again with the roar of power in my head. The fairies couldn't save me. Nixie … Sam …

"I love you, Foster," Cara whispered.

Light and warmth wrapped itself around me. The souls inside my head quieted as the healing took hold. It pulled my aura back together, repairing things that shouldn't be reparable. I felt the sword jerk out of my chest.

I heard the scream of the fairy, and my own scream joined

it. The light faded, and the screams died.

"It is done," Cara whispered. The fairy rolled off of me, snapping one of her wings beneath her own weight.

Foster stared at his mother. "I can heal you."

She shook her head once. "I … am done."

I looked up. Gwynn Ap Nudd stood beside a shattered throne, a pair of dark-touched to either side of him. He could have saved her. I was sure of it. Instead, he stepped backwards into a black vortex, his horned helm vanishing into the Abyss with the two vampires.

"What is that?" Mike hissed.

Shiawase stood above Vicky, his sword drawn. Something moved near the line of thrones, green eyes glowing amidst a body that looked like smoke and fur. I tried to focus on it, but Cara's voice drew my attention back.

"Damian … grow stronger. Don't face Nudd now. He knows not what he does, and he must … be stopped. The wolves said goodbye."

When I glanced behind me again, the creature was gone. I looked around for the Ghost Pack, but they were all gone. I already knew where they were: destroyed by the Demon's Sacrifice. There was a whisper of memory, a final goodbye from Maggie and Carter.

Jasper huddled up beside Cara as her face slackened. Her hands fell away from her chest and it was only then that I noticed the gore marks. Glenn had murdered his own wife.

"Cara?"

"Mom?" Foster whispered as he fell down beside the fairy. He touched his mother's pierced cuirass and winced as though he'd been burned. "Iron? No …"

227

Her body rose into the air, and I watched the fairy disintegrate. Power exploded from her fading form. Lances of white light shot through the walls around us, killing dark-touched vampires I hadn't noticed a moment before and crumbling the walls behind the throne. When Cara's armor crashed to the ground, empty but for her screams, only two figures remained standing.

I didn't need to know who they were. I understood that only devils resided in the enclave. Tessrian would have her choice of thrones.

I looked back at Foster, screaming over the motes of being that were all that remained of his mother, at the unconscious girl who would have been the Destroyer, at the ghost panda sworn to protect her, at the wounded demon who fought to save his love, and at the blood mage who risked god knows what to bring the fairies here. Carter and Maggie and Jimmy were gone, sacrificed to these fucking *things*. My *friends*.

In that moment, a rage settled over me. I felt the mantle of Anubis claim its new bearer. I understood the power that Ezekiel had once wielded, and I understood that the mantle had never been his to bear. It had always been mine.

The earth around me dissipated into little more than a cloud, swirling out and up only to slam closed over my head. When the darkness cleared, I saw with the eyes of the Jackal. Not the corrupted imitation Ezekiel had been, but the sleek obsidian helm of power that mantle was meant to be.

When I opened my jaws and cried out Cara's name, the Jackal roared with me.

"You dare stand in this place?" the first of the devils said. He was broad and thick where Prosperine had been slight and agile. He would die first.

I closed my right hand and the scepter appeared, long and golden and sharp enough to carve rock. The Jackal roared and, before the devil could move, the end of the scepter had already split his skull. A low sweeping kick shattered the knee of the other devil.

The second screamed while the first made wet sucking sounds.

"I can't heal!" The devil grabbed at his knee and recoiled. "What have you done?"

I breathed out as I turned the mantle to face the second devil. "My friends are dead and, because of it, you will never heal again. Warn your people." I released the scepter and it vanished, letting the first devil crash onto the stone steps.

"Enter our realm again, and I will reduce your world to ash. I leave you as gifts for Tessrian."

The devil cowered behind the shattered throne as the shadow of Anubis left them behind.

I heard whispers and slowly turned my head to the throne once more.

Two glowing green eyes opened in the gray rug to either side of the throne. I took a step back as the rug arched its back and stood. I didn't know what it was, but the massive shaggy gray form drifted forward. At the edge of the platform, I could see its human-like feet. The creature paused and leaned forward on a too-short arm. The head rotated from one side to the other, until it finally rotated in a full circle.

Apparently losing interest in me, the creature turned back to the devils. It wandered to the dying one and started *eating* it. The crunch was terrible. Bone and cartilage ground and shattered as the fur on the thing vibrated and shook.

I envisioned a wall rising between us, and so it was. This realm bent to the mantle's whim. I turned back to my friends, and let the head of the jackal decay around me. Trails of black dust fell down my shirt, staining the vampire skull and pooling at my feet.

I stared at the fairy. My friend; bent over the armor of his lost mother.

"Foster."

He looked up at me. I'd seen rage on the fairy's face more than enough times, but here it looked broken. His loss was a loss to us all.

"It was a *trap,*" Foster snarled and punched the dirt. "The marks carved by Ward reacted to the Key of the Dead because of your bloodline."

Mike leaned away from the words like he'd been struck a physical blow. "What? That's impossible. I would have known. Someone would have known."

"Glenn knew," Foster said. "He'd fed it to Koda years ago. That son of a bitch has more backup plans than … than …" The fairy let out a frustrated shout.

"How did Cara know?" Shiawase asked, sitting down beside Cara's armor. He kept a hand on Vicky's shoulder. Jasper rolled up beside the samurai, nestling into the crook of Vicky's arm.

"He told her," Elizabeth said. She sighed and fell onto her knees beside Foster. "That pompous ass told her."

Foster glanced at the blood mage. He leaned closer and started cleaning the blood from her arms. Sarah knelt on Elizabeth's other side and did the same. Her arms were beyond bloody. The depths she must have carved her flesh to open that portal made me cringe.

Elizabeth winced at every gentle touch. "Gwynn Ap Nudd has been working with Hern all along."

"Son of a bitch," I snapped. "Why tell her now?" I lowered myself to the ground beside Vicky. Her breathing was steady. I stared at her closed eyes, and dread crawled up my spine.

"Why now?" Elizabeth asked, wincing at Foster's gentle touch.

"He found out you were in the Burning Lands," Foster said. Dim light leapt from his fingers as he traced Elizabeth's wounds, sealing the deepest cuts.

"Don't heal the scars or the scabs. Those are for the Coven."

"I know," Foster said softly. "I can see the patterns."

"I can't get us out of here," Elizabeth said. "That was a one-way trip."

"The Seal has been restored," I said. "Mike can take us home."

"The Seal?" Mike asked, raising his eyebrows. "How?"

"I don't know. It just … I knew how to fix it. I think it's the mantle."

Sarah frowned. "There are old tales of mantles passing knowledge to each bearer. I've never known a god to ask them before."

I looked from Sarah to the empty armor on the cold stone. Tears burned at the back of my eyes. I turned away and crawled closer to Vicky. Three deep breaths. I reached out with my finger hovering above her eyelid.

"What has this price wrought?" Mike asked quietly.

I pushed Vicky's eyelid open and almost shouted in relief. "It's her. It's Elizabeth, I mean Vicky before she … it's her." I picked up her hand and held it between my own. "Welcome back, kid. Welcome back."

CHAPTER THIRTY-ONE

FOSTER PACKED CARA'S cuirass and helmet into my backpack after taking a few moments to heal the worst of our wounds. He carefully strapped the rest of the armor over his own. He said nothing of the Book of Blood that shared the space, but he did pull out a baggy filled with Frank's jerky.

I followed beside the fairy. "How bad would it have been?" I asked.

"It would have killed you and Sam and Vicky." He stuffed a thick strip of jerky into his mouth. "Maybe Mike and the others too."

"Even Happy?"

Foster gave a sharp nod. The panda snorted and walked beside Sarah. She'd insisted on carrying Vicky. As she was the least injured of the group, no one argued.

"Where's Bubbles?" I asked as we left the shattered outer wall behind us. I hadn't seen the cu sith since the start of the battle, and now it worried me.

Foster pointed toward the fortress near the horizon. "Up ahead. We never would have found you in time if she hadn't been with you."

A flickering flame waited against the soaring towers of the ninth fortress. Bubbles stared into the structure, unmoving until we grew close enough to touch her.

"You can stop," Foster said. "Good girl."

The burning cu sith spun in a quick circle, sending her braided tail out to slap against my knees before she leapt onto Foster. Bubbles whined and Foster slid to his knees, arms around the fiery cu sith.

"She's gone," he whispered into the cu sith's fur.

Bubbles flopped onto Foster's shoulder and rolled her eyes up to mine. She looked sad, like she knew exactly what had happened. I wondered if the cu siths simply fed off the emotions of those around them, or if Bubbles truly understood that Cara was gone.

"You did good," Foster said, running his hand through the bristly green fur. "You let her go home."

Bubbles sniffed and curled up on the stony earth.

"That's how her spirit returned to the ley lines?" Mike asked. "The cu sith was like a link home?"

Foster nodded.

I frowned and watched the cu sith panting beside the fairy. Without access to the ley lines, Cara's spirit never would have returned to our realm. She would have faded away to nothing here, never returning to the lines to reach the eternal sleep of Faerie.

"Take us home," Foster said, looking up at Mike.

Mike nodded and drew the Smith's Hammer from his belt. He started carving patterns into the stone around us until the fairy spoke again.

"Maybe there's still time to stop Sam."

My eyes snapped to Foster. "What?"

"They heard from Vassili. He's offered to treat with the Pit."

"Bullshit," I said, my heart lurching at the thought of Sam already being in more danger. "What's he want?"

Foster shrugged. "Tanks arrived in the city after you left. We don't know what the military is planning either."

"Fucking hell. What next?"

Foster ran his fingers through the cu sith's fur. A crease formed in his brow. "There are other things that worry me. Glenn's actions will shatter the Courts." Foster looked up at me. "To betray the Sanatio?" He shook his head. "I don't know, but it will be violent."

"Whose side are we on, then?"

Foster frowned and looked away.

"Ready," Mike said, breaking into our darkening conversation. "Now, this may not be the most pleasant trip you've ever taken, but I shouldn't have to set you on fire."

"I guess I should be happy for the little things?"

"Yes," Mike said an instant before he slammed the Smith's Hammer into the center of the circle. Fire raced across the design, looping through the knots and whorls before a pillar of flame shot up around us.

I waited for the burn as my stomach lurched to one side and heat surrounded me. Instead I felt acceleration like I'd been fired out of a cannon, and then nothing. The stop was as sudden as the start, and I fought against my urge to puke.

The room spun, and I slowly looked around. We were back at Death's Door, on the floor of the library upstairs.

"I have the spins," Elizabeth said, holding a hand over her mouth. "Oh god, this sucks."

Footsteps pounded up the stairs. A tuft of gray hair appeared at the end of the hall, and a fairy zipped past before exploding into Aideen's full-sized form.

"Damian?" Frank said. "You're back. Sam's been so worried." He pointed behind me. I turned to look and found Sam, one arm slouched over a chair. She was slack-jawed and snoring.

Bubbles hopped over me and pounced on my sister. Sam woke with a start, flipping the cu sith into the air. I could have sworn Bubbles was scowling at the peak of her flight, legs dangling for a moment near the ceiling, before Sam caught her and set her down.

"Damian?" Her eyes flashed around the group before locking on Vicky. The child was still sleeping on Happy's back. "How is she? Did it ... did it work?"

I nodded.

"Where's Cara? She went to help."

Silence overwhelmed the room.

"Foster?" Aideen asked, her voice not much above a whisper.

His head tilted forward as he shook it, his lips twitching into a frown. "She's gone."

Aideen winced and stepped around me. "I'm so sorry."

"What?" Sam said, jumping out of her seat. "Cara? No ... no!"

Aideen wrapped Foster up in her arms and they stayed that way for some time. Frank made his way over to Sam, and her tears cut me to the bone.

"What about Glenn?" Mike asked, breaking the silence. "Who do we ally ourselves with now?"

It brought me back to my earlier question. "Whose side are we on?"

"Nixie's," Aideen said, glancing up, "and possibly the commoners'. It may be time they learned how to kill the Fae."

"What?" Foster said, leaning away from his wife.

"We can't battle Faerie itself," Aideen said, placing a hand on either side of his face. "Not on our own."

I stared blankly at the fairy. Is that what this meant? We were going to go to war against Faerie? "We can't."

"Not at first," Aideen said, "but eventually. We need to see how the Courts fracture around the death of the Sanatio. If fortune is with us, we may have powerful allies to pursue the king."

"We need to be sure they know the truth," Foster said, his hands clenching into fists.

"And so they will."

My eyelids tried to close, and realized how exhausted I was. Elizabeth, the blood mage, was already snoring, leaning against Sarah, who in turn had smashed her face up against Mike the Demon.

"You should sleep," Aideen said. "We can talk in the morning about more of what has happened in your absence."

"All good things?" I muttered as I slid down to lean against the ghost panda.

"Rest now, and find peace in the child you saved."

I thought that seemed like a nice thing to say as my eyes fell closed. There was peace, briefly, before the nightmares came screaming back to greet me.

✦　✦　✦

I SAT AT the little Formica table in the morning, flanked by a blood mage, my sister's epic bedhead, and Frank. Mike and

Sarah had left. The fire demon wanted to find Koda and ask him what, exactly, I'd done to Sarah. Lord knows I didn't know. Vicky slept upstairs, still nested against Happy. The panda refused to move, but he did let me toss an order of hash browns down his throat. I didn't think that was standard panda fare. Maybe standard samurai panda fare?

Jasper rolled around the center of the table, his eyes locked on the tower of breakfast sandwiches Frank had brought in, while Bubbles sat stoically beside Sam.

"I need to check in with Ashley," Elizabeth said.

I took an excessively large bite of a sausage biscuit. "Ymmf tmmf cmmf wff?"

Elizabeth just stared at me.

"He asked if you want to come with us," Sam said, giving me an exasperated look.

"Oh, are you going to visit the Coven?"

I nodded.

"Good," Frank said. "Some of the amber Ashley ordered came in. We got some new tea for her too. You mind taking it with you?"

"Not at all," Elizabeth said.

Foster and Aideen glided out of the grandfather clock, gently landing beside the leaning tower of sandwiches.

"Morning," I said.

Foster nodded and started pulling a wrapper apart.

I glanced at Aideen and tried to ask how Foster was doing, without asking how he was doing. Aideen looked at the fairy and then back to me. She nodded slightly and smiled a bit. I hoped that meant good things.

Sam picked up another breakfast sandwich and unwrapped

it. Bubbles wiggled a little bit and sat up straighter. Sam held it out and a wet pink tongue rolled out to slap against the tabletop.

"Eww, no," Sam said. "That's not what I meant." She placed the sandwich on the cu sith's tongue, and Bubbles sucked it right in, snorting and smacking as she finished it in a few quick chomps.

It reminded me of Cara, being lenient and strict with the cu siths all at once. I'd never hear that stern voice again, never be silenced by one of her epic glares. I took another bite of food, but it tasted bland and lifeless. I took a deep breath and set the biscuit on the wrapper. It was going to be a long time before things were back to normal.

Jasper rolled up to Sam and stared.

"You want one too?"

A gaping black hole opened at Jasper's center, lined with silver gray fangs. His cohesive furball state broke down into piles of dust bunnies. Dust bunnies with a cluster of fangs. Sam tossed a sandwich in without unwrapping it. Jasper didn't seem to mind. Three seconds later he spit out a fully intact wrapper, with no trace of sandwich, before pulling himself back together.

"Things have gotten worse since you've been gone," Frank said.

I raised an eyebrow.

"The military presence in town is huge."

"We heard about the tanks," I said.

"That's only part of it. They placed watchtowers down by the river and up by the hospital. Manned twenty-four seven by snipers."

"What?" I said.

Sam nodded. "I've seen them."

"Is it just here?" I asked. "I mean, just in Saint Charles?"

Frank shook his head. "It's everywhere, really. If a Fae sighting has been reported, chances are good the military has moved to investigate."

"They treat us like an enemy," Aideen said. "They don't understand that we have lived beside them for millennia."

"Their ego probably stings from the failed bombing run on Falias," Elizabeth said as she wiped her fingers off. "Now they want to flex some muscle."

"They already had a presence in every major city," Frank said. "This seems unnecessary."

I agreed with him, wholeheartedly. "It's what governments do," I muttered. "Overreact and shoot things."

Foster looked up at Frank. "They'll have plenty to shoot when the dark-touched threaten their cities."

"How many are there?" Elizabeth asked. "Should we be worried?"

"We don't know how many crossed over," Aideen said. "The Seal was broken long enough for any number of them to be in our realm now."

I tried to imagine those things attacking humans. Commoners wouldn't stand a chance against a super-charged vampire that could heal itself from almost any wound.

"You never need to worry in the daylight," Foster said quietly, wiping his hands off on the corner of a napkin. "The sun is deadly to the dark-touched."

"What will Glenn do?" Frank asked.

"Without Mom there to stop him," Foster said, "he could do anything. I don't know. If he's working with Hern, they could be planning to expand Falias across the country."

The thought of that sent a chill down my spine. Enough people had died already. How many more would have to die for that? A small ocean of muttering sounded in my head, and it was only then that I realized the voices had been quieter, more like they had been in the Burning Lands.

Sam held out her hand to Foster and he climbed onto it. She held him up to her shoulder and he hopped off, settling into her wild tangle of hair.

"Your bed head is a disaster," Foster said, pushing a snarled knot of hair to the side.

Sam grinned. "Cut if off and I'll swat you."

"She's so cute when she's violent," Foster said.

Aideen sighed. "The key to my husband's heart, smashing things."

Elizabeth laughed and tossed a wrapper into the trash. "What about Vicky?"

The room quieted. I glanced toward the staircase at the back of the room. "I think she should go home."

CHAPTER THIRTY-TWO

THE BELL ON the front door jingled.

"I'll check it," Frank said. He froze at the saloon-style doors. "Sergeant?"

"Frank," a pleasant voice said. "I wanted to give you fair warning." The pleasant tone tightened and the man grunted in pain. "The commander is planning on issuing a curfew. You need to be locked down by ten o'clock tonight."

We all sat silently at the table, listening in to the conversation, until its pitch took a sharp turn.

"Is that blood?" Frank asked, pushing through the door. "You need a hospital. What the hell are you doing here?"

"We lost a unit by the river, not far south of the bridge."

I sprang out of my seat and followed Frank into the front of the shop. "Fuck."

The sergeant turned at Frank's insistence, revealing the slash tracing his shoulder and deepening as it reached his kidney. He had to be in shock, or he'd have been screaming.

"Aideen!" Frank shouted, his foot slipping on a thin trail of blood. "Oh Jesus, Aideen!"

The fairy ran in behind me. The sergeant's eyes glazed over. He barely took notice of the seven-foot fairy as she circled around him.

"Poisoned. This is no ordinary wound." She began whispering and tracing the edges of the cut. Green fluid pooled at the base of the gash before floating to the fairy's hand. "Who did this to you?"

"The river. It was the damndest thing. Just … I need to sleep."

"Hold him still," Aideen said. "The shock will fade when the healing begins."

"Can I help?" Elizabeth asked, moving up beside me.

Aideen shook her head. She frowned and framed the wound with her hands. *"Socius Sanation."* White light bathed the room, bright enough that the fixtures and people turned to pale outlines against a sun.

The sergeant screamed a moment later and wrenched away. His arm slipped in my grasp until I locked it down. He shook and cried out as the wound tightened and closed. He slid to the floor when the light faded. I helped Frank lower the sergeant.

"What … what was that?" he said, looking around frantically. "Aideen?"

"You are healed now, Sergeant Park."

The man looked torn between gratitude and horror. "Frank said I'll owe you a child. I can't do that!"

Aideen scowled at Frank.

Elizabeth snorted a laugh, and then covered her mouth with both hands.

"No, no," Frank said. "It was a joke. Relax, you don't owe anybody a thing."

I'd seen the sergeant before. I was sure of it, but Frank had an easy way with the man like they were at least acquainted. It was a mystery to me whether I'd had my nose buried so deeply in research that I hadn't noticed the military presence as much as I should have the last few days, or if Frank had a history with Sergeant Park.

"Tell us what happened," Aideen said.

Park's brow furrowed and he rubbed his forehead. "I don't know exactly." He struggled back to his feet. Frank grabbed him the stool from behind the register and the sergeant thanked him.

"What do you remember?" I asked. "You were saying something about the river."

Park nodded. "It was odd. Hell, what's not odd these days, really? We were on patrol down by the gazebo. There were surges of water, you know? They seemed to go against the wake of a boat that passed by. One of my men walked closer and the river ... it just rose up and swallowed him. It was one little part of the river, though. It wasn't a flood."

Park shivered and fell silent.

"What happened?" Frank asked.

Bubbles trotted into the room, flopping onto the floor next to Park's chair.

"She will not let anything happen to you," Aideen said.

Park showed an uneasy smile as he looked down at the cu sith. The man took a deep breath and his eyes met Frank's. "Two other soldiers tried to pull him out. The river took them too. The rest of us tried to run. It was like there was a translucent woman who rose up from the water. She cut Mitch's head clean off. It was ..." He closed his eyes and shivered.

Aideen and I exchanged a glance. I didn't dare say anything. I didn't want Nixie's people to be at the center of this.

"Come on," Frank said, apparently noticing the unease in the look between Aideen and me. "I'll get you back to HQ."

The sergeant slowly stood up. He looked at Aideen. "Thank you for this. I know you didn't have to do that. I won't forget it."

"Go in peace," Aideen said. "Remember there are good Fae and terrible Fae, the same as humanity."

Bubbles stepped aside when Frank slid up underneath Park's arm and helped him out the door.

The grandfather clock ticked ten times before any of us said a word.

"Water witches," Sam said. I turned to find her standing in the doorway, Foster perched on her shoulder. "He was talking about water witches."

"Yes," Aideen said. "But who and why? There has been no hostility toward the undines."

"The Queen," I said, crossing my arms.

Aideen started to speak and then hesitated. She sighed, watching Main Street and the river beyond.

"It makes sense," Foster said.

Elizabeth leaned on the edge of the counter. "Cornelius said he was surprised the Queen hadn't attacked Damian directly to get to Nixie and her people."

Aideen nodded. "Nixie helped save the European seaboard from that tidal wave. It was captured on film and in photos, and those images are now known to the world at large."

"What better way to discredit them?" I asked as I slammed a fist into my palm. "Murdering soldiers, leaving one alive enough to get back to his people?"

"He would not have survived that wound without a healing," Aideen said quietly. "It is a poison well known to the water witches. They bathe their blades in that awful tincture when they are at war."

"What can we do?" Sam asked.

Aideen turned back to Sam. "Nothing. Warn Nixie, use caution near the waters. If the Queen has learned of Cara's death, she may have decided to strike.

The words, so nonchalant in their delivery, cut me.

"I'd like to go home now," Elizabeth said.

I nodded. "You mind driving, Sam? We need to go see Ashley." I headed through the saloon-style doors to grab my backpack. I could only stare at the wreckage on the Formica table.

"What's wrong?" Foster asked as he glided over my shoulder and then burst into laughter.

A very bloated Jasper sat in the center of the table, and there wasn't a breakfast sandwich in sight, just a sad pile of slobbery, empty wrappers.

"He ate them all," Foster said.

"Well, he is a dragon."

The gray furball belched, and I swear the walls shook.

"A dragon with indigestion," Sam said.

"Why don't you stay here and sleep that off?"

The furball purred and then belched again.

"Don't forget the amber," Elizabeth said.

"Oh, yeah."

"He already forgot," Sam said. "You can see it in his vacant expression."

I smiled at my sister. I think she knew, with the mention of Cara's death, that I was starting to crack. Sometimes she could read me like a book, and sometimes I wouldn't have it any other way.

✦ ✦ ✦

WE ALL PILED into Sam's black SUV. It made a heck of a lot more sense than trying to shoehorn everyone into my '32 Ford.

"Call Hugh," Sam said as she steered onto Fifth Street. Foster clung to the edge of the dashboard like his life depended on it. It probably did.

I pulled out my phone. Every motion brought me closer to the loss of Carter and Maggie, and by the time the line started ringing, I was ready to crawl into a hole.

"Damian," Hugh said, his voice crackling as we crossed a dead zone.

"We're headed to Ashley's," I said. "Do you have time to meet us?"

The line was silent for a time until Hugh finally said "Yes. There is much we must do to honor the Ghost Pack's sacrifice, but I can visit briefly. I am not far from the priestess' home."

"We'll be there in about ten minutes, maybe less."

"I will see you there." Hugh clicked off the line.

"He doesn't sound too bad," Sam said.

I frowned and nodded. "Carter and Maggie were a big draw against the pack's magic." I ran a fingertip over my pack marks. "I had no idea I was weakening the River Pack."

"You think Hugh doesn't appreciate the time you gave to Maggie and Carter?" Foster asked from his perch on the dashboard.

"Alan talks about it all the time," Elizabeth said from the back seat. "He's going to miss his friends."

I closed my eyes and tried to sink into the rhythm of the road. We'd all miss them. It was going to be a rough change.

CHAPTER THIRTY-THREE

A FTER A WHILE, I looked at Foster. "You sure you don't mind leaving Aideen to watch the shop?"

He nodded. "I need to get out and do things. I don't … I don't need to be there right now."

The small driveway in front of Ashley's house was empty. I remembered ambushing her here one morning to buy a gift for Nixie. It had felt like dark times back then, but I'd had no idea how bad things were going to get.

I rang the doorbell and we waited. Footsteps sounded a short time later and the door cracked open.

"Damian?" Ashley said, pulling the door open wider.

" 'Tis I, milady."

Ashley scrunched up her forehead. "Isn't it a bit early for you? Isn't it a bit early for me to have to deal with you?"

"Ouch," Sam said, exchanging a smile and a hug with Ashley.

"It's always too early to deal with him," Foster said as he glided over the priestess.

"Come in," Ashley said, all of you. Her fingers trailed across Beth's forearm as the blood mage stepped inside.

I walked through the front door and my heart sank when I saw Alexandra in the living room. Could it have been her? Would she have attacked the sergeant?

"You are safe," Alexandra said, flowing across the room and embracing Elizabeth.

"Elizabeth was a huge help," I said. "How are you?" Well, that sounded awkward and unnatural. Way to play it cool.

"Her name is Beth," Alexandra said flatly.

Beth grinned at the water witch.

"And I am well, Damian. You should call Nixie. She has been very anxious about your trip into the Burning Lands. I would lecture you on adding stress to our future queen's life, but you have done an honorable thing."

"Yes, he has," Hugh said, stepping into the room. Before I could say a word, he opened his arms and embraced me. "Welcome home, brother, very well done."

I almost choked on the guilt rising up the back of my throat.

"Beth," Hugh said, turning to the blood mage. He extended his hand in greeting. His skin was dark beside Beth's pale and scarred arm. "Alan has said many great things about you. I believe you may be meeting his wife soon."

Beth fidgeted a bit and her eyes flashed around the room. "I don't do great with a lot of people in small spaces."

"Come over here," Ashley said, dragging Beth to a large club chair and squeezing in beside her. Beth kept her hand locked around Ashley's. "What are you all doing here?"

"Beth wanted to come home," Sam said. "Apparently sleeping on the floor at the Double D isn't her thing."

"I just wanted to get out," Foster said.

Ashley looked at the fairy as he settled on Sam's shoulder. "I'm so sorry, Foster."

Foster stared at nothing, and responded with only a short

nod.

Sam dragged one of the kitchen chairs into the living room and sat down beside Hugh. I flopped onto the couch next to Alexandra.

"Where is everybody?" I asked.

"Most of us have *real* jobs," Ashley said as she raised an eyebrow.

"Hey now, I own a store. That's a real job."

"The only person working a real job in that store is Frank," Sam said. "Don't even try to argue it."

I stopped on the verge of arguing, my finger in the air. I blew out a breath and sank back into the couch. "Fine."

"What was it like?" Alexandra asked. "The Burning Lands? In all my years, I have never seen them."

"Scary," Beth said. "I saw oceans of fire in the time I was there, and a throne room for their devils. I don't understand how anything can survive it."

"That about covers it," I said, not mentioning the trials, or the geryon, or the dark-touched. There were a few things I didn't feel like talking about yet. I raised my eyes to Alexandra as she ran her fingers through a tangle of long black hair. "When we got back, one of the Army patrols had been killed by undines."

"One of them bled green poison," Foster said.

Alexandra froze. "What?"

"Any idea who could have done it?" Sam asked. She managed to relay the question without making it an accusation. All I said was 'hi' and it sounded like an accusation. Sam had much better people skills in some things, but at least I didn't eat them.

Alexandra looked away. "There are not many undines with

the blades to poison a man."

"I thought it was common," I said.

The water witch shook her head. "The flower only grows in Faerie, its roots bound in Magrasnetto ore. The last I heard spoken of it, there were none left alive."

"But there are already weapons out there," Beth said. "Do they lose their power, or is the poison always there?"

"It will be lost eventually, but it takes millennia for it to be worked out of the blade. In a mortal's eyes, the poison would never leave."

"Who has access to them?" Ashley asked. "Are they common, like Damian thought?"

"They are rare. Most of them are known to be under the guard of Nixie's clan. Or so they were before she split from the Queen."

"So the queen has them?" I asked.

Alexandra nodded. If that were true, someone *could* be trying to set the Queen up. The only real fallout I was concerned about was the assumption that the attack came from Nixie's people.

"They could be trying to frame you."

Alexandra narrowed her eyes. "I do not understand this term."

"Blame you for someone else's crime," Beth said. "But who would do that?"

Alexandra leaned back in her seat. "The Queen, I am afraid."

Ashley stood up and squeezed Beth's shoulder. "Can I get you all a drink?" Sam and Alexandra declined.

I jumped in my seat when something hammered at Ashley's

door.

Foster hopped up from Sam's shoulder with his sword half-drawn.

"I will answer it," Alexandra said as her graceful steps carried her into the hall. "Calm yourself."

Foster left his sword unsheathed.

The screen squeaked and I heard a deep voice.

"Jonathan?" Alexandra asked.

"Is Samantha here? Is she okay?"

"Yes," the undine said.

Sam hopped up and walked toward the foyer, almost running into Jonathan when the wisp-thin vampire zipped into the room.

"What are you doing here?" Sam asked.

"Looking for you. You didn't answer your phone."

Sam patted her back pocket and a sheepish frown crossed her face. "It must be in the car. What's wrong?"

"We found him."

"Who? Vassili?"

Jonathan nodded.

"Where?"

"You could at least introduce yourself," Ashley said, settling back into the chair beside Beth.

Jonathan stared at her. I watched his aura surge toward Ashley, wrapped in green and yellow bursts of power amidst the black and white ribbon. I almost laughed when I realized what he was doing. Apparently I did laugh a little bit because Jonathan's gaze snapped to me.

"What is so humorous?"

"I don't care how much mojo you put behind that trance," I

said, tapping the edge of my glass. "She's not going to go on a date with you."

"That is not what I …"

Elizabeth planted a kiss on Ashley's lips before sliding her arm through the other woman's and staring at the vampire.

"Oh."

Sam sat up a little straighter. "Wait, he can't turn her into a thrall because she's gay? But he's gay too, so what gives?"

"People of this time are obsessed with labels," Alexandra said. "Ashley is Ashley and Jonathan is Jonathan. Why do they need more of a name than that?"

I tipped my glass to Alexandra.

"He could still enthrall her," I said, "just not with the sexy time vampire mojo."

I looked at the room at large. They all stared at me. "What?" I snapped. "I read it in a book somewhere."

"Somehow I think the phrasing may have been different," Jonathan said. He turned to Ashley. "I do apologize, Priestess. I am … I am not myself quite yet."

"It's fine," Ashley said. "I take no insult. Please, join us, would you?"

Jonathan rubbed his hands together and nodded. I scooted closer to Alexandra when she sat down again so the vampire had room to join us on the couch.

"What did you find out about Vassili?" Hugh asked, pulling everyone's attention to him as he sipped on a small cup of tea. He raised his eyebrows slightly. "I am not that interesting."

A small smile crossed Jonathan's face and he relaxed a fraction. "He's been sighted twice in twenty-four hours. Near Rivercene last night, and again at the southern towers of Falias this morning."

"Who saw him?" Sam asked.

Foster slowly sheathed his sword. "Do we trust them?"

"To say the least," Jonathan said with a sharp incline of his head. "The innkeeper called Vik late last night."

"Why there?" Beth asked.

"The Seal," Alexandra said. "When the Seal was damaged, the dark-touched could have come through any of the gateways. But why would Vassili suspect Rivercene? The legend of its Guardian is well known."

"It is an ancient path," Hugh said, "capable of transporting great numbers. It was not coincidence that Philip and Ezekiel made their way to Rivercene. The power in that place is substantial, and there is much reward to be had with that risk."

"The dark-touched have been sighted in the southern and northern parts of the state," Ashley said, her hand flexing near her hip where the nine-tails usually hung. "We may be ready here, but one of the covens near Kansas City ..." She glanced down before raising her head with murder in her eyes. "They're all dead but two of the witches."

"They are under the watch of the Wichita Pack now," Hugh said. "They will not have a representative at the gathering tonight because of it. A small group of dark-touched was sighted near Piedmont, as well. It sounds as though Camazotz and Zola's predictions were correct."

"Why don't we have Edgar roast them all?" Sam asked. "He *is* Ra, for fuck's sake."

"It is not the same," Alexandra said. "Edgar can certainly destroy some of them with a direct attack, but they will not die merely by being exposed to the light of his arts."

"Edgar is Ra?" Beth asked, leaning forward. "Like, literally, Ra? The sun god?"

"How else could you explain the sheer pompousness of that man?" Ashley asked.

"I just think it's funny that Ra wears a bowler," I said.

Beth huffed out a quick breath. She pulled down the waist-band of her jeans and revealed an impossibly intricate tattoo on her outer hip that stretched up to her ribcage. I stared at the eye of Ra. Beth's scars traced the symbol, and the alternating patterns of scars and ink were mesmerizing.

"That is a beautiful design," Alexandra said. "You do not strike me as a follower of the old religions."

Beth shook her head.

"You wear it as a symbol of destruction." Alexandra frowned slightly. "It is an apt thing for your art. You cannot use your power without destroying your flesh."

Ashley ran her fingers over Beth's tattoo and pulled her shirt down to cover it. "It's beautiful."

"There are many followers of Ra still in the world today," Alexandra said. "I do wonder what they would think if they knew he watched over them in a more traditional sense than as a long-absent deity."

"Who else saw Vassili?" Sam asked, turning her focus to the other vampire.

"The green men outside Falias," Jonathan said.

I choked on my yawn. "Green men? Here?" I'd heard of their legend, but I'd never met one. They were the highest order of Fae warriors.

"It may have been a mistake to bring them here," Alexandra said. "Glenn may have overestimated their loyalty. The green men are fierce warriors, but they are philosophers at heart. We may be able to use that to our advantage. Nixie would know more about them."

"I need to call her," I said. Alexandra's reminder had been stuck in my head for the last several minutes, and the mention of Nixie's name had me distracted again.

"Use the old well at the edge of the woods," the undine said. "So long as Ashley does not mind. It is the closest body of water connected to the river."

"The river isn't that far," Ashley said. "Goddess knows Damian could use the exercise with the crap he eats."

I looked at everyone in turn. "No one's going to argue that? No one?"

"I once saw you live off beef jerky for a week straight," Sam said. "Oh, and I remember when we were kids, you coated a stick of butter in brown sugar and started eating it."

I could *feel* the eyebrows go up around me.

Hugh nodded and released a slow laugh. "The freezer at Howell Island is half filled with chimichangas."

"That's for emergencies!" I frowned at the werewolf. "What if we had to live there? Besides, you're exaggerating. It's a quarter full, at most."

Hugh smiled and sipped his tea.

CHAPTER THIRTY-FOUR

I HEADED OUT into the backyard once the food shaming was done. I breathed in the warm, muggy air. It still felt cool after I'd so recently spent time in the Burning Lands. As I approached the well, a deer stood still, finally sprinting away when I undid the latch on the ancient stone and lifted the cover with a metallic squeal.

The Wasser-Münzen felt cold in my hands. I tightened my backpack before throwing a leg over the edge of the well. The stone was smooth, almost polished. For a moment, I saw only the black obsidian walls of the Burning Lands fortress.

I squeezed my eyes shut to banish the vision and made my way down the ladder rungs set into the walls. It wasn't until my feet splashed down that I realized I probably should have taken my shoes off. Darkness waited at the bottom of the well, even with the sun lighting the curve of the wall far above. I slid the disc into the water and waited.

Something scampered up the wall, diving in and out of the narrow shadows between the bricks. Still, nothing moved in the water. I'd almost given up when the surface started bubbling. Nixie's form rose up, a beautiful translucent shadow.

"Why did you not come to Faerie with Gaia as soon as you returned?"

Her question was more blunt than I was used to hearing. "Is

everything okay?"

She looked away before nodding. "I was only worried about you. I did not enjoy learning of your return from my witches rather than you."

"Noted," I said with a smile.

She turned to me, and I could just make out the narrowing of her eyes. "Why aren't you here?"

I took a deep breath. "We're at Ashley's, as you probably knew already."

She nodded. "I have spoken to Alexandra here many times."

"We freed Vicky, Nixie. We did it, but the price …" I shook my head. "They're gone, Nixie." My lips trembled in the shadows of that well, and I finally let the loss break me. "Cara's dead. Carter and Maggie and Jimmy … I didn't even fucking like Jimmy, but now he's dead." I raised a hand to my eyes when the tears started.

"I'm sorry," Nixie said.

I tried to speak, but only a choking sob passed my lips. I punched the stone wall of the well and felt my knuckles split. Nixie didn't argue that the wolves were already dead. She understood, on some level. I remembered the realization she'd had at Ashley's, how her killings had brought great sadness into the world.

"You saved the child."

I smashed the palms of my hands against my eyes and rubbed the tears away.

"Vicky will live, and Sam will live. You will have the chance to save more people, Damian. Cara was proud of you."

"Glenn has to die," I whispered. "Cara's dead because of

him."

Nixie stared at me in silence for a time. "There are some things we should not discuss over the Wasser-Münzen. Tell me of the Burning Lands, Damian. I have heard they have a cold beauty."

I sniffed and blew out a breath. "More like a hot, muggy beauty. A lot like Missouri in the dead of summer.

"I do enjoy the heat, though I still have no desire to visit the Burning Lands."

"They aren't exactly friendly," I said.

"You only saw the circles, Damian. That is like visiting this realm and only seeing a castle's dungeon and its grandest hall."

"No one uses dungeons any more."

Nixie gave me a flat look.

"Point taken," I said. "I saw an Utukku there."

"They still speak fondly of you here. Did they try to kill you in the Burning Lands?"

"Yes ..." I said, drawing out the word and crossing my arms. "I know it wasn't an actual Utukku. I mean, it wasn't the Utukku I know." I frowned. "You know what I mean. It was an imposter."

"A geryon," Nixie said.

I nodded.

Her form rose slightly and she glanced over her shoulder. "They were formidable adversaries before they were banished to the Burning Lands. I once saw a geryon create a false Atlantis in the Wandering War. She trapped many that day. What did the geryon trick you with?"

"She killed a dark-touched for us, in a hall made to look something like the Royal Court in Faerie."

Nixie frowned. "Was it an actual vampire? Or only a simulacra?"

I thought about that. "I have no idea. Some of the dark-touched pieced themselves back together even after we dismembered them."

Nixie nodded. "They are resilient, but I do not believe they are resilient to that degree. They are powerful, and incredibly fast."

I grimaced at the thought. What if those hadn't been actual dark-touched? What if the dark-touched we'd face had been geryon all along? What if there was something worse waiting for us? "Wouldn't Mike know?"

Nixie shrugged. "It is possible, but he may have been pre-occupied with his lover."

I cursed and leaned against the stone wall. "Yeah, he definitely was. Either way, they're gone and we're here."

"That does make it a better day."

"Did you know about the strikes against the military here? By water witches?"

"What?" Nixie snapped. "What do you mean?"

I told her about Sergeant Park and the poisoned blade. I told her how Aideen had saved him, and how I had been worried when the first undine—at least the first of our allies—I had seen here was Alexandra. Nixie finally cut me off.

"It was not Alexandra. She would never touch a poison blade. She has lost too much to them. Do not speak of this further. I will talk to my people here, though I doubt your suspicions are wrong."

She turned away and her image started fading into the well. "I love you."

"I love you too, Nix. Be safe."

And then she was gone.

✦ ✦ ✦

MY PHONE RANG as I walked back into Ashley's. I stopped at the door and wiped the grime from my face before sliding off my wet shoes and socks and finally answering.

"Hello?"

"You could have at least spared this old woman a text message," Zola said, biting off the last couple words.

It was good to hear her voice again. The screen door squeaked as I entered the house. I paused in the front room where Ashley had a plush couch and a bookshelf filled with old photos.

"We're back." The smile on my face faded. "Cara didn't … she's …"

"Ah know, Damian. Ah'm sorry for that, truly, but our work is not done yet. We need to meet."

The conversation in the other room died. You never really got to have a private conversation when there were vampires and werewolves around. I paced back to the couch and sat down.

"What is it?" I asked.

"Who is there?"

"A lot of people. We're at Ashley's with Hugh and Sam and—"

"Ah don't need a roll call, boy, though that is convenient. Go south to the cabin. Ah'll meet you there."

"Alone?"

"No, boy, bring Hugh and Samantha. The fairies too, and

your staff."

"I cannot," Hugh said. "Tonight we say goodbye to Maggie and Carter, and I must prepare. There are many packs from many places set to join us. I would like you to attend."

"I wouldn't miss it," I said. "We'll head straight there after we finish up at the cabin."

Hugh nodded with a slow incline of his head. "It will be a good thing for you to witness. You must understand the lives they have touched, even after their mortal forms were long lost."

"Is Cornelius's apprentice with you?" Zola asked.

"Beth? Yeah, she's here."

"Bring her."

"Why?" Ashley asked.

I was surprised Ashley picked up on the conversation. Either I had the volume turned up way too high, or she was getting some side effects from training in her non-traditional witch arts.

Zola sighed. "Bring Ashley too. She'll know soon enough."

The line went dead.

"What does she want us all at the farm for?" Ashley asked. "And why not just tell us over the phone?"

I shrugged. "You know as much as I do. I have no idea."

"Will we all fit in my car?" Sam asked. "Or do we need to take separate cars?"

"Who all's going?" Beth asked.

"Me," I said. "Sam, Foster, you, Ashley … Alexandra?"

The water witch shook her head. "I am traveling to Howell Island with Hugh. There is much to be done in preparation for the ceremony. I am here in Nixie's stead, unless you wish to walk the Abyss with her."

As tempting as it was, I already knew water watches had a tentative relationship with the Abyss. Any realm without water was a threat to their very being.

I shook my head. "I won't put her through that, even if she wanted to risk being away from Faerie."

"She will be there in a sending. She will be there in heart."

"And that is all she need do," Hugh said, smiling at Alexandra. "I appreciate you both making an appearance. It says much for the changes in our world, and the future we must embrace."

"Of course, Honiokaiyohos."

"Well," Foster said, "if Alexandra is through showing off the fact she can say Hugh's name, we should go."

CHAPTER THIRTY-FIVE

S AM'S SUV RUMBLED down the gravel road. It was like driving on smooth glass compared to my old '32's bouncing over the rocks and ruts.

"Ugh," Beth said from the backseat. "What is that?" I turned around in time to see her shiver.

Ashley stayed silent beside her, keeping her fingers laced together with Beth's.

Sam steered the car around a bend and I pointed out toward an old field. "There used to be a sawmill here, a whole town, actually. Lost but for the ghosts, now."

I watched the woods go by and listened to Sam curse about all the scratches she was going to have on her black SUV. It felt right. It felt like coming home.

The woods thinned and Sam pulled into a wide field that ran up to a short hill. The cabin stood outlined by the glow of a fire in the woods behind it. Sam steered us up the hill and parked beneath the old oak.

"How big of a fire is that?" Foster asked. "It's still daylight."

I shrugged.

"This is the middle of freaking nowhere," Beth said as she climbed out.

"It was a lot of fun when we were kids," Sam said. "I could have lived down here for years."

I smiled at my sister and climbed out the passenger door. I loved the smell of the country, or the lack thereof. Clean air and clear skies waited above us in the early evening. A breeze rustled the branches behind me and brought the scent of the bonfire with it. I looked at the darkening sky, already able to see the brightest stars far to the east.

"How long until we have to be back to Howell Island?" I asked.

"Four hours or so," Foster said, standing on Sam's shoulder. He cocked his head to the side. "Something else is here."

"Like Aeros?" I asked, and I immediately wanted to see the old rock pile. I raised my Sight and scanned the area. I didn't see anything out of the normal in the ocean of dead auras. "I don't see anything."

"Let's find Zola and see why she wants us all here," Ashley said, breaking her silence.

Sam led us and I walked beside the priestess. I found myself looking at the tree where the Ghost Pack had eviscerated Zachariah, the bare earth that concealed Azzazoth's corpse, and the repaired railing on the left edge of the porch.

"You okay?" Ashley asked, her hand grasping the handle of her nine-tails.

I looked at the priestess. Concern wrinkled her forehead. I smiled and looked back to the cabin. "I am, and you won't need that here."

Her hand jerked away from the weapon, as though she hadn't realized it was in her palm.

"Zola!" I shouted when we reached the short steps to the porch.

"In the back," came her somewhat muted response.

I stepped out in front of Sam, and led the group around by the well. I didn't want to walk by the shed or Azzazoth's corpse. We'd come so close to losing Sam to that demon. I'd lost too much today.

The lawn was freshly mowed. Part of my brain was happy about that, because the last thing any of us needed was a nasty bite from a copperhead snake. We rounded the cabin and I slowed at the edge of the back porch.

Zola waited on one of the stones Aeros had raised during our battle with Philip. The forest still hadn't grown back where Zola's incantation had burned it through, taking Philip out of this world once and for all.

A bonfire flickered and cracked in the crater inside the circle of stones. Orange light and shadows made twisted shapes out of Zola's braided hair as the wind rattled the charms against each other. She adjusted her cloak and watched us.

"Why did you call us here?" Ashley asked, and the bluntness of her question surprised me.

It didn't faze Zola at all. She scanned the group and her eyes settled on Foster. "Ah'm sorry to hear about Cara."

The fairy glided toward her and settled on another stone. "Thank you."

"And as to your question, priestess," Zola said, turning back to Ashley, "Ah wanted you to meet someone. Do not fear him, for it is not us he hunts."

A shade moved in my periphery. I turned to focus on it and found only darkness, with two glowing red eyes. The hunched form straightened and stepped out of the shadow of the cabin.

I had met many men and many creatures. This man walked with an easy grace that promised a world of violence. He wore clothes not so different from our own, but his jewelry spoke of another time. Golden fibers, braided and looped to form a thick rope, hung from his neck and shoulders, silent as he moved toward us.

The hilts of two green stone daggers peeked from sheaths under either arm. His shirt hung open, and beneath the golden ropes waited an intricate tattoo; a circle surrounded by stone idols, and within the circle sat a hunched man, bearing another idol on his back.

I knew who he was, without hearing his name. Zola had known him for a long time, and Mike had known him even longer. Edgar had perhaps known him the longest.

"Camazotz," I said.

He slowly inclined his head. "I am." His voice was deep, and his accent subtle enough that I couldn't place it. "Please, join us. There is much we need to discuss."

"This is a weird day," Beth said, following Ashley and me to the stone circle.

I took up a seat beside Zola while Sam sat across from me. Ashley and Beth settled onto one of the wider stones. Camazotz strode up to the center stone and sat down, his back perfectly straight.

"Welcome back," Zola said, smiling at me. "Well done."

I offered a weak smile in return. "Thanks."

Camazotz leaned forward slightly. "There are not many who can claim to have journeyed to the Burning Lands and returned. There are even less who are still alive that can claim it. You have done great things in this past day, Damian, but you must prepare. The dark-touched are upon your world, and they are an insidious threat."

"We fought them in the Burning Lands."

Camazotz gave a quick shake of his head. "You fought ghosts and visions." He looked toward the forest before turning to Zola. "Has Aeros arrived?"

The ground shook and crumbled before the bonfire. Filaments and stone rose before the embers of the crackling fire, shifting the earth until it became the Old God, his pale green eye lights eerie in the shadows formed by the bonfire.

"Yes," Zola said.

I snorted a laugh. "That sarcasm will get you killed one day. At least that's what you used to tell me."

"This is an odd sight," Aeros said, his gaze sweeping around the circle. "The bat children are restless, Camazotz."

"I will take them to a cave soon enough," Camazotz said. "We need only find where the dark-touched will strike next, and I will move them. Thank you for watching over them."

I had heard stories of the bat children. I wasn't sure if I wanted to meet them or not. Human-like forms with bat heads and wings were way off my creep meter.

"You saved the child," Aeros said, drawing my attention back to him.

I nodded at the Old God.

"Thank you."

I tried not to frown at the old rock's words, but I didn't know why he was thanking me. He didn't owe me; he hadn't sent me on a suicidal march through the Burning Lands.

"Where is she now?" Aeros asked.

"Happy and Jasper are keeping her company back at the shop," Foster said. "She's been sleeping like a rock since we got back." Foster blinked. "Was that insulting? I didn't mean for that to be insulting, but now that I think about it, I'm trying really hard not to laugh."

I grinned at the fairy and Ashley chuckled.

I looked over at the priestess and the blood mage, and felt really, really bad for not warning Beth. She looked pale, her eyes locked on the Old God.

"Oh, Beth," I said. "I'm sorry. This is Aeros." I gestured to the rock pile.

The Old God turned his head to the grinding sound of boulders. "It is good to meet you, apprentice of Cornelius. Thank you for helping my friends."

Beth blinked. "It's … I … yes. It's good to meet you. Cornelius has spoken of you, but … you are far more imposing in person."

"Alright people," Foster said, tapping his wrist. "We're on a schedule."

"Tell us about Kansas City," Zola said. "They need to hear what has happened."

"I find it is best not to anger the fairies," Aeros said.

"Please," Zola said. "They need to know."

"It has some impact on your undine alliances," Camazotz said with a nod to Zola. "The few dark-touched would have had the power to destroy the coven on their own, there is no doubt in that, but they should not have been able to find them."

"What do you mean?" Ashley asked, gripping the edge of her stone seat.

"The coven was allied with some of the native Fae. There have been problems with Mishupishu in the rivers there, and the coven was providing their help in tracking the creatures. As thanks, the Fae concealed the coven's riverside home."

"Native Fae?" I asked. "You mean like Native American? You mentioned the Mishupishu."

Camazotz nodded. "I had hoped Hugh would join us, but I understand why he could not. He will be able to tell you more, but I will share with you what I do know.

"The woodsmen were the first to bring word of the attack. The mere fact they were willing to expose themselves speaks volumes to the betrayal of the undines."

"Woodsmen?" Beth asked. I had to give her kudos for not cringing when every eye in the circle turned to her. "Like lumberjacks?"

Aeros responded with one word. "No."

Beth raised her eyebrows when he didn't continue.

"It takes him a while to think sometimes," I said. "You could cook an egg on his forehead, though."

Camazotz barked out a laugh, and it caught me completely off guard. "You jest with a stone guardian, an Old God that could flatten you at your strongest. I had heard stories from your master. I thought them exaggerations."

The rock pile sighed and turned to Beth. "One day his name will be upon the walls of my home." His eyes flicked to me, and I could have sworn the old rock winked. "The woodsmen are known as green men in Faerie."

"What?" I asked.

"See," Sam said. "Shut your smart-ass mouth and you might learn something."

"That's beside the point," I said, narrowing my eyes.

"Children," Aeros said. "Please be silent."

I exchanged a grin with Sam, and waited for the Old God to continue. He didn't.

"That's it?" I asked.

"Yes."

"That's not good," Foster said. "The green men are peaceful and solitary. For one to make themselves known …" He shook his head. "Not good."

Aeros rumbled to life. "The green men can be violent creatures. Peaceful unless provoked. They are unequalled sentinels."

"And they saw nothing," Camazotz said. "What creature could move through those woods out of sight of the woodsmen? The undines, yes, but it doesn't sound like the undines were the only killers."

Camazotz frowned and rubbed a necklace bead shaped like golden skull between his fingers. "There was an ancient tribe around what became Kansas City. It was one of the few that welcomed Fae and humans alike. They married many languages, and you would find Siouan, Algonquian, and a great deal more. Though many would call it a lost tribe, their children were like no others, and their descendants remain some of the most powerful shapeshifters in the world today."

"Is that what attacked the coven there?" I asked. "A shapeshifter? They could have hidden from the woodsmen?"

"I do not know enough," Camazotz said. "If I visit the grounds, I may be able to make some sense of it."

"Then go," Zola said. "If we don't know what's attacking our allies, we could lose this battle before it begins."

Allies? We didn't know them. Then I remembered I was sitting next to Ashley. She would have known any witches in Missouri. These people could have been more than allies; they could have been her friends. She might have been their priestess. Sometimes it was good to keep my mouth shut.

"The authorities have no idea what happened," Camazotz said. "All they know is that there are bodies along the river."

"And with everything in Falias right now ..." Foster shook his head. "This isn't going to end well."

"It has already progressed more than you know," Camazotz said. "The water witches, the same undines that led the dark-touched to the coven, killed the detectives at the scene, spouting some nonsensical rhetoric about Faerie's right to rule the commoners."

"The surviving witches didn't escape," Ashley said quietly, leaning forward to stare at her boots. "The undines let them escape." Her fist turned white as she squeezed the handle of the nine-tails.

"Yes," Camazotz said. "It is difficult to spread the message when everyone is dead."

"The undines in Saint Charles," I said, "they must have had the same motives."

"Same motives?" Foster said as his wings flared out. "It was probably the same Fae."

"What water witches?" Zola asked. "We've heard nothing about Saint Charles."

I ran a hand through my hair. "They killed an Army unit earlier. Left one man alive." I frowned. "Cut by a poisoned blade, he would have died without Aideen's healing."

"Another strike at the authorities," Camazotz said. He nodded slightly. "It's an aggressive ploy, but the balance between the Fae and the military is tenuous at best."

"There is only one Fae who benefits from that misdirection," Zola said. "The Queen is bringing her war to us."

"Nixie's queen?" I said as the blurrier parts of the puzzle started clicking together in my head. "Then the attack in Saint Louis could have been a setup for Alexandra. If she drove a wedge between us, one of Nixie's closest allies would be suspect. Fuck."

"Alexandra," Beth said. "She doesn't know. She's not safe!"

"Where is she?" Zola asked.

"She went with Hugh." Beth looked at me, and then Zola. "I've known her for years. She'd never do that."

The old Cajun nodded. "I believe you." I recognized Zola's tone. She was suspicious of any Fae, and not without good reason. "The important thing is that she is safe. Hugh will tell her more of the Kansas City attack than we know."

Aeros shifted and shook the earth. "Alexandra is cunning and quick. You need not fear for her."

Beth traced the line of on old scar on her forearm. "I hope you're right."

"You are safe too, child," Zola said.

"Aside from all the Fae that want us dead," Sam muttered.

I blew out a breath. "Oh, and I thought that was Camazotz sitting next to you."

The Old God smiled and crossed his arms. The eyes on his tattoo glowed red for a split second. My skin crawled.

CHAPTER THIRTY-SIX

I LET THE door to the cabin slam behind me as I walked back out to the stone circle. "I told you we had some." I held up a box of graham crackers, chocolate bars, and marshmallows. Six long poles made for grilling S'mores were tucked under my arm, and I kicked a case of bottled water out next to Zola.

"Why don't we stop for some real food on the way home?" Sam asked. "We have time if we leave now."

"Dell loves his S'mores," Zola said, taking one of the poles Dell had left at the cabin and a water from me. "Samantha is right. You should get a decent meal. Drink as much water as you can before the ceremony tonight."

I opened a few of the chocolate bars and laid them out. "Oh, funny story I forgot to mention, Zola. I met Graybeard in the Burning Lands."

She spat water onto Aeros and froze. The Old God blinked.

I laughed through a smile. "You know he captains the Bone Sails in the Sea of Souls? Not bad for a dead parrot."

"A dead *parrot*," Zola said, regaining her composure. "You used a soulart on that bird when you were what? Eleven? Twelve? Andi didn't need more strangeness in that house. It was a choice between sending him to the Burning Lands or killing him. Again."

"So you sent him with Ronwe."

"How did you …" Zola started to ask as she narrowed her eyes, and then she sighed. "That bird always did talk more than he needed too. Ah'm still not telling you why that demon owed me a favor. Ah gave her my word, Damian. Let us say Mike is not the only demon to have had a change of heart in his existence."

I could respect that, even if it didn't answer all my questions. I'd have to pick at it again when I got her alone. "Have you heard from the Old Man?"

"Yes," Zola said. "Ward has joined him in Falias. Ah do hope they are safe."

Camazotz harrumphed. "Leviticus is likely safe, no matter his situation. And they have Edgar. He is an excellent ally in a conflict such as this."

Zola gave a quick nod and shoved her pole into the campfire. "Either way, we cannot afford to divide ourselves between Missouri and Falias. Not without more allies."

Aeros's eyes flared. "You want me to join Leviticus?"

"No," Zola said. "Ah want you to guard the commoners from their own military. People have been killed. People who have no ties to this conflict."

"I will be seen," the Old God said.

"Yes, and Ah hope that is all it takes to end the bloodshed."

"Where?" I asked, wondering where Zola wanted Aeros to be.

"Near Main Street. Take up a post at the corner of Adams Street by Death's Door. Block the tanks."

"The commoners may see that as an act of war," Camazotz said. "Or they may attack Aeros out of fear."

"No," Zola said. "His presence will *prevent* attacks. And if they do attack him? You think some paltry tank can face an Old God? Rubbish. You saw what the Leviathans did to those weapons."

A part of me could only stare at Zola, watching her take charge. Camazotz leaned forward, listening to her words. He clearly valued her opinion, and it made me wonder what had led the pair to this point. How had they known each other?

Another part of me traced the darkened scar on the Old God's arm, where Gurges had cut Aeros in our final conflict with Philip, when we lost Cassie. I took a deep breath. Too many questions and not enough answers.

"What of the dragon scales in your satchel?" Camazotz asked, turning to Ashley.

The priestess straightened in her seat and leaned away slightly. "What?"

"I can feel them," Camazotz said. "I have not felt rune tiles such as those since the wars of old."

Ashley squeezed the black leather pouch at her side. "Mike gave me some, along with several rune tiles." Her eyes flicked to Zola. "He said to keep them away from you."

"Ah swear that demon can't take a joke," Zola said.

"You were totally going to destroy those," I said. "I remember when he bought them at that farmer's market. You weren't joking."

"Perhaps," Zola said, not really responding to my statement. "They are dangerous things, Damian. Far more potent than an ordinary chunk of Magrasnetto."

"Have you been warned about their power?" Camazotz asked. "Any strike you make from the Blade of the Stone will be amplified tenfold."

I remembered the cloud of death that had eaten away cars and men and stone when Ashley struck with that art. I tried to imagine what ten times the power would look like, and I shivered.

Beth pulled a pole out of the fire and started picking at a S'more.

"I hope to never use them," Ashley said. "But understand that I won't let my coven be destroyed by Fae, or anything else."

"Some believe your coven was lost the instant you took up the nine-tails," Camazotz said. "Legend of your powers has grown and rumors have spread far to the west and south. Far enough that I knew of it before Zola told me you were an ally."

"They are *fools*," Ashley said. "My coven is my family, and the few who could not stand it have already left."

"Be wary of strangers who come to visit your coven," Camazotz said. "I speak this only as a warning. There are powerful Fae who would see you cast out."

Ashley stared at Camazotz for a short time, the only sound the crackling of the bonfire and the grinding of stone when Aeros moved his head.

I lifted a smoking pole out of the fire and made the mistake of sitting it next to Foster.

"Gimme."

"Hey now—"

He'd stuffed three bites into his face before I could so much as finish a sentence. "It's so good." The fairy inhaled and I could see his pupils widening. "I need more. Just one more bite. Maybe two. Nice weather tonight. Who built the bonfire?"

I groaned and dragged my fingers down my face.

"Hey bug," Sam said, "how about we go on patrol?"

"Patrol?" Foster said as he zipped into the air. "Yes! Yes! Patrol! March, two, three, four."

Sam mouthed *you're welcome* as she walked toward the cabin, a pale blur zooming around her head.

"Some things do not change," Camazotz said. "The Fae can't handle their sugar." He looked away from Sam and Foster and focused on me. "It has been a long time since Anubis walked upon the earth," Camazotz said.

I picked up the remnants of my S'more and started chewing on it. A bit charred, but still gooey and chocolatey and smoky.

"What does he mean?" Beth asked.

"Damian is the seventh son of Anubis," Ashley said.

"What? Like the god?" She laughed a little, blowing her breath out through her nose.

"Ezekiel was Anubis," I said quietly.

"No. He was not." Camazotz pointed at me. "He may have been worshipped as a deity, but he was not. You are a true inheritor, a mantle bearer. Ezekiel was a corrupted monster in every way."

"He originated the bloodline," I said, sticking another S'more into the bonfire. "That's all I've ever heard."

Camazotz slowly shook his head. "The god who was Anubis died long before Ezekiel's time. He set the bloodline in motion. Ezekiel was the first to inherit the gifts, and Leviticus the second.

"There is an old magic in the world, Damian, bound up in prophecy and time and what some would call destiny. You can embrace it, or let it destroy you. It can consume everything you are, or open the door to worlds you cannot yet imagine."

"Destiny," Zola said, drawing out the word. "There is no destiny here. There is only life. Pray you learn that before the end."

"A series of coincidences, if you will," Camazotz said. "Nonetheless, events that were set in motion thousands of years ago are affecting us today. How do you not call that destiny?"

"It doesn't matter," I said.

Camazotz started to protest, but I cut him off.

"No, listen. It doesn't matter if this is destiny or coincidence or events setup by some sadistic pre-ordained puppet master. I'll fight to protect the people I love, and I'll die for them if I need to. That's all I need to know. That's all anyone needs to know."

Camazotz frowned at me.

"Ah said you'd like him," Zola said.

A small smile lifted the god's lips.

"He's one of the greatest friends I've ever had," Ashley said. "I've seen him kill for his friends, and I've seen him do everything he could to save them. There is no one I'd rather have at my side."

I turned to Ashley, nearly speechless. "Thank you," I finally said.

Ashley nodded and squeezed Beth's leg.

I held out a fully toasted S'more to Camazotz. He frowned at the gooey mess as he pulled it out of the holder.

"Trust me," I said.

"Don't always trust him when it comes to food," Ashley said. "He'd eat a tire if it was seasoned right."

"Umm, no I wouldn't," I said. "Rubber comes from plants. That basically makes tires really durable vegetables."

Camazotz bit into the graham cracker and chewed. He nodded and held up the sandwiched marshmallow. "It is a good food, but I have yet to find anything that rivals the cacao drinks of ancient times."

"Perhaps because it was a gift of worship?" Zola asked. She lowered her voice and raised an eyebrow. "When they were worshipping you? Ah would suspect that might earn your favor."

"Not the traditional ceremony, but yes. It happened at times."

"Gifts," Aeros said. "I have never understood the need for physical gifts. I awake in the morning to see the earth and the sky. There is little more I need."

We sat there for a time, quietly eating our S'mores and listening to Sam shout at Foster in the distance.

"Gaia offered a gift," I said into the silence.

"What kind of gift?" Zola asked.

"I don't know, exactly, but she says I can take her power to help fight the dark-touched."

Camazotz leaned back into his stone seat. "Take the powers of a Titan into a mortal body?"

"At what price?" Zola said. "It could kill you both."

"It gets stranger. She said the only being that knows how is Tessrian."

Zola frowned. "We still have her bloodstone?"

"I already talked to Tessrian and promised to set her free, to lead her back to the Burning Lands."

"Why?" Zola asked. "It is a generous pledge, but what favor do you owe that demon?"

Part of me was relieved Zola hadn't started screaming.

Maybe I expected that more because we were at the cabin. "Tessrian told me how to use the Key of the Dead to enter the devil's enclave." I glanced between Zola and Camazotz. "And Gaia says Tessrian knows how to transfer Gaia's power to me."

A slow smile showed on Camazotz's face. "You intend to return her to the Burning Lands, so long as she shares that with you."

I nodded.

"A bold manipulation that may only serve to get you killed."

"Welcome to my average weekend," I muttered. Someone squeezed my shoulder and I jumped. Sam stood behind me, watching Camazotz. Foster snored on her shoulder.

"Tessrian will have no real concept of time inside her prison," Zola said. "Remember Gaia's offer in case we need it for the coming battle, but for now it is not worth the risk."

"Agreed," Camazotz said.

Beth watched me until I lifted a brow. Then she stared at Camazotz before turning her attention to Zola. "This is what you do? Plan ways to hurl yourselves into the paths of oncoming trains?"

"An apt analogy," Camazotz said.

Zola nodded. "I rather like that."

Beth shook her head. "Cornelius was right. You're all crazy."

"You have no idea," I said before I paused. "Well, I guess you have some idea now. Welcome to the club!"

"We should go," Sam said.

I nodded. "I only have one other question. What do we do with Vicky?"

"What do you believe is right?" Camazotz asked.

So I told him, and the ancient god smiled.

✦   ✦   ✦

"WHY DID WE rush out of there?" Beth asked once we were on the highway and closing in on Farmington. "We have almost two and a half hours."

"Catfish Kettle," Sam and I echoed at once. I glanced at my sister and we both laughed.

"Should we get it to go?" Sam asked. "I'm not sure if we really have time to stop."

I nodded. "I'd rather get to Howell Island early. I hope you don't mind a little greasy food in the car."

"No," Sam said. "Vik can scrub it out."

"You're going to have the Lord of your Pit scrub the greasy food stains from your upholstery?" Beth asked.

"Yep."

"You'll get used to their antics if you stay with us," Ashley said.

"I'm not going anywhere," Beth said. She squeezed Ashley's hand and leaned on her shoulder.

Foster ripped a huge snore and woke himself up. "What happened? Where are we?"

"You ate my S'more," I said flatly.

"Oh, yeah," The fairy said, flexing his wings. "It was good."

Sam steered us through the small town of Farmington and parked in front of the Catfish Kettle. Foster insisted on riding on Sam's shoulder. She finally gave in. "I'll be right back. Damian, stay here. I know they know you."

The door slammed closed.

"They know you here?" Beth asked.

I smiled and nodded. "Yeah, I used to pig out here with Zola. They have a picture of me on the wall."

"Quite the legacy there," Ashley said.

"Shut up, witch."

Sam came back a few minutes later, loaded with fried catfish nuggets, hushpuppies, and four drinks precariously balanced in one hand. I leaned over and pushed her door open.

We ate as we drove back to Saint Louis. By the time the White Castle in Festus passed our windows, the weight of what was coming fell heavy on my shoulders. We were saying goodbye to Carter and Maggie for the last time.

CHAPTER THIRTY-SEVEN

I CLOSED MY eyes when we neared Highway Forty. It was effortless now, reaching out to Happy. Not so long ago, it took every fiber of my being to find him across the city. Now it was more like flipping on a radio.

"Happy."

I could see him there, on the second floor of Death's Door with Bubbles nestled at the foot of a chair. Vicky was curled up and nestled into the stuffed leather with a blanket over her. I looked closer and realized it wasn't a blanket at all. Jasper was spread out, keeping her warm.

"How is she?"

Happy looked away from Vicky and it felt like he was looking into my eyes.

She still sleeps, though she has stirred many times. She is well, Damian. I will watch over her. Honor the Ghost Pack.

I nodded and let the vision fade.

"Let's go," I said, and Sam steered us onto the highway, heading straight for Howell Island.

✦ ✦ ✦

"I'VE NEVER SEEN so many cars here," I said as Sam parked on the grass below the levee. There was nothing hidden about the pack tonight. A fire turned the woods to orange and black shadows in the distance, and visions of the Burning Lands came screaming back.

"Aideen's already here," Foster said. He closed his eyes and smiled. "I can feel her. I'll see you inside." He launched himself off the roof of the SUV, gliding over the steep incline of the levee before diving into the tree line.

"Is that Frank's car?" I asked, eyeing the old green Challenger. I caught sight of the license plate—FNGLVR—and groaned. "Never mind."

"You love it," Sam said, putting an arm around my shoulders. "Come on, now you're just procrastinating. Let's go see Hugh."

I took a deep breath. She was right. I didn't want to do this. I wanted to see Carter materialize in front of me again. I wanted Maggie's golden glow to light up a room one last time. I didn't want to bury them again.

Sam ushered me forward.

"Should we be here?" Beth asked. "It seems like we shouldn't. I didn't know them that well, or at all, really."

"You know Alan," Ashley said with a tired smile. "We should be here for Alan, if nothing else."

Beth followed in silence.

"What's in the trees?" Sam asked as we made our way onto the island. The humidity on the river was overwhelming, and muffled voices sounded deeper in the woods. Something that looked like canvas stretched across the canopy above us. I smelled the leather mixed with river water.

"I have no idea," I said. We followed the curve of the trail and the voices grew louder. I took a slight right at the gnarled old tree. It was a good reference to find the clearing where the pack gathered, but tonight I didn't need it. This was one of the few times I'd been on the island when the voices whispered louder than the river.

I focused on the path ahead of us and the ley lines burst into view, blinding in their intensity. When I'd last seen them, they were strong, but they were candles beside the sun compared to the energy running through the island now.

My heart jumped when I saw a golden werewolf around the next corner. A moment later I realized the fur wasn't golden because it was dead. It belonged to an eight-foot-tall werewolf who was very much alive. "Wahya?"

"Brother." His voice was throaty and deep. I hadn't seen him since the battle at Gettysburg. If his appearance—crowned by a sharp snout and sharper fangs—wasn't enough to strike terror into the hearts of his enemies, his voice was up to the task.

I extended my arm to trade grips, and the werewolf pulled me into a hug instead. I tried not to sneeze as I got a faceful of golden fur.

"How are you here?" I asked. "I thought you were managing the werewolves' interactions with Falias near Gettysburg."

"I flew in this morning," Wahya said. "I will leave again tomorrow, but this is a celebration I could not miss. We honor Carter and his pack for all that they were, and all that they've done."

I could feel the pressure at the back of my eyes. I nodded to Wahya and squeezed his arm. He handed me a silver flask. "For the dark times. It is my own recipe, though many do not appreciate it."

It fit neatly into my jeans pocket. "Thank you."

He didn't say more, merely stood to the side to allow us passage.

"He's huge," Beth whispered.

"I hear quite well," Wahya said from behind us. "But thank you, tiny blood mage."

The clicking sound I heard next may have been Beth's teeth snapping closed, or it may have been the shifted wolves' claws around us. I wondered why only a few were shifted and the rest still looked human.

I would have said more, but I was too busy staring at the slightly raised earthen platform where Haka and Hugh stood before Camazotz and Zola.

"How are they already here?" Beth whispered behind me.

"No clue."

"Thank you for coming," Hugh said, exchanging a forearm grip with Camazotz. "It means a great deal to us."

"Our alliance will never fade so long as I live, Hohniokai-yohos. I remember what your people sacrificed to aid my children."

Camazotz bowed slightly before leading Zola off into a crowd of werewolves. Zola raised an eyebrow as she glanced at me over her shoulder. There were werewolves and Fae and gods in a circle here, not so unlike our gathering around the bonfire at the cabin, but the mood was far more somber.

Haka hopped off the low platform and walked over to us. Hugh followed.

Hugh made no motion to grab my arm. He wrapped Ashley up in a brief bear hug. "Welcome, priestess."

"I'm so sorry for your loss," Ashley whispered. She kissed Hugh on the cheek and he patted her back before releasing her.

He turned to me and knocked my offered arm to the side, instead crushing me in a short hug. "Welcome home, Damian."

Haka mimicked Hugh, slapping me on the back hard enough to crack ribs. "I can't believe you're alive."

"Thanks for the vote of confidence, kid."

He smiled and stepped back beside his father.

"How's the pack since the ..." I hesitated. "Since it's not being drained anymore?"

"You have seen the island for yourself," Hugh said. "Did you not notice the life and the energy all around you? The pack magic is stronger than it has been in a very long time."

"It wasn't just you," Haka said. "The Ghost Pack was a drain, sure, but every pack's magic was choked off when the Fae first cut Faerie off from the world. Thousands of years, now."

"Haka, go tend to the guests," Hugh said.

Haka glowered at his dad and stalked away.

"Was that true?" I asked.

Hugh sighed and gave a sharp nod. "He talks a great deal when he is sad. Some of us are not taking this loss as well as others. How is the child?"

"She's sleeping, but Happy seems to think she's okay."

"Good. That is good." He turned to Beth. "Alan has told me much about you. You are welcome at our home anytime you choose, as is your master."

"Thank you," she said.

Hugh smiled at the unmasked surprise in her voice. "Samantha, it is always good to see you have not had to kill your brother yet. I applaud your patience in all matters related to him."

287

"Smartest damn werewolf on the planet," Sam said with a huge grin.

"Please, find a seat, or stand if you wish. We begin soon."

Hugh walked past us to greet another couple coming in beside Wahya.

"I see Alan," Beth said. She squeezed Ashley's hand and started weaving between the werewolves. Some stared at the scars on her arms, while others took no notice of the blood mage in their midst.

I glanced up at the great canvas dome reaching across the forest's canopy. At its center stood the fire pit, not so far from the entrance to the wolves' underground lair.

A golden light glinted in the shadows near the bunker. I did a double take as I realized it was Edgar, fully armored. I made my way over to him, slipping behind wolves I didn't know and others I did. He was gesturing widely and speaking in hushed tones.

"It's based on a sweat lodge, but I've never seen anything so large before," Edgar said.

"And that's why the entrance faces due east?" I hadn't realized the man beside him was Frank until he spoke.

Edgar nodded. "It's amazing." He looked up as I approached.

Sam drifted over to Frank. The smile that lit up the man's face made me happy for them both.

"Weren't you in Falias?" I said, turning my attention to Edgar.

"I would not miss this, Damian. Carter was an old friend. I'll return to Falias when the ceremony ends. Is Nixie still coming?"

"Oh, shit," I said, fumbling at my backpack. I pulled out the Wasser-Münzen. "She'll be here in a sending."

"You should call her now. Hugh will be starting soon."

"Where?" I asked. "If I head out to the river, no one will see her."

Edgar pointed to the opposite side of the clearing. "The wolves carved an inlet for her. Alexandra is already there."

I could just make out her waist-length black hair in the firelight. "Do you think she already contacted Nixie?"

"Perhaps," Edgar said, "but Nixie will wait to appear until you call. It is a symbol of the alliance between the wolves and the witches, an alliance you helped to forge."

"Beth will be glad to see Alexandra here." I started toward the water witch, and then paused, looking back at Edgar. "I'm glad you're here. You should say hi to Beth when you see her. I think she'd like to meet you."

Edgar nodded. "I will bear that in mind."

I didn't tell him anything else, but I heard Ashley sigh behind me. She stayed with Sam and Frank, talking quietly to Edgar. It always amazed me how one person whispering could be so quiet, but a hundred whispers became a rolling thunder.

"Cornelius," I said as the old blood mage stepped out of the woods beside Alexandra. "Beth's around here somewhere with Alan."

"I am glad to hear that," he said.

"As am I," Alexandra said, looking over my shoulder into one of the groups.

"I feared what might become of her when she opened the portal into the Burning Lands," Cornelius said. "I'm thankful you helped her, and I'm thankful Adannaya trained you so well." He walked away without another word, heading toward Beth and the smiling werewolf beside her.

"Hugh is about to start," Alexandra said. "Summon her."

I bent down and slid the blue obsidian into the water. "I'm pretty sure she'd kick your ass if she thought I was trying to 'summon her.'"

Alexandra narrowed her eyes and I gave her a weak smile. The water boiled around my hands.

"It's time," I said into the bubbles.

Nixie appeared in an instant. There was no slow rise of the bubbles, no ceremony. One moment she wasn't there, and the next, a translucent vision stood beside me.

"Thank you both," she said, looking from me to Alexandra. "We have lost great allies, and I wish to honor them all."

Hugh stepped back up onto the raised earthen platform.

I'd half expected the werewolves to be naked. It felt like they did everything naked, but here they wore simple skirts and jerkins. Most were cracked and dark like ancient leather, but a few were modern. The shifted wolves wore silver-colored medallions, though I didn't know why.

Frank stood beside Sam. They waited with Ashley and Edgar at the edge of the woods.

I saw faces I didn't recognize, and some that surprised me greatly. Gosha, ally of Wahya, who had fought with us at Gettysburg. Carter's lost love, Caroline, Alpha of the Irish Brigade. She stared into the flames and did nothing to hide the tears flowing down her cheeks.

The wolves closest to the fire sat down, and the motion moved out in a cascade. I settled in between Alexandra and Nixie, crossing my legs and catching glimpses of the other guests as I could.

Alan sat down across from Alexandra, his eyes red and puffy. Beth stayed at his side. We exchanged a short nod.

Hugh was the last to join us on the earth, now dressed in only a pair of modest leather shorts and two feathers tied into his braided hair.

He raised a hand and the entire assembly quieted. "Let us begin this very day …" Hugh paused and frowned at the flames licking the side of the fire pit. "I suppose this is not a day for our traditional prayers." He took a deep breath and looked skyward, as though he could see through the canvas and into the stars above.

"The Ghost Pack is no more, and their spirits no longer speak with words for our ears. Their entirety was taken to free the child, Vicky, but every soul honored the River Pack in saving her, and in removing the Destroyer from our world."

"I will miss them," Alan whispered, echoing a murmuring tone throughout the group. He wore a smile, but it didn't mask the sadness beneath it.

"Twice did Carter and Maggie die to save the pack," Hugh said, raising his voice and speaking in a slow rhythm. "Twice did we lose the best of us, but they died in good company. They pass with honor into the next life, escorted by thirty of our brothers and sisters."

I almost fell over. My hand shot out to stabilize my failing posture. "Thirty?" I whispered. I leaned forward, fighting a weight in my chest that threatened to choke me.

"Hush, Cub," someone hissed. "They knew the price. The decision was unanimous."

I didn't know who'd spoken. I didn't care. I'd destroyed

thirty souls to save Vicky. I'd killed thirty ... I'd ... I almost gagged on the emotions tearing up my mind, and I couldn't stop the tears from running down my face.

Hugh began naming them. Some part of my mind registered that. I didn't know some of the names, but Carter and Maggie and even Jimmy cut me like a blade.

Why didn't I know I'd killed thirty wolves? How? How was that possible? I dug my fingernails into my shaking palms and bit my tongue. What was wrong with me?

"Remember them," Hugh said. "They have saved a child who will be able to grow old, and live, and one day join them in the Spirit World. Our friends will not be waiting there, longing for those lost. They will not journey to find the ghosts and the worm pipe. We are at peace, as are they."

The worm pipe. Zola told me that story once, or some version of it at least. It was a sad tale, and a potent warning about failing to move forward with your life. I thought it was a bit heavy-handed, coming from Hugh, like he was trying to lecture me. I raised my eyes as Caroline broke down, sobbing into Gosha's shoulder.

I was a fool. Hugh didn't mean it for me alone. He meant it for all of us around that fire, and all of us who would never join the pack again.

The drums were quiet and deep at first, playing a steady rhythm while several of the wolves slowly bobbed their heads to the beat. My eyes didn't lift from the dancing fire in the middle of the gathering. It swelled and receded, and I could have sworn it moved in time to the music. A wood flute added a simple run of notes, deliberate and sad. The winds picked up around us, snapping the canvas above with a deep throbbing boom. Another set of brighter toms joined the sound and the world moved as one.

I don't know how long we sat there, but the humidity and heat and flame built until the air itself felt as though it might catch fire. The music stopped when the colors in the pit were no longer those of a wood flame. I didn't have to raise my sight to see the spiral of blue and gold fires dancing in that place. They bent and twisted and shaped themselves into something else. It looked like an ancient face for a time, etched with deep lines and a patient frown.

Something rustled in the trees above us, and the very trunks shifted. Everyone's gaze turned skyward, and the canvas dome split at its widest part. An enormous eagle-like head eased through the opening.

I stared at the Piasa Bird, and heard the whispers around the fire.

Thunderbird.

Water dripped from the thunderbird's beak. It touched the fire, and the flames exploded into the sky. It was only then that I realized the Piasa Bird wasn't wet, it was tears dripping into the flames. The fire looked to be standing up, holding wavering hands out to the Piasa Bird. My pack marks burned and I glanced from them back to the scene before me. This was the spirit of the island. I knew it without being told. It mourned with us, bound as it was in pack magic. Lightning flashed around the thunderbird's eye before he lifted his head out of the canopy and released an ear-piercing cry.

Then there was only silence.

"The war is not over," Hugh said into the quiet. "We will lose more wolves. We will lose more friends like our brave

Cara, Sanatio of the Sidhe. More of our allies may become enemies before the deed is done, but remember too our enemies that have become allies.

"Remember the water witches."

Alexandra came to her feet and Nixie rose to stand on my other side.

"Remember the blood mages."

Cornelius and Beth stood, and Alan stood with them, wrapping each in one of his massive arms.

"Remember the vampires and the gods."

Edgar and Sam and Camazotz stepped up beside Hugh.

"They are friends to us. They are as close as blood can be without being blood. Protect them as though they were your own. Fight with them as though they were your children, for they have done the same for us."

Hugh turned his gaze to me. "Remember the boy Carter watched over, and the man he would become. Remember the master who trained him."

Zola stepped up in front of the earthen platform.

"Remember Maggie's words of kindness about a being that should have been a sworn enemy," Hugh said, his voice rising as he held his hand out to Zola. "Remember our brother, our necromancer. Remember his journey to the Burning Lands to save that child! Without his help, Carter and Maggie's greatest wish would have died out before they took their flight into the Spirit World. Now they rest easy in the knowledge a child will live, and the Destroyer—she has met her end!"

I stood up, tears coursing down my face.

"Stand with us," Hugh said, his voice rising to a thunder. "Stand and show our allies the strength of wolves. Show them the love for our families! Show them our power!"

Hugh shifted, fur and muscles exploding from his form. I expected his clothing to tear off, but it stretched to fit the wolf as his jaws opened toward the sky, and a terrible, mourning howl cut into the night.

The mass shift that followed battered my senses. There was so much power pulled through the pack marks and the fire and the island itself that I thought the earth might split open. Another scream joined that earth-shattering howl. The scream of thousands of souls inside my head. They'd been quiet for so long, I'd hope they'd been quieted forever.

What would that take, though? To be silenced forever? Would they have to be destroyed like Carter and Maggie and the rest of the Ghost Pack? Sent into an oblivion from which they'd never have vengeance for their deaths?

If I had some say in it, they'd help me destroy Gwynn Ap Nudd and bring Hern to his knees. They deserved blood from those Fae, and I swore it as I drew the focus from my belt and channeled in that cacophony of power.

A golden sword erupted from the hilt, licking at the sky beside the flames of the pit, and the wolves grew louder.

CHAPTER THIRTY-EIGHT

A FTER THE CEREMONY ended, a few of us sat around the pack's massive couch in the underground bunker, clad in heat and sweat. I rolled the Wasser-Münzen between my hands before tucking it into my backpack. Beth and Ashley joined us, with Hugh and Edgar and Zola. Sam and Frank sat quietly beside Alan. I was surprised they hadn't left to go home. I was still shaken up from watching Wahya carry Caroline away from the fire. She was hurting bad, and Hugh explained why.

"She buried her husband outside Falias two weeks ago," Hugh said. "The loss … it is something I truly cannot imagine."

"She lost both men she loved in the span of two weeks?" Sam asked.

Hugh closed his eyes and nodded. "I am afraid she may become reckless with the Irish Brigade. Time will tell. Wahya has offered to help. It is a rare thing for an Alpha to allow someone from outside the pack to help."

"Wahya's not exactly a normal wolf, though, is he?" I said.

Hugh shook his head. "No."

Edgar looked up. The golden mail hanging from his helmet chimed against his breastplate when he moved. "What of the dark-touched at Rivercene?"

"I have not heard from the innkeeper," Hugh said. "I assume that means things have been quiet. I expected to hear more by now, but she may have kept her distance, knowing the ceremony was tonight. Camazotz is on his way now."

Beth stared at Edgar, her eyes tracing the hieroglyphs carved in the man's armor beside ancient runes and symbols that had long been forgotten.

"Edgar," I said.

He looked at me. "This is Beth."

"I know Beth," Edgar said. "Do not trouble me over who the Watchers did or did not pursue."

"Beth, this is Ra."

Edgar raised his eyebrows and I heard a sharp intake of breath from the blood mage.

"Oh my god, I mean lord, I mean … it is such an honor to meet you. I've read so many of the old stories, your stories, and they just, they just."

Edgar's head fell and he let out a deep sigh.

I grinned while Beth continued to gush about Edgar's past life. When she was close to five minutes of breathless rambling—which was amazing in itself—Edgar turned his head to me and smiled. The more Beth spoke, the more it became obvious that she was a scholar, well learned in Ra's mythologies, and even the stories that were not mere stories.

"You flatter me," Edgar said. "It is good to know that some people still carry the old stories close to their hearts."

Beth pulled up the edge of her shorts, revealing the deep scars around the eye of Ra. "Reading about you got me through some tough places." She tugged her shorts back down. "I'm sorry for being so crazy right then," she said, unable to wipe the smile from her face. "It's just, I mean, thank you. For talking to me, and for helping my friends and the love of my life." Beth grabbed Ashley's hand and squeezed.

Ashley raised Beth's hand and kissed it before covering it with her own.

"Thank you," Edgar said, "for lightening the mood at this dark hour. One day, perhaps when the war is done, I will tell you the stories no one knows. From times when the Old Gods roamed the earth, and only the immortals stood defiant."

"I know those stories," Hugh said.

Edgar crossed his arms and leaned into the couch. "Indeed, you know several, but perhaps not all."

We stayed there for a time, bantering with small talk and stories of the lost wolves. One thing I was sure of, we were all going to miss Carter and Maggie.

✦   ✦   ✦

I WALKED TO the back of the shop after Sam and Frank dropped me off on the side street. Camazotz was off to Rivercene. I wasn't sure where everyone else was going. I'd have moments of clarity where I remembered how important it was that we'd saved Vicky, and then the Ghost Pack's death would come crashing down onto my heart once more.

I leaned against my old '32 Ford and pulled Wahya's flask out of my jacket. I smiled at the face carved into it, a green man. The wolf either had uncanny timing, or a terrible sense of humor. The whiskey burned going down, and I felt its warmth spread out across my gut. It was woody and strong and slightly smoother than paint thinner. I winced and said, "Damn, Wahya. What the hell?"

"Well, well, well. If it isn't the necromancer with all the dead friends."

I froze before I realized it was our obnoxious deadbolt talking. I narrowed my eyes. "I would have thought you'd change back."

"Why? Because one fairy died?" The ugly little face twisted into a frown. "Maybe if *all* of Faerie died. Hopefully her son will be next."

I stood up and walked toward the door.

"Let's be reasonable, now," the little face said, apparently realizing the error of his ways.

I smashed the toe of my boot into the deadbolt's face. It grunted and snapped open. I hurried inside before I acted on a strong urge to shoot the fucking thing in the face, and slammed the door behind me.

One more shot of whiskey calmed me a bit. I closed the flask and slid it into my backpack.

Foster and Aideen sat on the little Formica table. Foster's wings shuddered and Aideen laid her head on his, wrapping him up in her arms. I didn't interrupt. There wasn't anything I could say right now. He'd lost his mom. Aideen cast me a sad smile and nodded to me.

I held up my hand and started up the stairs.

Shiawase waited in one of the overstuffed leather chairs, an old book propped up in his hands.

Vicky looked peaceful there, tucked into the chair next to Shiawase, but my concern that she hadn't woken up continued to grow. I needed a shower, but dammit, if the kid was stuck here asleep, I could stay here one more night.

"I can see the worry on your face," Shiawase said, looking up from his book as I walked up beside Vicky. "She is safe here, and I will not abandon my post. When she awakens, you will be the first to know."

He hadn't left her side in days. I guessed if anyone would know, he would. "Thank you. I think I'll just sleep here, if it's all the same to you."

"I am in your home," Shiawase said. "The choice is yours."

I pulled my backpack off, flopped onto one of the deep leather chairs, and sighed.

Something heavy and bristly hit my thigh. I cracked an eye open to find Bubbles staring at me. I smiled and scratched her head. She chuffed and laid down on my feet. I probably wouldn't be able to feel them in a few minutes, but I didn't ask the cu sith to move.

Jasper chittered from across the table.

"Good job, furball. Good job." I closed my eyes again, almost welcoming the escape of another nightmare.

✦   ✦   ✦

MY HEART HAMMERED in my chest and I awoke, reaching for the hilt of the focus, ready to cut through a possessed River Pack to save Sam. The voices thundered through my mind, screaming their own fears as pins and needles stabbed at my legs.

I took three deep breaths and wiped the sweat from my forehead. Bubbles snored, her bulk half-crushing my feet. Shiawase was out like a light. It was one of the few times I'd actually seen the ghost sleep. I rubbed my face and gently slid my numb feet out from under Bubbles.

Water. I needed water. I pulled the Book that Bleeds out of my backpack and placed it inside the hidden chest before wobbling around the cu sith on half-numb legs. I glanced back at the motley crew sleeping in my reading nook. I hoped they would get more rest than I had.

I found a Frappuccino in the small fridge in the back room instead. There was no way in hell I was going to try to sleep again after that. The grandfather clock ticked nearby. I'd never see Cara here again, and the recurring thought made the tock sound like thunder. I had to get away.

Aideen glanced up from her perch on the register when I walked into the front room. "There is a green man at Rivercene who wishes to speak with the Dead God."

"The what?" I asked, wondering if maybe I was still asleep and my nightmare was taking a new turn.

"You," she said. "The green men hold on to old traditions and, to them, necromancers are Dead Gods."

My groggy brain slowly pieced things together. "A woodsman? From Kansas City?"

"I don't know if he's from the city, but yes, he is a woodsman. I considered waking you earlier, but the innkeeper offered to entertain the green man for a while. We all needed the rest."

"Is Foster awake?" I asked. "Do you think he'd want to go?"

"It might be easier to walk the Abyss with Gaia," Aideen said. "I'm not sure if the woodsman will wait until daylight. Foster is sleeping."

I nodded. "How is he?"

Aideen tilted her head to the side. "Better than I expected, but he is trying hard to hide his pain. I fear what he may do out of vengeance."

"Think he'll go after Glenn?" I asked as I opened my backpack.

"I hope not."

"If he does, he won't go alone. We have Nixie's people, and the wolves."

"We can talk more, later," Aideen said. She gave me a pained smile.

"Of course," I said. "I'm sorry to bring it up now."

I held Gaia's hand. Before I stepped into the Abyss, I said, "Take care of him."

"Take care of your own, Damian. We need you."

The world turned black.

CHAPTER THIRTY-NINE

"Where can I take you?" Gaia asked.

"Rivercene," I said.

Gaia looked at me as the path materialized beneath our feet. "You wish to accept my offer?"

"No," I said. "I need to speak with the innkeeper. I'm guessing you can get me past the Guardian there?"

"As I am the Guardian? Yes."

We walked in silence for a time, passing nightmares and starry vistas along the way.

"I don't see as many of the Old Gods as we used to," I said, staring out into the darkness.

"Many have left the Abyss," Gaia said. "Though you repaired the Seal from the Burning Lands, many creatures escaped into other planes."

I remembered some of the tree-like tentacles and mountainous creatures we'd passed. The thought of encountering any of them outside the Abyss—while they weren't slowed— was terrifying.

Gaia slowed. "We are here."

I took a deep breath. "Ready."

She said no more. The stars collapsed in on themselves as I was torn from the Abyss. I landed on the front steps of Rivercene, facing the distant river as I slammed into the wood ass-first.

"Ow," I said, grabbing my ass. "Ow ow ow." The voices were a cacophony inside my head. Whatever was here, they didn't like it.

"Damian?"

I looked up and found the innkeeper staring at me as I slowly stopped rubbing my ass.

"Oh, don't stop on my account," the innkeeper said, squinting at me under the porch light. "I'm surprised you survived the Burning Lands. Thought for sure that fire demon would get you killed. Must be slipping in my old age."

"It's good to see you too," I said as I adjusted my backpack and leaned forward, resting my arms on my knees. The transition out of the Abyss hadn't been smooth, and the world still spun a bit.

I blew out a breath and looked past the innkeeper. The skies weren't as clear here as they had been at the cabin, but the night sky was still stunning compared to the city. Some vague movement flickered through my peripheral vision, and then it was gone. I didn't remember the tree line being so close to Rivercene. One of the shadows moved in the darkness.

It occurred to me that I might be seeing things, considering the screaming voices in my head, but the harder I looked, the more I could make out.

A creature stepped into the light, and I had no doubt it was the woodsman. It was taller than Foster, nine feet, maybe more, depending on how its leafy branches and constantly shifting vines bristled. It stepped onto one of the flagstones with a thud, and the rock cracked.

"Dammit, you overgrown bush!" The innkeeper snapped. "I

told you I didn't mind if you waited here, so long as you didn't break anything."

"The stone is now two," the woodsman said. "It is not broken. It is of the earth, and the earth cannot be broken."

The innkeeper squeezed her forehead. "Gods but I hate these things sometimes." She turned to me. "Damian, this is—" Her words cut off into a brief clicking that sounded like wooden sticks banging together.

"What?" I whispered.

"That's his name," the innkeeper said with a sigh. "Call him green man, or woodsman. They all answer to those names."

The woodsman bent down onto his knee so his emerald eyes were just above my own. The tightly wrapped vines that formed his face stilled as though they had decided on their form.

"Hmm," the woodsman said as he looked me over. "You are the Lord of the Dead Gods. I did not realize that."

"He means the mantle," the innkeeper said. "Melodramatic lot, they are. Tell him what you saw so we can all get some sleep. Tell him what you told Camazotz."

"Very well," the woodsman said. He settled onto the ground at the bottom of the short stairs leading to the front door.

"Is Camazotz still here?"

The innkeeper shook her head. "He went on to Kansas City, after he heard this tale."

I stopped asking questions and instead focused on the woodsman.

"We have long been friends with the witches by the river. They respect the land and the trees and find peace in the waters."

"The coven?" I asked, unsure if he meant the undines or the green witches.

"Yes. They were an ancient group. I have known them in one form or another for thousands of your years. The old Fae, before they were driven into hiding in the wars, were one with us."

I wasn't sure if the woodsman meant they were one with nature, or if the old Fae were actually green men.

"But the old stories are not why I have come to find you. It is the old enemies that have led me to walk in the light."

"He means show himself," the innkeeper said. "Just talk like a normal person, yes?"

The woodsman turned his head to the innkeeper and then returned his focus to me. I didn't think he gave half a damn what the innkeeper thought. I kind of admired him for that.

"What are the old enemies?" I asked.

"Ancient creatures, monsters some would say. Flying heads, baykok, mishupishu, skinwalkers, and the water witches. We have heard stories of Sharp Elbows, a two-faced nightmare once thought no more than story."

"All at the coven?" I whispered.

"No," the woodsman said. "But they have been seen by the eyes of the green men and, by their gaze, I know these things to be true."

"You should have told Camazotz," the innkeeper said. "You only told him of the dark-touched.

The woodsman's eyes flashed to the innkeeper. "He did not ask after the old enemies."

"Never mind," the innkeeper said, pinching the bridge of

her nose. "I'll get a message to him."

"What destroyed the coven?" I asked. "How did the survivors escape?"

"The coven fell at the attack of the dark-touched, the night dwellers, and the sea witches." The woodsman's hands curled into fists and his voice angered. "They killed that which was under the protection of the green men. It will not be forgotten."

"How did they escape?"

The woodsman's fingers cracked and he slowly uncurled his fist. A slow-moving sap oozed down his knuckles. "They did not." He drew the sap up into a small spike on the back of his hand. "The dark-touched allowed them to flee at the request of a flame-haired undine."

"A redheaded water witch?" I asked.

"Yes." The woodsman cracked his hand again and spread more sap across his knuckles.

"I would have expected him to say her head had been on fire," the innkeeper said. "Thank you for speaking plainly, woodsman. I know this must pain you."

I swallowed a laugh. I was pretty sure the innkeeper was being a total smartass, and wondered how the woodsman would respond.

"Nothing can pain me so much as the betrayal of the Fae," the woodsman said. "A betrayal that cut out the heart of my brethren and left their friends dead and drawn across the earth."

The innkeeper sat down on the stairs beside me. "Let him talk for a while," she whispered.

The woodsman launched into a five-minute tirade about the injustices of the Fae and the impotence of their king. I raised an eyebrow when the woodsman grew quiet, and spoke of things I'd never expected to hear from a green man, a people known for their calm and peace.

"We will not stand idly by while the False King sentences our allies to death. He will answer for allowing the return of the dark-touched and I will smite him for the injustice he inflicts in the name of peace. When the veil falls, we march to war, and Hern dies with him."

The innkeeper made a series of clicking sounds. "The world's gone mad when the woodsmen promise war." She clicked out another pattern with her tongue that I recognized as the green man's name.

The woodsman raised his emerald eyes to her and spoke quietly. "Prophecy is destiny, and destiny does not barter."

The innkeeper tilted her head to one side. "I'd forgotten that. I apologize. I meant no disrespect."

"None was found."

"What now?" the innkeeper asked.

"I will return to my city, but my brothers remain to stand watch, as they have since our mother was buried beneath this place." The woodsman returned his gaze to me, emerald eyes catching the moonlight in a series of flashes. "It has been most good to meet you, Lord of the Dead Gods. I hope to meet you again on better terms, for it is the dead that feed the new growth, and the new growth that feeds the living."

"What should I call you?" I asked. "I won't remember your real name."

The woodsman looked at the nearby tree stump where we'd once hung a man as bait. "Call me … Stump. It is a good and sturdy name."

I bit my lips and slammed my brain on the emergency stop button for my sarcasm. It was a close thing. "Stump. It was an honor to meet you."

"And you," the green man said as a pale light swelled in the grasses around his feet. He sank into the earth without another word, and then he was gone. The nearby tree line shifted closer to the river. I couldn't be sure how many woodsmen surrounded Rivercene, but it was significant.

"Why didn't they help when Ezekiel was here?" I asked.

"Not their fight. Now, if one of you idiots had gone into the cellar. Well, let's just say it would have become their fight."

A breeze rolled across the fields around us, setting the trees to swaying. I knew the woodsmen, the green men, were not a common sight, but I might never look at a tree the same way again.

"Come in for tea," the innkeeper said, regaining her feet. She looked up at the sky. "Perhaps coffee. The sun will be rising soon. There is something I would discuss with you in private."

I nodded in agreement. The thought of being alone with the innkeeper sent a frisson of excitement down my spine. She was a mystery in many ways, and maybe I could learn something more of her.

The screen door squealed when she opened it, and I reached out to hold it for her. The innkeeper put an old key in the front door and twisted. The lock clicked and she twisted again. This time it kachunked in the frame and the innkeeper pushed her way inside.

"Come in."

CHAPTER FORTY

I FOLLOWED HER through the doorway. Every voice, every sound inside my head cut off. I could hear my own heartbeat, and I didn't move for almost a minute, basking in that glorious silence.

Nothing had changed since I'd been there before. The grand old wooden stairs still flowed up the right side of the hall, flanked by a wide, sweeping bannister. I took a deep breath and smiled, looking across the hardwood floors at the aged portraits on the wall and the beige Victorian chairs below them.

I studied the piano in the living room off to the left. Mike had forged a wardstone for it, setting a protection on the home unlike anything I'd experienced elsewhere. Ghosts were hidden from me here, hidden from all who might harm them. I'd been told it was for their own safety, but I wondered.

The innkeeper's footsteps grew distant. I took one last look at the marble fireplace on the far wall, one of many inside Rivercene, and turned back to the hallway. I couldn't see the innkeeper, but I figured she'd gone to the kitchen. I made my way past the upright piano tucked beneath the staircase and the curio filled with old photographs and antiques.

The kitchen was just as crazy as I remembered, with an enormous fireplace in the wall. The dark hardwood floor extended into the mouth of the fireplace now, and I frowned.

"You don't light fires anymore?"

"Of course we do," the innkeeper said, filling a perfectly modern coffee maker on top of the contemporary cabinets. "Take a seat." She wandered over to the ancient five-shelf spice rack and pulled one of the jars off. "Powdered creamer?"

"Black is fine," I said.

"No no, powdered creamer is my guilty pleasure. None of that greasy taste left on your tongue like real cream. Try it." She sprinkled a bit in each mug and stirred them up.

I stared into the fireplace, remembering the roaring fire I'd seen there in the past. Had the floor looked like that back then? I couldn't remember. Remembering the fire brought my mind tumbling back into the Burning Lands and the hellish seas within it.

"It is not so unusual for things to get worse before they get better," the innkeeper said as she handed me a steaming cup of coffee.

I looked away from the fireplace and studied the green mug. "Lately it feels like all things do is get worse."

"And imagine if you hadn't been here to stand in the way." She sighed and frowned at me. "And really, you just stormed the Burning Lands and put an end to the Destroyer. I'd think you'd be less of a brat right now."

I barked out a laugh and sipped my coffee. The creamer took some of the edge off, but it still had a nice bitter warmth. "You're way too much like Zola." I sat the mug down and glanced at the fireplace. "I'm worried. Vicky's been asleep since we got back."

"How is the Devil's Knot?"

I looked at the innkeeper.

"Didn't even check it, did you? Well, if your sister's still alive, I'm sure the knot is intact. Ward knows the price of making mistakes. You picked an excellent craftsman, there. I've seen more than one fool get themselves killed with less dangerous things."

"What did the woodsman mean about his mother being buried here?" I asked, sipping from the cup again. "Did he mean Gaia?"

The innkeeper nodded. "Gaia has made you an offer."

I froze with the steam from the hot coffee tickling my nose. "How did you know that? Did Camazotz tell you?"

The innkeeper shook her head. "I am … tied to Gaia in some ways. When the Mad King's spells push her to act, I am aware of the compulsion, and I am often aware of what that act will be. Do you intend to accept?"

I started to say *hell no,* but did I really mean it? If it meant helping Sam? Keeping my family safe? Could I really throw out the idea completely? I shrugged. "I'm not sure. She says it would help me battle the dark-touched, but what would her awakening mean?"

"She has never awoken. I don't know, but for her to leave the post of Guardian in this place, it could have dire consequences."

"Doesn't everything?" I muttered.

The innkeeper's wrinkled face smiled. "That it does."

I took another drink of coffee and leaned back in the chair. "What about the things the woodsman was talking about? I don't know what half of those are. Sharp Elbows? Baykok?"

"If you are lucky, you may never find out. You are more likely to face the shapeshifters. Have you ever seen a skinwalker?"

"Considering they're shapeshifters, I wouldn't know even if I did, right?"

The innkeeper frowned and bobbed her head from side to side. "Perhaps if they were fully shifted it may be difficult. Here." She leaned over to a short bookcase against the wall and pulled out an old leather photo album. "Hugh left this here a very long time ago, when he was friends with the captain who owned the home."

"Werewolf Hugh?"

"Is there another Hugh we both know, you idiot?" she snapped. The innkeeper cleared her throat and unhooked the two latches on the edge. Runes ran in a circle on the thick leather cover and the hinges creaked when she cracked open the photo album. Her voice resumed its easy cadence. "Now, magic has always had a place in this home. There is a Nexus beneath us that is tied to a gateway far older than that of the Wandering War. Magical things have always been drawn here because of it."

She flipped through the thick pages, each framing an old black and white photo in an arched window. The innkeeper stopped and turned the photo album toward me. I flinched. Even though it was black and white, the skinless skull and muscled grin peering out was a nightmare incarnate. The man held his own face in one hand.

"What the fuck?" I whispered.

"Here." She turned the page and a cougar's skin had been pulled over the skull. The photo next to it showed a twisted creature in mid-transformation, the cameras of the time far too slow to capture the movements. She turned the page again, and a perfectly formed cougar sat in a circle of reeds near a pond.

"They are powerful," she said. "Their strength goes beyond the forms they take."

"How can you even identify them if they've already shifted?"

"There are ways," the innkeeper said. "Their power comes from a dark place within the earth, and its magic will look strange to your Sight."

"I can't walk around all day with my Sight up looking for skinwalkers."

"No," the innkeeper said, "and that is what helps make their camouflage so perfect."

"And the Nexus?" I asked. "There's one in my shop, you know? But we don't have a sleeping Guardian protecting it."

"It's not the Nexus here that requires a Guardian. It is the old gateway, built well before a time when men or Fae realized how dangerous the gateways could be."

"Why not destroy it?"

"It cannot be destroyed by any means we know of. It will outlive the earth, you understand? When there is nothing left of our world, it will latch onto the bloated sun and let the Eldritch wander free into our universe. We won't much care by then, being dead.

"But the Nexus spawned other gateways around Missouri, and a few in nearby states. The dark-touched know of them, and you will have to destroy them."

"I plan on it."

"Not the vampires, boy, the gateways themselves. All manner of vile things can march through those damned things when the Seals are damaged. We can't destroy the old gateway here, but the lesser gateways are vulnerable."

"Can anything destroy it?" I asked.

The innkeeper paused. "There are things, yes, but if those creatures ever reached this plane, the gateway would be the least of your worries." She sipped at her coffee. "Actually you'd be dead, so you wouldn't have many worries at all."

"What kind of things?" I asked.

"They share some distant lineage with your dragon."

"Jasper?"

"No, your other dragon." She gave me a flat look. I wondered if she'd taught Zola to make that face. "No one knows. There have been only two sightings across the realms. One of those realms no longer exists."

"How does anyone know it was there if it was wiped out?"

The innkeeper sighed. "Realms can be observed from the outside, you know? You don't have to be standing inside one when it's annihilated to know it was annihilated. Did you know Falias was mostly destroyed by Ezekiel in Faerie?"

"Yes ..." I said, looking for the trap.

"Were you there to see it happen?"

I pursed my lips. "No."

"Indeed."

"How do you stand just being called innkeeper? Don't you want people to use your name?"

"Adannaya warned me about you and your questions. I should have known, after the last time you came here."

"I can't help it," I said. "It's so quiet in here. It's like I'm remembering all the things I wanted to ask before I had a small country crammed into my brain."

She settled back into her chair. "You can thank the fire

demon's wardstone for that." She drummed her fingers on the table. "Very well … I come from a time where a name could get you killed. Even your master changed her name while she was on the run. Sarah and …" She frowned. "Whatever the hell Philip was calling himself back then."

I turned the coffee mug on the table, trying to frame a more personal question. "What was Zola like back then?"

"Hard," the innkeeper said without pause. "Brave, noble, compassionate. One of the strongest women I ever met. Still is." She tapped a finger on her mug. "I've seen terrible things in my life, Damian, some worse than the rise of Falias, though none that took more lives. I've seen tragedies and darkness the likes of which I hope never scar the realms again, but what she endured?" The innkeeper shook her head. "No human, no living being, should be afflicted with that kind of hell. Broken out of her bonds by a lover who would become a madman? A man she'd have to kill with her own hands centuries later? If there are Fates among the stars, they are cruel creatures indeed."

She took a sip of coffee. "From here, they headed to Stones River. I think you know how that turned out. Trapping a demon and losing friends to another, your great-great-grandfather, in fact, if memory serves."

The innkeeper looked out the window and sighed. "Sun's coming up. You want some food?" She released a quiet, sharp laugh without looking at me. "Never mind. I'll whip something up right quick."

✦　✦　✦

I LET MY fork clatter down onto the plate, victorious over a soufflé that should have fed four. "Thank you. I can't believe I ate all that."

"Haven't eaten much since you got back from the Burning Lands, have you?"

"I guess not, now that I think about it."

"Not unusual. The transitions can upset your basic brain function a bit."

"As long as it's not serious."

The innkeeper smiled. "Not at all."

I grabbed her plate and stacked it on top of my own before standing up and walking to the sink.

"You don't need to do that."

"You didn't need to cook," I said. "I can wash a few dishes." I scrubbed out the pots while I stood at the sink, wondering how many people had stood there over the centuries. How many had lived in the old house? How many had died here?

"How long have you been here?" I asked, casting a glance over my shoulder. "I mean, how long have you lived here?"

"I knew what you meant, boy. I've watched over Gaia longer than I care to admit, but I know my limits. I can't stop an army of dark-touched. One day they'll come, and things will change."

I set the last of the plates in the dish rack and dried my hands. I took a deep breath and asked, "Can we see her?"

The innkeeper looked me over and glanced at the pack I'd left on the chair. "Leave your backpack here. I don't want that arm any closer to her than it already is. Gods only know what the Mad King did to it."

The innkeeper stood up and stretched. "Are you coming?"

I scrambled to hang up the towel. "Yes!"

CHAPTER FORTY-ONE

I FOLLOWED THE innkeeper outside, stepping onto a small
porch that faced east. A sliver of morning sun washed away
the stars at one edge of the world, while the other edge waited
in darkness. We took the wooden stairs down to the yard, and
from there it was only a few steps to the cellar.

Paint had chipped away from the old wooden door. "Is it
rotten?" I asked, wondering at the damage along the top and
bottom edges.

"No," the innkeeper said, "it was constructed hastily. It's
likely the sturdiest thing on this property." She pulled the
ancient brass key ring off the clip on her belt and unlocked the
door.

The key looked simple, with only a couple teeth at the end.
"Looks like it would be easy to pick."

She let out a short laugh. "Unlikely. There is a binding magic between the key and the door. Only if Rivercene is under
attack can that door be opened without the key. You'll have to
duck."

The innkeeper picked up a lantern just inside the doorway.
Zola used the same kind down at the cabin sometimes, a gas
light, painted green. She twisted a valve and snapped her
fingers. A spark came to life inside the lantern, and the small
bulbs inside glowed, casting a circle of light around us.

"Close the door behind us, would you?"

I ducked through the doorway and walked down three stone steps before pulling the heavy door shut until it clicked. A web of light peeked through the cracks near the top of the door. The only other light was the lantern's glow.

"They didn't make this for tall people," I said, trying to keep my hair out of the cobwebs and the critters scurrying through them.

It felt like we'd barely started walking when the innkeeper came to a stop and turned slightly to her right. "This is Gaia." She gestured to a raised patch of earth.

The shadows resolved the more I stared. It wasn't earth. There were feet sticking up near us. Roots bound the body to the floor, wrapping Gaia multiple times in a faint green magic. Her face lay hidden in shadow, and her left hand lay palm up. I stared at her right arm, which ended suddenly, her forearm missing.

The innkeeper walked closer to Gaia's head.

Even through the gray desiccated flesh I could tell it was her. The same long flowing hair she wore in the Abyss was here, only covered in dust and dirt.

"Was she never buried?"

"She was," the innkeeper said. "They stumbled onto her back when they were building this place."

"Why not bury her again? Why leave her out in the open like this?"

"Oh, they tried. Any more dirt than what you see on her now will flow away like water. I assume it has something to do with the Mad King's magic, but I can't say for sure. We don't know much about the Titans."

I stepped up beside the body. When I was farther away, I hadn't realized how large Gaia's figure actually was. I knew she was tall, but now I suspected her body was taller than that of the woodsman I'd recently met.

"I always imagined Titans to be the size of buildings."

"Some were," the innkeeper said. "Being of their bloodlines didn't guarantee any sort of size or power. They are like us in that way, I suppose, inheriting traits from their ancestors, but you can never be sure which traits they'll be."

I stood beside Gaia's head. She looked peaceful, covered in a fine layer of dirt as she was. I could hear her soft voice in my head. "Do you think her offer is safe? Or do you think it's a trap of some kind?"

"It could be either. Depending on how enthralled she was by the Mad King's magics, it could be a trap and she'd never know it. What a weapon against the dark-touched you could wield, though, Damian." She shook her head. "Well, I suppose we may never know."

Part of me hoped we wouldn't, another part of me wanted to climb back into Tessrian's prison and find out how to awaken the Titan and claim her gift. The lantern light swelled and dimmed.

✦ ✦ ✦

"WHAT WILL YOU do now?" the innkeeper asked when we returned to the kitchen.

I shook my head. "Head back to Saint Charles? Regroup with everyone, I guess. I don't know." I looked down at the photo album. "I need to call Hugh. Do you mind?"

"Not at all. If you need me, I'll be in the bedroom on this

floor. It's been a long week, and I must sleep while the dark-touched do. Prepare yourself, Damian. They are like nothing you've fought yet."

"Thank you," I said. "For the food, and for showing me Gaia."

The innkeeper nodded and disappeared into the hallway.

With the backpack slung across my shoulder, I wandered to the front room, pausing briefly to study the old curio. Most of it was the same as last time, but now one of the pictures of Zola and Philip was propped up against the back. They looked happy, and it made me glad that Zola had gotten some measure of happiness out of that bastard.

I called Hugh as I settled in by the old piano at the front of Rivercene, staring at the faceless skinwalker's photo.

"Yes?" Hugh answered. He sounded tired.

"Did I wake you up?" I asked. "I'm sorry."

"No, cub. I have not yet slept."

I wasn't sure if that made me feel better, or worse. I just launched into what I knew, so I could let Hugh do what he needed to do. "The woodsman saw a skinwalker with the undines."

"That is troubling," Hugh said. "They have remained hidden so long some of us hoped they'd died out."

"Camazotz doesn't know, but the innkeeper is sending him a message."

"You have returned to Rivercene?" Hugh asked.

"Yes."

"Did she tell you of the gateway?"

I ran down everything the innkeeper and the woodsman had told me, filling in as much detail as I could for Hugh. I didn't tell him about Gaia. The vision of her body frozen forever in that shallow layer of dust and dirt wouldn't leave my mind.

I ran my fingers around the page where the skinwalker photo was embedded. "How did you get this picture of the skinwalker, Hugh? Cameras back then weren't exactly fast."

"It was not me," Hugh said. "It was left at the home of a slaughtered pack. I kept it until there was a need to warn the family at Rivercene. I suspect it was left as a warning to others who walked their path."

"You mean this guy posed with his face off long enough for the picture to turn out?"

"Yes."

I shivered. "Ugh."

"Sharp Elbows concerns me, Damian."

"Why?" I asked. "I would have thought the underwater panthers were about ten times as scary as some guy with sharp elbows."

"You will change your mind."

I waited, and he didn't elaborate. "What should we do?"

"Wait for Camazotz to investigate. He will be able to tell us more about the attacks than the woodsmen. Camazotz has fought a great deal of dark things in his long life. You should—"

Happy's voice boomed inside my head. *She is awake.*

I barely said goodbye to Hugh before I hung up and grabbed my backpack. It was rude to leave the innkeeper like this, but I thought she'd understand. "Thank you!" I shouted as I swung the heavy front door open, slamming it behind me before I darted down the stairs.

I laced my fingers between Gaia's. One step I was hurtling

toward the river, and the next I was in the Abyss. I didn't wait for the golden motes of power to congeal.

"Vicky's awake. Get me to Death's Door, *now.*"

We ran, or at least I ran. Gaia matched my pace with an easy stride. It wasn't more than a minute before she spoke.

"I can send you into the store from here, but the landing will be unpleasant."

"Do it."

She released my hand, and I fell. The sensation was wrong. I wasn't falling down, I was falling in a forward arc like I'd been fired out of a trebuchet. The darkness and stars of the Abyss flickered around me before spinning violently to one side. My face hit hard, and it took me a moment to realize it was carpet singeing the stubble from my cheek.

The room tilted, and then spun. I slammed my palms into the floor and took three heaving breaths.

"Damian?"

Her voice. Vicky. I raised my eyes and found the girl curled up on the floor beside Bubbles. Shiawase stood to the side, his sword raised almost as high as his eyebrows.

"What was that?" Shiawase asked. "It was like thunder, and the room shook. I feared an attack."

"You said she was awake." I slowly brought myself up to a knee. "I told Gaia to hurry."

Vicky hit me like a cu sith, wrapping her arms around my neck. "Is it really over?"

"I think so, kiddo. You're safe." I couldn't lie to her. I couldn't tell her I knew with one hundred percent certainty that it was done, but for now, she was safe. I squeezed her tight, but when I tried to let go, I found her arms locked around me.

"I felt them go," Vicky said. "They all said goodbye. Did you know that? Could you hear them? They all said goodbye to me before they killed the devil." She shook in my arms. Bubbles bounded up beside me and nosed at Vicky's arm.

"I'll miss them and Cara," I said, and the words caught in my throat. We'd lost so much, but here, back at Death's Door, Vicky was finally safe.

"I just want to go home," Vicky whispered into my ear.

I nodded, but I couldn't form the words to say yes.

✦   ✦   ✦

"I GOT YOU a present," Vicky said.

I leaned against the bookshelf beside her. "Really?"

She nodded and pulled a folded piece of black fabric out of her Hello Kitty backpack, handing it to me.

I laughed when the T-shirt fell open and the vampire skull stared back at me. "It's like you knew I'd burned the other one by accident."

"Other two," she said. "Sam got extras. She said you're why she can't have nice things."

I tried to think of a rebuttal, but I drew a blank. "Thank you."

She hugged me and said, "I'm tired."

"Get some sleep, okay? When you wake up, you can see your folks. How about that?"

"I'd like that." She nestled up against Bubbles, and Jasper rolled out from behind the chair, tucking himself under her arms. By the time I got back to my feet and sat down on one of the chairs, she was well on her way to sleep.

"I will miss her," Shiawase said when Vicky's breathing

changed.

"We'll still see her," I said. "Somehow." I couldn't imagine not talking to the kid again, but how did you explain that to her parents? Oh hi, I was friends with your murdered daughter while she was a ghost, but hey look I brought her back! Cue awkward police conversation.

"It will be different, now," Shiawase said. "Change reveals itself to be the only absolute."

I crossed my arms and took a deep breath. "You going to stay in Forest Park? It sounds like Aeros will be moving into the neighborhood soon. You're welcome to stay here."

"Thank you, Damian, but I am rather fond of my home. I do not know how the red pandas would entertain themselves in my absence."

I smiled at the samurai. Vicki snored, and it was time to go.

CHAPTER FORTY-TWO

I STOOD OUTSIDE the house with the sleeping child curled up in my arms, wondering if this was really the right thing to do. I laid her on the porch and tucked the edge of her blanket around her before ringing the doorbell and sprinting away like some idiot kid on Halloween.

The bushes made a fairly crappy hiding place, but I didn't think I'd need a very good one. "You watch over her, yeah?" I told the pile of gray fluff on my shoulder. Jasper vibrated, his black eyes staring into the night.

The door creaked open.

"Hello?" a small voice said from the doorway. The man sounded broken, like life had taken one too many things from him and left nothing to fill the void.

He finally glanced down. His hand shot out and slammed into the door frame, supporting his trembling body. "Elizabeth? Elizabeth! *Oh my god!*"

A second shadow appeared at his side, and Elizabeth's mother screamed as she collapsed over her lost child. Sometimes there are no words. You can only cry out as the world tears your entire being into pieces and smashes it back together again.

"Mom?" a groggy Vicky said. "Mommy!"

I stared at that frantic reunion, an outsider who wanted

nothing but the best for that poor child. Their cries and love made me think Carter and Maggie had known exactly what they were doing. What wouldn't I sacrifice to bring that kind of love into the world? What wouldn't I sacrifice to *keep* that kind of love in the world?

I'd battle the dark-touched, and the Old Gods, and I'd see Gwynn Ap Nudd cast down from his throne and buried by his own people. For Cara, for the Ghost Pack, for my family.

I hoped I'd never see Vicky again, but part of me hoped I'd see her in the morning. I watched the tuft of gray dust flow into the house behind the family.

When the door clicked closed, I wiped the tears from my eyes and whispered, "Love you, kid."

Note from Eric R. Asher

Thank you for spending time with the misfits! I'm blown away by the fantastic reader response to this series, and am so grateful to you all. The next book of Damian's misadventures is called Rattle the Bones, and it's available now.

If you'd like an email when each new book releases, sign up for my mailing list (www.ericrasher.com). Emails only go out about once per month and your information is closely guarded by hungry cu siths.

Also, follow me on BookBub (bookbub.com/authors/eric-r-asher), and you'll always get an email for special sales.

Thanks for reading!
Eric

Please enjoy the following excerpt from

Rattle the Bones

The Vesik Series, book #6

By Eric R. Asher

Much has been lost in the conflict with the Fae king and his allies, a conflict we hadn't known we were in until one of our own fell at his hand. And while a great Seal between realms may have been rebuilt, dark things slipped through in the chaos, creatures who would over- run this world. Our allies are many. Our enemies are terrible. And someone ate my last chimichanga despite the fact I had clearly marked it with a note that said it was mine.

"O F ALL THE things I thought might happen, that wasn't even close to being one of them." I stared out the window at the front of Death's Door, watching Aeros and the swarm of children surrounding him.

Zola patted my shoulder.

I slowly shook my head and marveled at the scene across the street. Aeros had been here less than a week, taking up his post at the corner of the parking lot. He'd intimidated the military patrols, as we'd hoped, but the kids had been a surprise.

A boy slipped as he reached the Old God's shoulder, and I hissed, expecting to see him smack into the ground. Instead, a pillar of rock rose beneath him, cutting his fall short. Aeros glanced at the boy, and I could see the Old God's craggy mouth moving.

The boy jumped off, laughing, and joined his friends by the curb. One of the girls made it up to Aeros's shoulder and swung her legs to hang over his chest. They'd turned the old rock pile into a playground.

"You think he misses Vicky?" I asked.

"We all do, Damian, but she's with her family again, and her bond to the Destroyer is broken. There's not much more we can ask than that."

I agreed wholeheartedly.

A man walked around the corner, dressed in a three-piece suit and bowler.

"Edgar?" I asked, watching him as he walked toward the front door.

"Ah've been expecting him," Zola said. "Took him long enough."

The bell on the front door jingled a moment later, and Edgar stepped inside.

"Waiting for him to flatten one of those kids?" the Watcher asked.

"You know damn well he would *never* do that to a child," Zola snapped.

Edgar held up his hands. "My apologies. I had no intention of starting an argument."

"Especially when you'll lose," I said.

Edgar shot me a sideways glance, but he didn't deny it. "Are

Foster and Aideen around? I'd like to speak with them."

"It's barely been a week since they lost Cara," Zola said.

"Something's happening in Falias. There's been fighting inside the city over the past few days, and no one seems to know why." Edgar hesitated, glancing toward the back of the shop before nodding. "They're the only Fae I trust right now. The loyalties split between Glenn and Hern are confusing, and judging Fae intentions is little more than a guess."

"Let me see if Foster and Aideen are up for visitors," I said to Edgar. I walked toward the back, passing the glass countertops on the right and the large display case of gemstones off to the left. The saloon-style door creaked as I pushed my way past it.

Foster sat on the edge of the grandfather clock beside Aideen, his rage disturbing the ley lines around the clock, sending out sickly black waves from his aura. He had been like this for a week, teetering between rage and guilt, and I felt much the same. Cara shouldn't have had to lay down her life for mine.

Bubbles and Peanut sniffed the air from where they were both crammed into their underground lair's entrance.

"You hear all that?" I asked.

"We did," Aideen said. She turned to Foster and placed a hand on his cheek. "It is time, my love. The seven days are over."

Foster kissed his wife and slid off the edge of the grandfather clock, exploding into his full size. He sang, and the ringing notes sent shivers down my spine.

Seven days have passed, oh king.

Seven days I've seen.

Seven days I held the lost.

Seven days unseen.

Foster slammed the saloon-style doors open, and Aideen joined him. I'd heard the mourning song before. When Cassie died at the farm, something sang it for weeks in the depths of the woods.

In seven moons, the deeds be done,

Sheathed inside the king.

In seven lives, we know the boon,

What now forever sees.

I followed the fairies out into the store. Foster stared at Edgar, and the immortal stared back.

"Did you know?" the fairy whispered. "Did you know what Gwynn Ap Nudd intended to do to my family? My *mother*?"

"Gods no!" Edgar said, stepping back as if he'd been struck. "There was no hint of it. I'm not even sure he'd intended it himself. He acted when an opportunity presented itself."

"She wasn't an opportunity." Foster bit off each syllable.

Edgar froze, and I stepped between them.

"That's not what he meant," I said, holding up my hands. "Foster, please, I don't want to scrub Edgar's brains out of the cracks in the hardwood."

The fairy shifted his eyes from Edgar to me and slowly raised his eyebrows. "That is rather difficult, trying to clean the blood out of those little cracks."

"Probably worse than armor," I said, nodding vigorously.

The stony look on Foster's face relaxed a fraction.

Edgar took his bowler off and ran his finger around the brim. "As much as we argued over the years, I considered Cara a friend. I may have kept some things from you in the past, but never something like this."

"I need a fight," Foster said, his voice verging on a growl.

Zola rapped her cane on the hardwood floor. "You'll have them in spades."

Foster frowned and glanced at Zola.

Aideen stepped up beside him and laid a hand on his sword arm. "What do you know? Is it Nudd?"

"Edgar can tell you. So long as you don't stab him, of course."

The front door opened to the quiet jingle of bells. We all turned to face it.

Frank froze as he stepped inside. "Uh, hope I'm not interrupting." He held up a bag of White Castle. "I have breakfast."

Sam blipped through the door behind him. "Yes, *we* have breakfast."

A minute later, we were all seated around the old Formica table in the back room. Frank divided up the breakfast sandwiches. He'd bought enough for a small army. Clearly, he knew me.

Foster and Aideen sat to either side of a sandwich in their smaller forms, slicing off bits of bread and egg to build their own miniature breakfast.

"Nice to see you outside the clock," Sam said.

"The seven days of mourning are a tradition in our family," Aideen said.

Foster nodded. "She means thanks for not sticking your nose in any more than you did." He stuffed his face with a bite of his breakfast sandwich.

Sam gave him a small smile.

"Thanks, Frank," I said after a bite of warm gooey cheese. "But not Sam."

She narrowed her eyes at me.

Frank nodded and glanced at Edgar.

Edgar wore a frown. He stared at the boxed breakfast sandwich. "This is … food?"

"You've never had White Castle?" I said, unable to keep the disbelief from my voice. "Be sure to take it out of the box first. That's just decoration."

Zola snorted a laugh beside me, the gray metal charms braided into her hair tinkling as she moved.

"It is square, virtually a cube of meat and cheese…" Edgar took a bite of his sandwich and chewed deliberately. He swallowed, frowned, and took another. He looked uncertain, but his sandwich kept getting smaller.

"Tell us," Foster said, after finishing one of his mini sandwiches. "What did Zola mean about fights?"

Edgar looked up from his square sandwich and glanced at his watch. He grimaced and said, "It's time. Turn on your television."

I hadn't tried to turn on the little television in the back of the shop in years, and was surprised when the tube whined and came to life. "What station?"

"I'm sure it doesn't matter," Edgar said.

A few flips of the dial on the front of the old set proved him right. Every station showed a stand of microphones and a sea of cables running away from the platform. Soldiers in uniform flanked the stage, and my stomach started to sour.

A reporter stepped into the frame. I snorted when I saw who it was.

"Well," I said. "she sure knows how to step into some shit." She'd been there when a leviathan rose from the Ohio River, when Ezekiel had executed Watchers along the Brookport Bridge. And yet she was still here, still reporting. I had to give her credit for that.

"This is Emily Beckers, coming to you live. We're awaiting the first public address of the Fae. Stay with us for this historic moment."

The light dimmed on the small screen, like a storm front had rolled in front of the sun. As it brightened again, two distinct forms took shape behind the microphones. The feed fell silent, and the cameras zoomed in on the newcomers.

"Fucking hell," I muttered.

Glenn stood there, one arm raised in greeting to the crowd. He could have passed for a Watcher, wearing a finely tailored suit as he was. The only thing that looked out of the ordinary was the antlered helm he carried beneath his arm.

"Glenn *and* Hern?" Aideen said.

Foster sat down in the middle of the table and stared. "Hern … what are they doing?"

Sam was stock still on Frank's lap. "He killed Cara." Her hands paled as she clenched her fists.

"They're working together," I said. "They have to be."

Foster leaned toward the television, his fingers strangling the hilt of his sword.

"Greetings," Glenn said, wearing a smile that made him

look more like a long-lost grandfather than a murdering psychopath. "I am the leader of the Fae city known as Falias, and yes, some will even go so far as to call me their king. That's too impersonal a term, as we are here to form an understanding between our communities. So while my given name may be Gwynn Ap Nudd, I implore you to call me Glenn."

"I think I just threw up a little bit," Sam said.

"Shh," Foster said, waving at her to be quiet.

"You lost a great many souls when our fair city was wrenched from its home. Please realize, I lost friends and family too in that great cataclysm. But you must understand, it was not me. It was not even one of the Fae."

Murmurs filtered through the audience. They hadn't shown the crowd before, and when the camera panned across them, I was taken aback at the sheer scale, the risers constructed to either side of the stage like some grand stadium. Like some terrible simulacra of the Royal Court.

"Though we of Falias may be powerful, we were not able to stop our shared enemy. In that very conflict, I lost my wife."

Foster screamed at the television. "You son of a bitch! I'll gut you from groin to lung just to heal you and start again!"

"Not long ago, your military felt their best course of action was to drop bombs on our fair city, killing more innocent families. Children." Glenn hung his head and shook it slowly. The camera switched to a horror-struck middle-aged man and a younger woman, maybe his daughter, with one hand over her mouth. Glenn was playing the crowd like a goddamned fiddle. "It was an act of fear, but it is an act I can forgive. By the end of our short speech here, rest assured those bombs that did not find their targets will be returned, undamaged and ready to be deployed at more … appropriate threats.”

A massive green cylinder appeared in front of the podium, looking like a water tower laid on its side and capped with a cone.

Murmurs and shouts rose up from the audience.

“We are only returning what was lost,” Glenn said. He stepped to the side, and for a moment a black-cloaked figure stood hunched behind him, a hood pulled down to cover a helmeted face, and then it was gone.

“That’s a damn daisy cutter that just appeared,” Frank said. “That bomb could kill everyone there.”

Emily stepped onscreen again. “We’re taking you live to an aerial view from our news chopper.”

The image flipped to something I could scarcely wrap my head around.

“What you’re seeing are dozens of unexploded bombs, carefully laid out behind the stage.” Emily turned, and looked to be scanning for someone. “It’s unknown where these bombs came from, but we’re currently speculating that the Fae—”

Someone put their hand up in front of the camera, and the screen flashed back to a stunned-looking newsroom.

I flipped the channel. It was the same on every one.

“Well,” I said. “Glenn knows how to make an impression.”

“Peace,” Glenn said when the picture returned. “There is nothing to fear in this place.” He waited for the crowd to quiet.

Aideen crossed her arms and watched from Zola’s shoulder.

“It was not so long ago that I was at war with one of my allies. This man, here.” He gestured for Hern to step forward. “Our own realm has been scoured by battle, scarred by it. But we have put our differences aside, Hern and I, to work for the betterment of all people."

The crowd's murmurs broke into a polite applause.

"So please," Glenn said, "do not fear us for our differences, but do use caution around the outskirts of our city. There are … bad neighborhoods, much like you have inside your own cities. I would not wish for any of you to be harmed, and it would not do for that to be a reflection on Falias itself.

"Hern will answer your questions about safety, and help guide us into a new era. A time of peace between your realm and our own. An era when our children may play together, grow old together, and bring peace to this fractured world."

Something in the crowd shifted, and their polite claps broke into a raucous applause, the sound little more than static on the television.

Edgar took a deep breath before slamming his palm on the Formica table. "That was brilliant. That was bloody brilliant. If he plays this right, and I have little doubt he will, Gwynn Ap Nudd will look like an ambassador of goodwill between the commoners and Fae."

"He's a monster," Frank said. He huffed and leaned back in his chair. "Edgar's right. It was a perfect setup. Too perfect. What's his game?"

Zola leaned forward and rested her chin on her knuckles. "Keep your opponent off balance, until the time is right."

Hern stepped up to the microphone. "Thank you, Glenn. As my colleague said, you may ask me whatever you wish. We will be conducting tours of Falias, as I understand many of you would like to meet some of the local Fae who are now your neighbors."

"It doesn't even sound like Hern," Aideen said. "How long? How long have they been planning this?"

"There *are* dangerous beings from our world. They are not Fae, but please use caution if you would happen to encounter anyone claiming to be a necromancer, vampire, or a witch. It is believed the group responsible for the tragedy in the East is based in Saint Louis. Thank you for your time today." He inclined his head and walked off the stage.

Zola growled.

"He just put the entire world on alert," Sam said. "*For us.*"

"Yeah," I said, turning the television off. "Shit."

Edgar rubbed his forehead and turned to Aideen as she hopped onto the table. "There has been more fighting in Falias the past two days. I hoped you or Foster may have some idea of why."

"Our numbers are building at the Obsidian Inn," Foster said. "There is more fighting because there is more resistance."

Aideen wiped down her sword and sheathed it. "What do you wish to do?"

"We go to Falias." A savage smile lifted the corners of Foster's mouth.

Rattle the Bones

The Vesik Series, book #6

Available now!

Also by Eric R. Asher

Keep track of Eric's new releases by receiving an email on release day. It's fast and easy to sign up for Eric's mailing list, and you'll also get an ebook copy of the subscriber exclusive anthology, *Whispers of War.*

Go here to get started: www.ericrasher.com

The Steamborn Trilogy:

Steamborn

Steamforged

Steamsworn

The Vesik Series:

(Recommended for Ages 17+)

Days Gone Bad

Wolves and the River of Stone

Winter's Demon

This Broken World

Destroyer Rising

Rattle the Bones

Witch Queen's War – coming fall 2017*

*Want to receive an email on the day this book releases? Sign up for Eric's mailing list.

www.ericrasher.com

Mason Dixon – Monster Hunter:

Episode One

Episode Two – coming summer 2017*

*Want to receive an email on the day this book releases? Sign up for Eric's mailing list.

About the Author

Eric is a former bookseller, cellist, and comic seller currently living in Saint Louis, Missouri. A lifelong enthusiast of books, music, toys, and games, he discovered a love for the written word after being dragged to the library by his parents at a young age. When he is not writing, you can usually find him reading, gaming, or buried beneath a small avalanche of Transformers. For more about Eric, see: www.ericrasher.com

Enjoy this book? You can make a big difference.

Reviews are the most powerful tools I have when it comes to getting attention for my books. I don't have a huge marketing budget like some New York publishers, but I have something even better.

A committed and loyal bunch of readers.

Honest reviews help bring my books to the attention of other readers.

If you've enjoyed this book, I would be very grateful if you could take a minute to leave a review on the platform of your choice. It can be as short as you like. Thank you for spending time with Damian and the misfits.

Connect with Eric R. Asher Online:

Twitter: @ericrasher

Instagram: @ericrasher

Facebook: EricRAsher

www.ericrasher.com

eric@ericrasher.com

Made in the USA
Monee, IL
27 March 2023

30622356R00204